owtw

Amy's Diary

charmz

MORE GRAPHIC NOVELS AVAILABLE FROM charmz™

STITCHED #1 "THE FIRST DAY OF THE REST OF HER LIFE"

STITCHED #2 "LOVE IN THE TIME OF ASSUMPTION"

G.F.F.s #1 "MY HEART LIES IN THE 90s"

G.F.F.s #2 "WITCHES GET THINGS DONE"

CHLOE #1 "THE NEW GIRL"

CHLOE #2 "THE QUEEN OF HIGH SCHOOL"

CHLOE #3 "FRENEMIES"

CHLOE #4 "RAINY DAY"

SCARLET ROSE #1 "I KNEW I'D MEET YOU"

SCARLET ROSE #2 "I'LL GO WHERE YOU GO"

SCARLET ROSE #3 "I THINK I LOVE YOU"

SCARLET ROSE #4 "YOU WILL ALWAYS BE MINE"

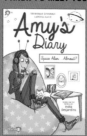

AMY'S DIARY #1 "SPACE ALIEN... ALMOST?"

SWEETIES #1 "CHERRY SKYE"

MONICA ADVENTURES #1

ANA AND THE COSMIC RACE #1 "THE RACE BEGINS"

SEE MORE AT PAPERCUTZ.COM

Amy's Diary

The World's Upside Down

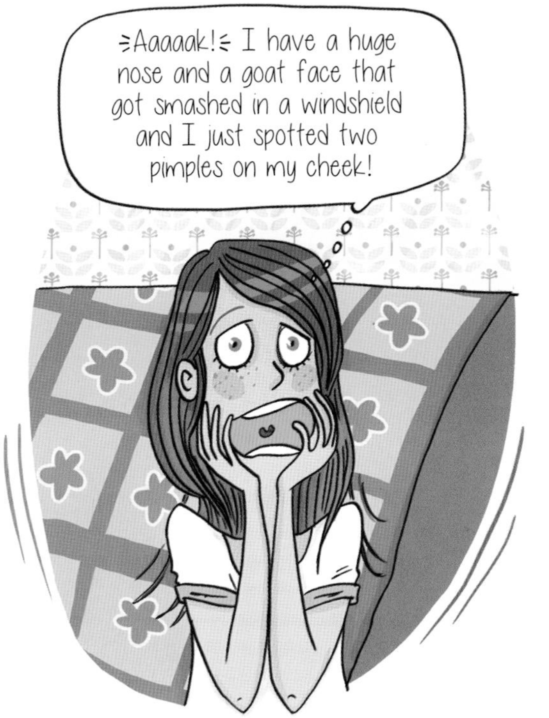
≠Aaaaak!≠ I have a huge nose and a goat face that got smashed in a windshield and I just spotted two pimples on my cheek!

Based on the novels by INDIA DESJARDINS

Adaptation — VÉRONIQUE GRISSEAUX

Illustration — LAËTITIA AYNIÉ

charmz

NEW YORK

Véronique and Laëtitia, an awesome team that's totally captured Amy's universe.
Elsa Lafon, my partner in crime from the other side of the Atlantic.
Florence, Annabelle, as well as the whole team of Michel Lafon and Jungle.
—India

To my grandmother, who was as cool as Amy's and who left for the stars too soon…
A big thanks to the terrific team forever and ever for entrusting me once again with the adventures of the ever so appealing Amy.
—Laëtitia

Thanks to Laëtitia, Annabelle, Mélanie, and Estelle,
and an especially BIG thanks to India for once again entrusting her Amy to me in this second volume!
—Véronique

Amy's Diary

"The World's Upside Down"
Le journal d'Aurélie Laflamme [AMY'S DIARY] volume 2 *"Le monde à l'envers"* © 2016 Jungle/Michel Lafon. All Rights Reserved. www.editions-jungle.com. Used under license.

English translation and all other material © 2019 Papercutz. All rights reserved.

Based on the novel by INDIA DESJARDINS
VÉRONIQUE GRISSEAUX—Comics Adaptation
LAËTITIA AYNIÉ—Art, Color, Design
JOE JOHNSON—Translation
BRYAN SENKA—Lettering
LÉA ZIMMERMAN—Production
JEFF WHITMAN—Managing Editor
JIM SALICRUP
Editor-in-Cheif

Charmz is an imprint of Papercutz.
Papercutz.com

Hardcover ISBN: 978-1-6299-1857-0
Paperback ISBN: 978-1-6299-1856-3

Printed in China
July 2019

Charmz books may be purchased for business or promotional use. For information on bulk purchases please contact Macmillan Corporate and Premium Sales Department at (800) 221-795-7945 x5442.

Distributed by Macmillan.
Frist Charmz printing.

MAY

Letting the dust settle

- Sunday, May 7th:

3:05pm:
I'm fourteen, almost fifteen, and I'm a "chocoholic." I looked in the dictionary, and this word actually exists. Usually I have to invent words to define myself and that constitutes the hundred thousandth reason why the human race and I aren't birds of a feather.

3:10pm:
It's Easter's fault, there's chocolate everywhere!
When the chocolate melts in my mouth, just before I swallow it, I forget all my worries. I feel like my taste buds are dancing on my tongue, that they have tiny arms they're waving in the air shouting at me:

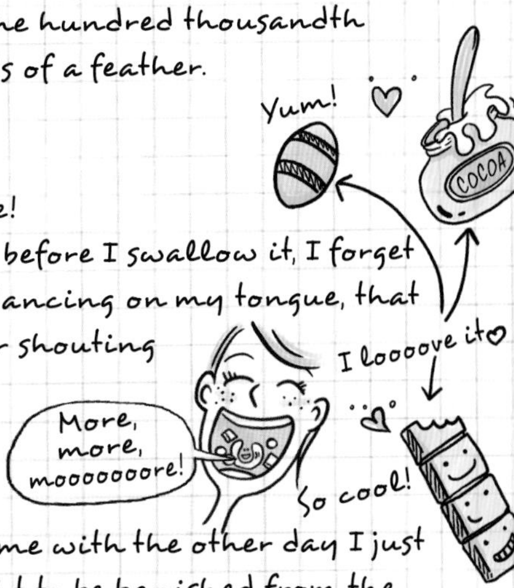

Yum!
COCOA
I loooove it
More, more, mooooooore!
So cool!

3:38pm:
Right now, there's an expression my aunt hit me with the other day I just can't stand anymore (an expression that ought to be banished from the face of the earth), it's: "there are plenty more fish in the sea." Since things ended with Nick, I can't count how many adults have told me that. Like that'll make me feel better! Grrrrrrr!

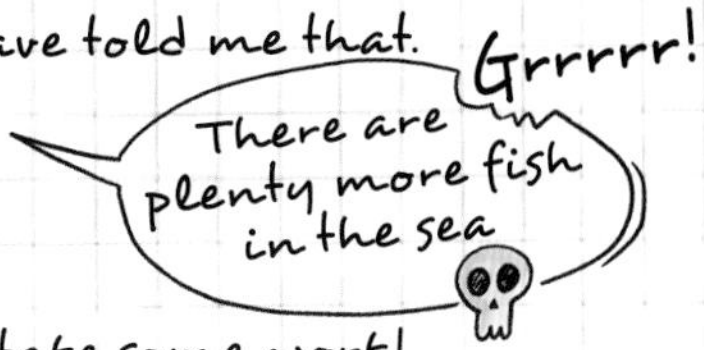

Grrrrr!
There are plenty more fish in the sea

3:48pm:
I've decided to become more mature... Hmm, that'll take some work!

4:32pm:
My mom thinks I'm "on edge" lately. Pfffff!
She's one to talk. When my dad died five years ago, she went into a zombie-like lethargy.
She's got to understand I'm... in the middle of a broken heart!

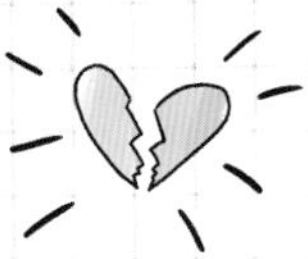

5:00pm:
My mom's going off on a month-long road trip with her boyfriend: Frank Blay. He's one of the most annoying people on this planet...
Since I hate camping, my mom agreed I wouldn't spend the summer in a pop-up camper with them. The deal: Spend the summer at my Granny Von Brandt's. I'm not happy about it, but it won't be as bad as being in some forest without toilets with a good chance of coming across bears. Luckily chocolate exists, otherwise I'd think life totally sucked.

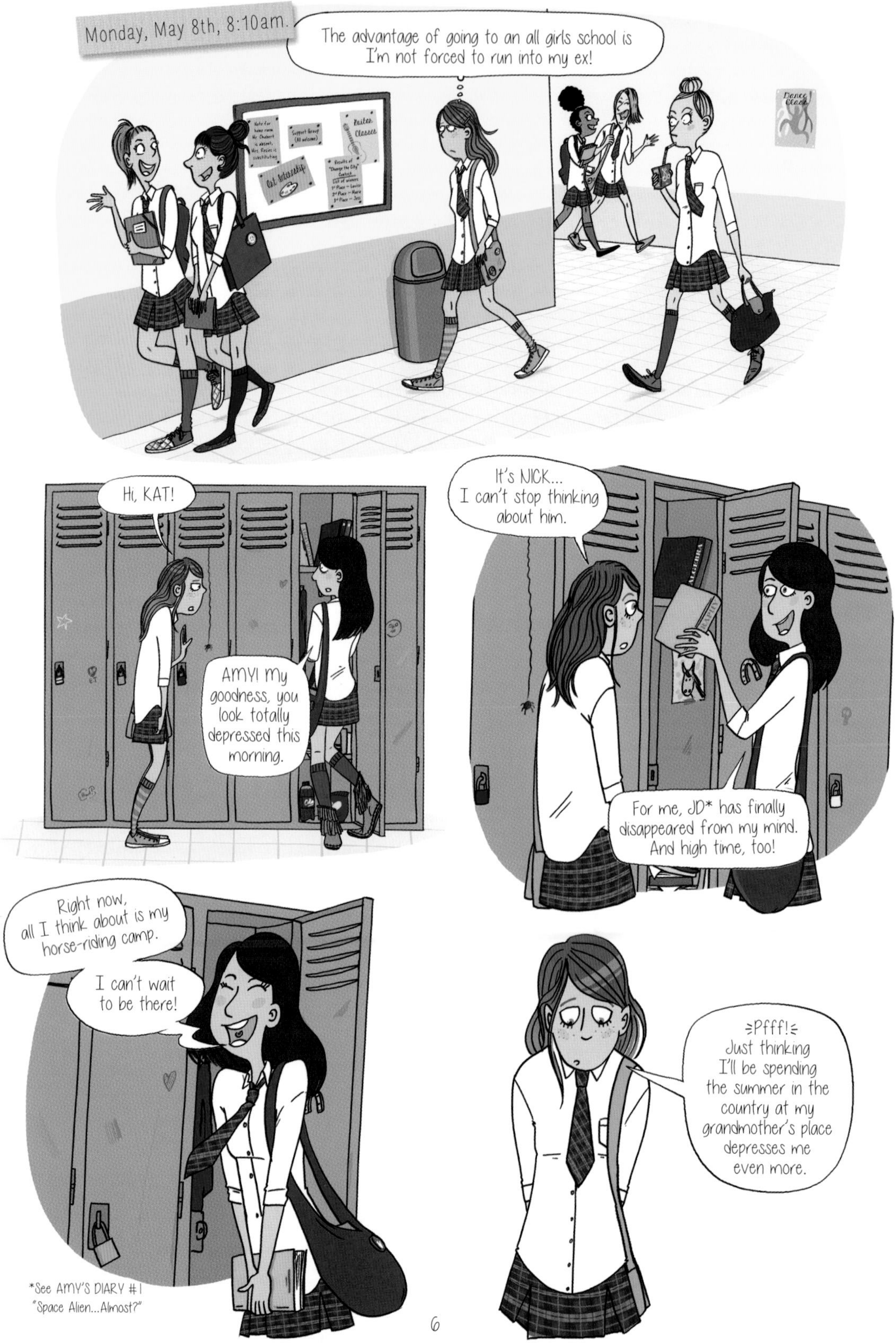
Monday, May 8th, 8:10am.
The advantage of going to an all girls school is I'm not forced to run into my ex!
Hi, KAT!
AMY! My goodness, you look totally depressed this morning.
It's NICK... I can't stop thinking about him.
For me, JD* has finally disappeared from my mind. And high time, too!
Right now, all I think about is my horse-riding camp.
I can't wait to be there!
Pfff! Just thinking I'll be spending the summer in the country at my grandmother's place depresses me even more.

*See AMY'S DIARY #1 "Space Alien...Almost?"

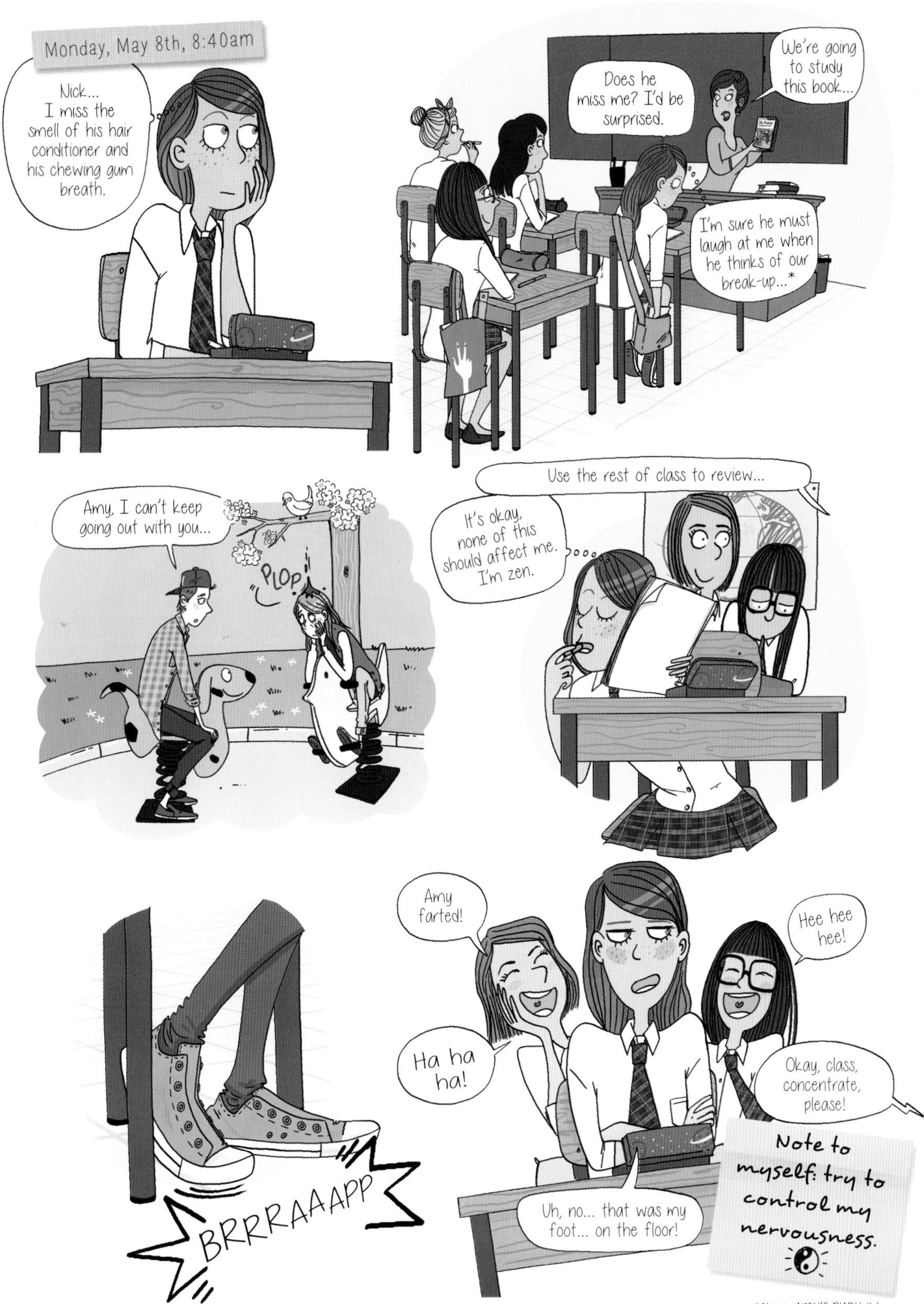
Monday, May 8th, 8:40am
Nick... I miss the smell of his hair conditioner and his chewing gum breath.
We're going to study this book...
Does he miss me? I'd be surprised.
I'm sure he must laugh at me when he thinks of our break-up...*
Amy, I can't keep going out with you...
PLOP!
Use the rest of class to review...
It's okay, none of this should affect me. I'm zen.
BRRRAAAPP
Amy farted!
Hee hee hee!
Ha ha ha!
Okay, class, concentrate, please!
Uh, no... that was my foot... on the floor!
Note to myself: try to control my nervousness.

*Also in AMY'S DIARY #1.

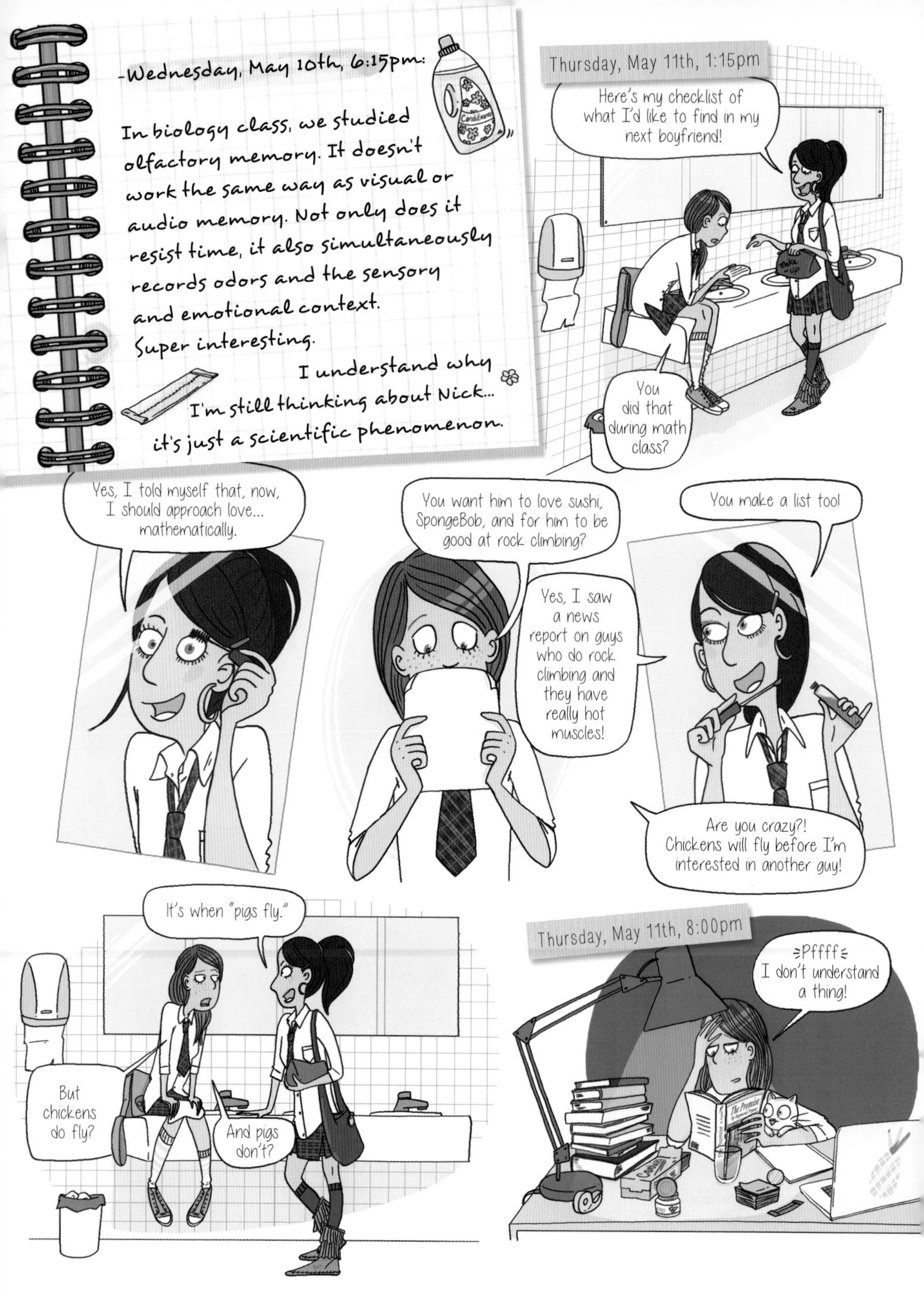
-Wednesday, May 10th, 6:15pm:
In biology class, we studied olfactory memory. It doesn't work the same way as visual or audio memory. Not only does it resist time, it also simultaneously records odors and the sensory and emotional context.
Super interesting.
I understand why I'm still thinking about Nick... it's just a scientific phenomenon.
Thursday, May 11th, 1:15pm
Here's my checklist of what I'd like to find in my next boyfriend!
You did that during math class?
Yes, I told myself that, now, I should approach love... mathematically.
You want him to love sushi, SpongeBob, and for him to be good at rock climbing?
Yes, I saw a news report on guys who do rock climbing and they have really hot muscles!
You make a list too!
Are you crazy?! Chickens will fly before I'm interested in another guy!
It's when "pigs fly."
But chickens do fly?
And pigs don't?
Thursday, May 11th, 8:00pm
Pffff
I don't understand a thing!

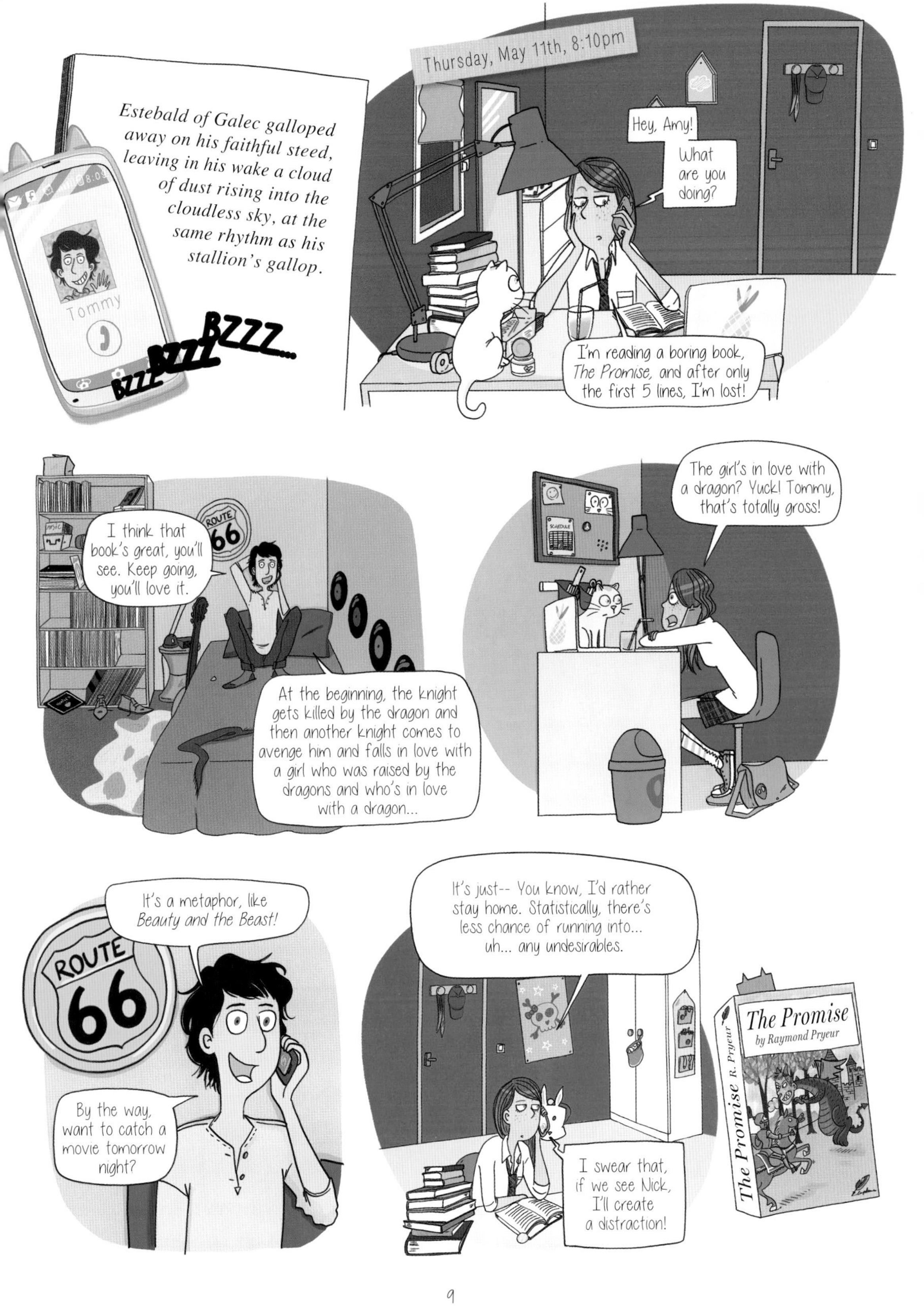
Estebald of Galec galloped away on his faithful steed, leaving in his wake a cloud of dust rising into the cloudless sky, at the same rhythm as his stallion's gallop.
Tommy
BZZZ BZZZ BZZZ...
Thursday, May 11th, 8:10pm
Hey, Amy!
What are you doing?
I'm reading a boring book, *The Promise*, and after only the first 5 lines, I'm lost!
ROUTE 66
I think that book's great, you'll see. Keep going, you'll love it.
At the beginning, the knight gets killed by the dragon and then another knight comes to avenge him and falls in love with a girl who was raised by the dragons and who's in love with a dragon...
The girl's in love with a dragon? Yuck! Tommy, that's totally gross!
It's a metaphor, like *Beauty and the Beast*!
ROUTE 66
By the way, want to catch a movie tomorrow night?
It's just-- You know, I'd rather stay home. Statistically, there's less chance of running into... uh... any undesirables.
I swear that, if we see Nick, I'll create a distraction!
The Promise
by Raymond Pryeur
The Promise R. Pryeur

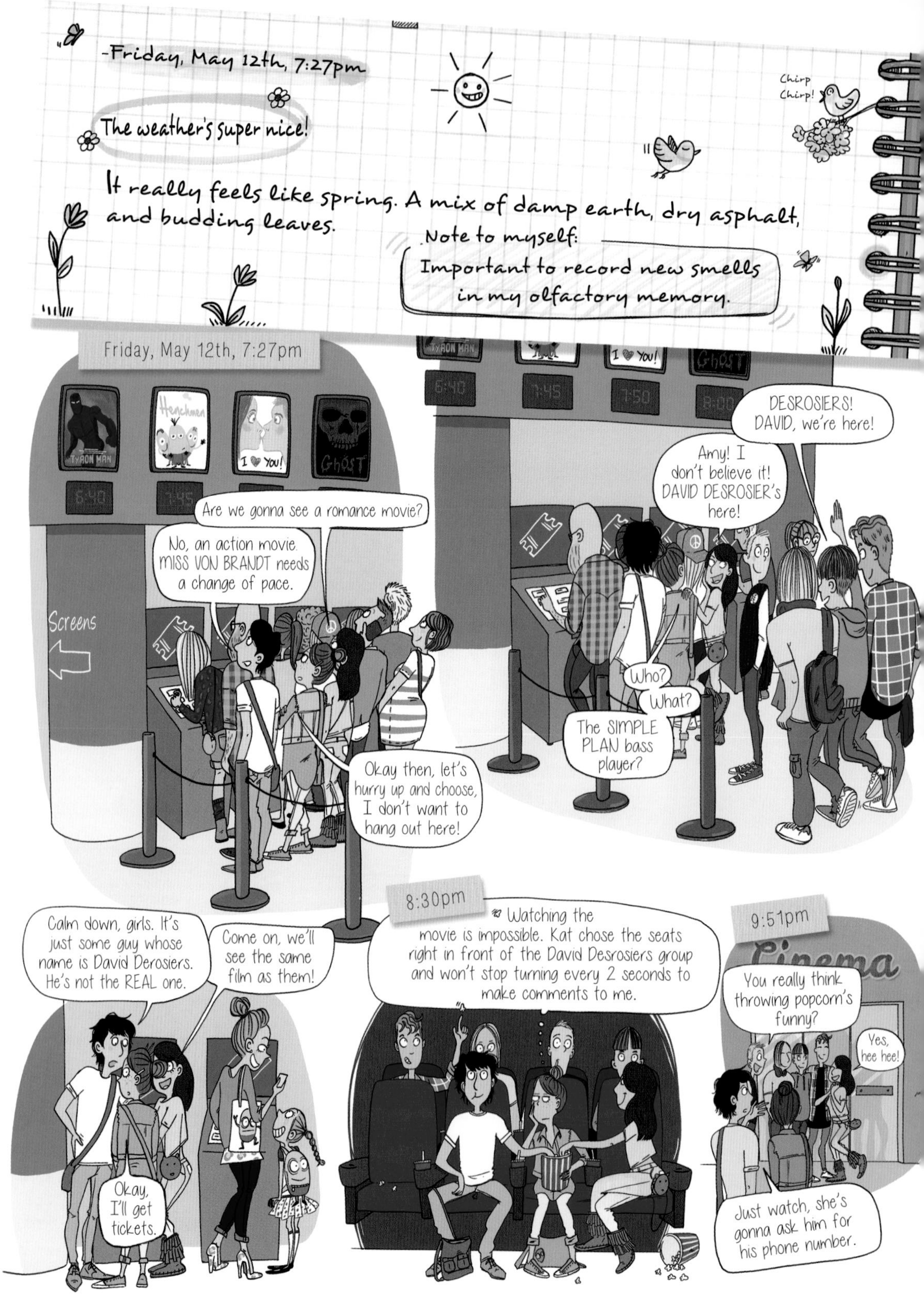
-Friday, May 12th, 7:27pm
The weather's super nice!
It really feels like spring. A mix of damp earth, dry asphalt, and budding leaves.
Note to myself:
Important to record new smells in my olfactory memory.
Chirp Chirp!
Friday, May 12th, 7:27pm
Are we gonna see a romance movie?
No, an action movie. MISS VON BRANDT needs a change of pace.
Okay then, let's hurry up and choose, I don't want to hang out here!
DESROSIERS! DAVID, we're here!
Amy! I don't believe it! DAVID DESROSIER's here!
Who?
What?
The SIMPLE PLAN bass player?
Calm down, girls. It's just some guy whose name is David Derosiers. He's not the REAL one.
Come on, we'll see the same film as them!
Okay, I'll get tickets.
8:30pm
Watching the movie is impossible. Kat chose the seats right in front of the David Desrosiers group and won't stop turning every 2 seconds to make comments to me.
9:51pm
You really think throwing popcorn's funny?
Yes, hee hee!
Just watch, she's gonna ask him for his phone number.

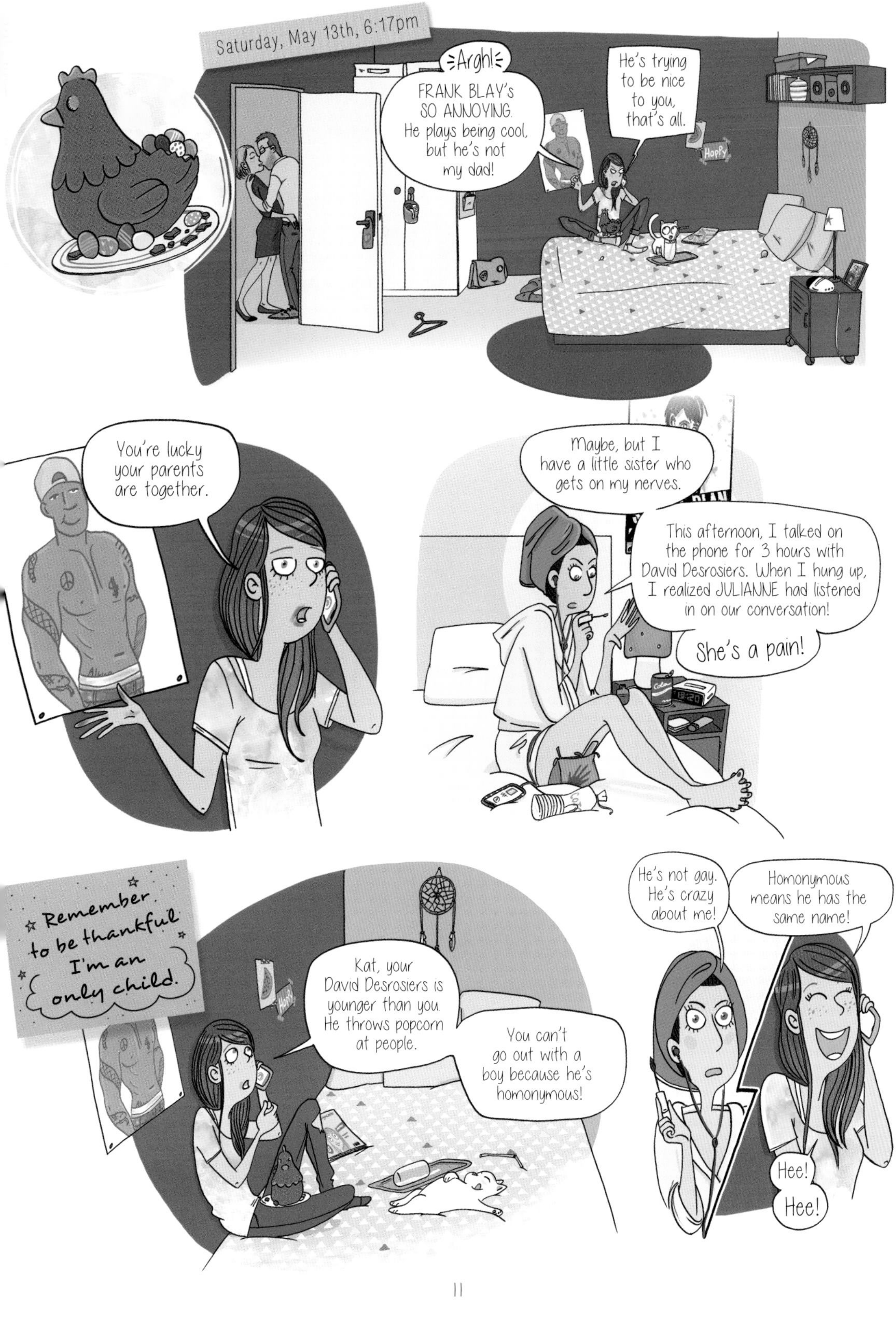

Saturday, May 13th, 6:17pm
Argh!
FRANK BLAY's SO ANNOYING. He plays being cool, but he's not my dad!
He's trying to be nice to you, that's all.
Happy
You're lucky your parents are together.
Maybe, but I have a little sister who gets on my nerves.
This afternoon, I talked on the phone for 3 hours with David Desrosiers. When I hung up, I realized JULIANNE had listened in on our conversation!
She's a pain!
Remember to be thankful I'm an only child.
Kat, your David Desrosiers is younger than you. He throws popcorn at people.
You can't go out with a boy because he's homonymous!
He's not gay. He's crazy about me!
Homonymous means he has the same name!
Hee!
Hee!

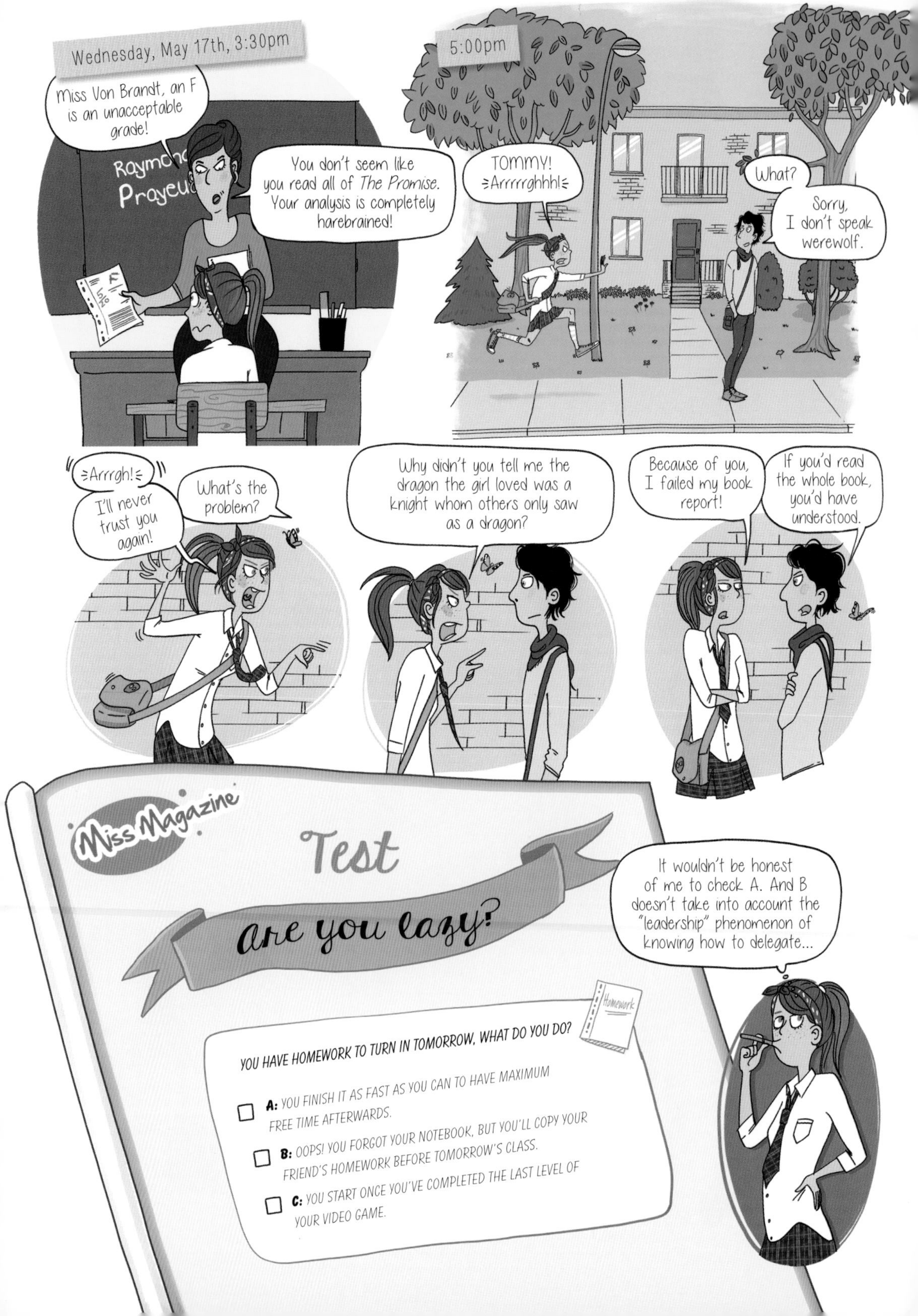
Wednesday, May 17th, 3:30pm
Miss Von Brandt, an F is an unacceptable grade!
You don't seem like you read all of *The Promise*. Your analysis is completely harebrained!
5:00pm
TOMMY! Arrrrrghhh!
What?
Sorry, I don't speak werewolf.
Arrrgh! I'll never trust you again!
What's the problem?
Why didn't you tell me the dragon the girl loved was a knight whom others only saw as a dragon?
Because of you, I failed my book report!
If you'd read the whole book, you'd have understood.
Miss Magazine
Test
are you lazy?
Homework
YOU HAVE HOMEWORK TO TURN IN TOMORROW, WHAT DO YOU DO?
A: YOU FINISH IT AS FAST AS YOU CAN TO HAVE MAXIMUM FREE TIME AFTERWARDS.
B: OOPS! YOU FORGOT YOUR NOTEBOOK, BUT YOU'LL COPY YOUR FRIEND'S HOMEWORK BEFORE TOMORROW'S CLASS.
C: YOU START ONCE YOU'VE COMPLETED THE LAST LEVEL OF YOUR VIDEO GAME.
It wouldn't be honest of me to check A. And B doesn't take into account the "leadership" phenomenon of knowing how to delegate...

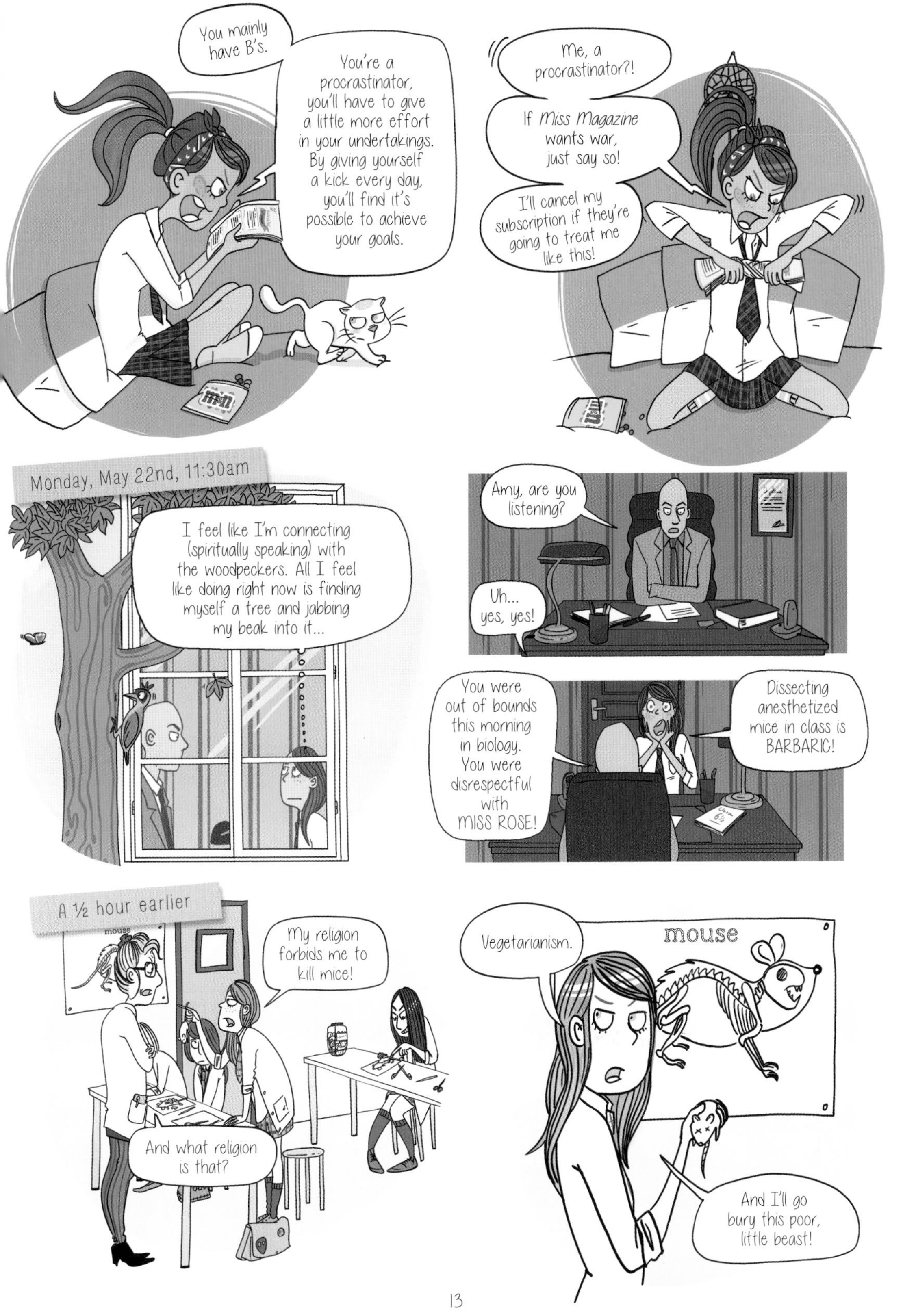

You mainly have B's.
You're a procrastinator, you'll have to give a little more effort in your undertakings. By giving yourself a kick every day, you'll find it's possible to achieve your goals.
Me, a procrastinator?!
If *Miss Magazine* wants war, just say so!
I'll cancel my subscription if they're going to treat me like this!
Monday, May 22nd, 11:30am
I feel like I'm connecting (spiritually speaking) with the woodpeckers. All I feel like doing right now is finding myself a tree and jabbing my beak into it...
Amy, are you listening?
Uh... yes, yes!
You were out of bounds this morning in biology. You were disrespectful with MISS ROSE!
Dissecting anesthetized mice in class is BARBARIC!
A ½ hour earlier
mouse
My religion forbids me to kill mice!
And what religion is that?
Vegetarianism.
mouse
And I'll go bury this poor, little beast!

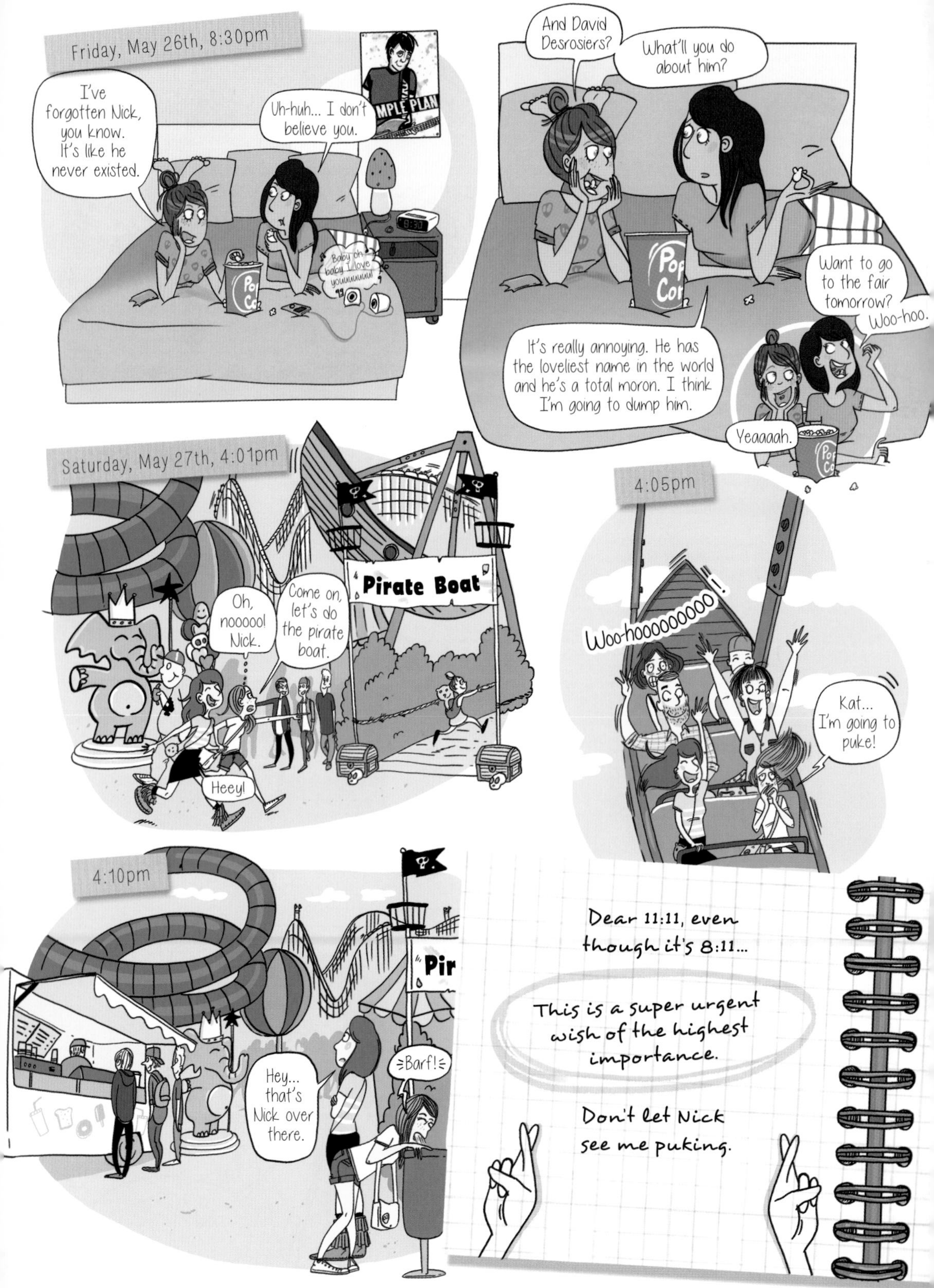

Friday, May 26th, 8:30pm
I've forgotten Nick, you know. It's like he never existed.
Uh-huh... I don't believe you.
And David Desrosiers?
What'll you do about him?
It's really annoying. He has the loveliest name in the world and he's a total moron. I think I'm going to dump him.
Want to go to the fair tomorrow?
Woo-hoo.
Yeaaaah.
Saturday, May 27th, 4:01pm
Pirate Boat
Oh, nooooo! Nick.
Come on, let's do the pirate boat.
Heey!
4:05pm
Woo-hoooooooooo!
Kat... I'm going to puke!
4:10pm
Hey... that's Nick over there.
Barf!
Dear 11:11, even though it's 8:11...
This is a super urgent wish of the highest importance.
Don't let Nick see me puking.

JUNE

A real suitcase

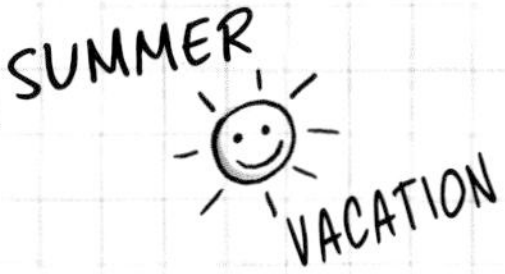
SUMMER
VACATION

- Saturday, June 3rd:

3:05pm:
I'm going to get a nose job. I feel totally over my break-up with Nick. Apart from this slight detail about my olfactory memory (which will be settled as soon as I convince my mom about the benefits of a minor surgical intervention).

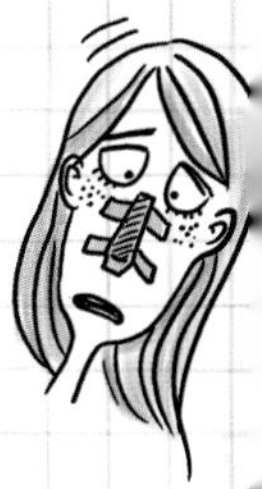

3:15pm:
My mom told me "NO" about the nose surgery and she went on to say: "I know you're hurting right now. Nick was your first love. You have plenty of time to find another one!"
I stopped her immediately when she ended her sentence with:

"There are plenty..."

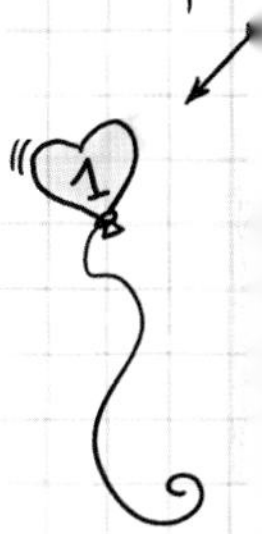
1

4:00pm:
How did I end up on my hands and knees cleaning my closet? I don't know.

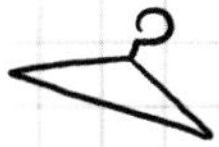

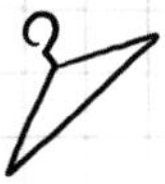

Yes, I do. It's because my mom told me:
"You should do some cleaning. When you straighten up your bedroom, you straighten up your life."

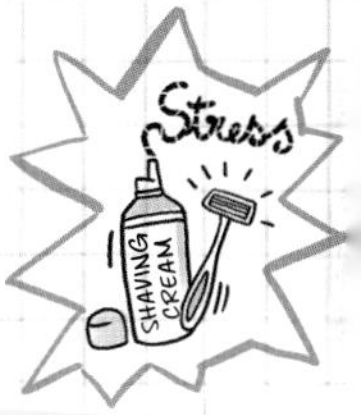
Stress
SHAVING CREAM

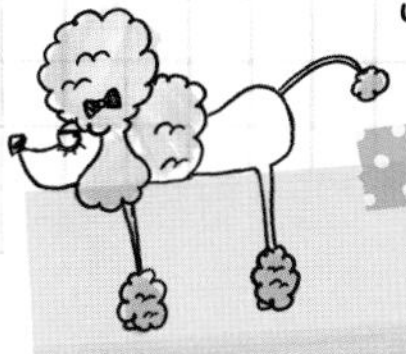

Hypothesis:
I'm sure she pulled out her theory of "straightening up your life" to manipulate me! She totally takes me for a slave.

Deep Hypothesis:
Unless she considers me to be intelligent because she has to hit me with stupid theories to get me to do housework. Hmm...

I'm a respected slave.

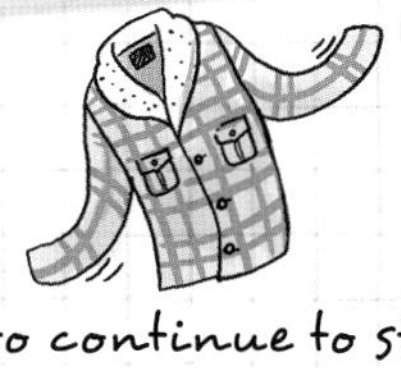

- Sunday, June 4th:

10:20am:
I just opened my closet to continue to straighten things up. It's crazy the stuff you find.

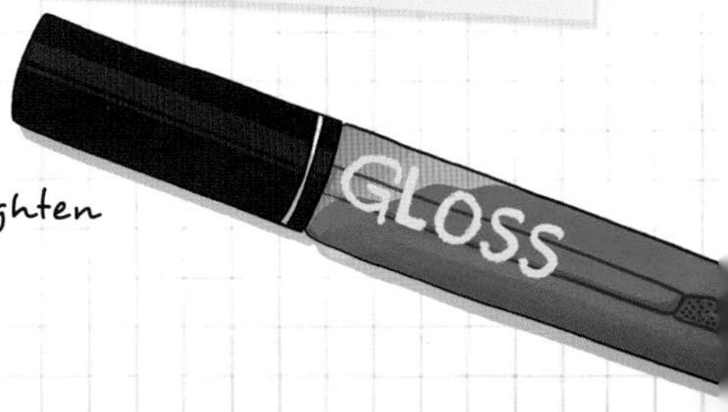
GLOSS

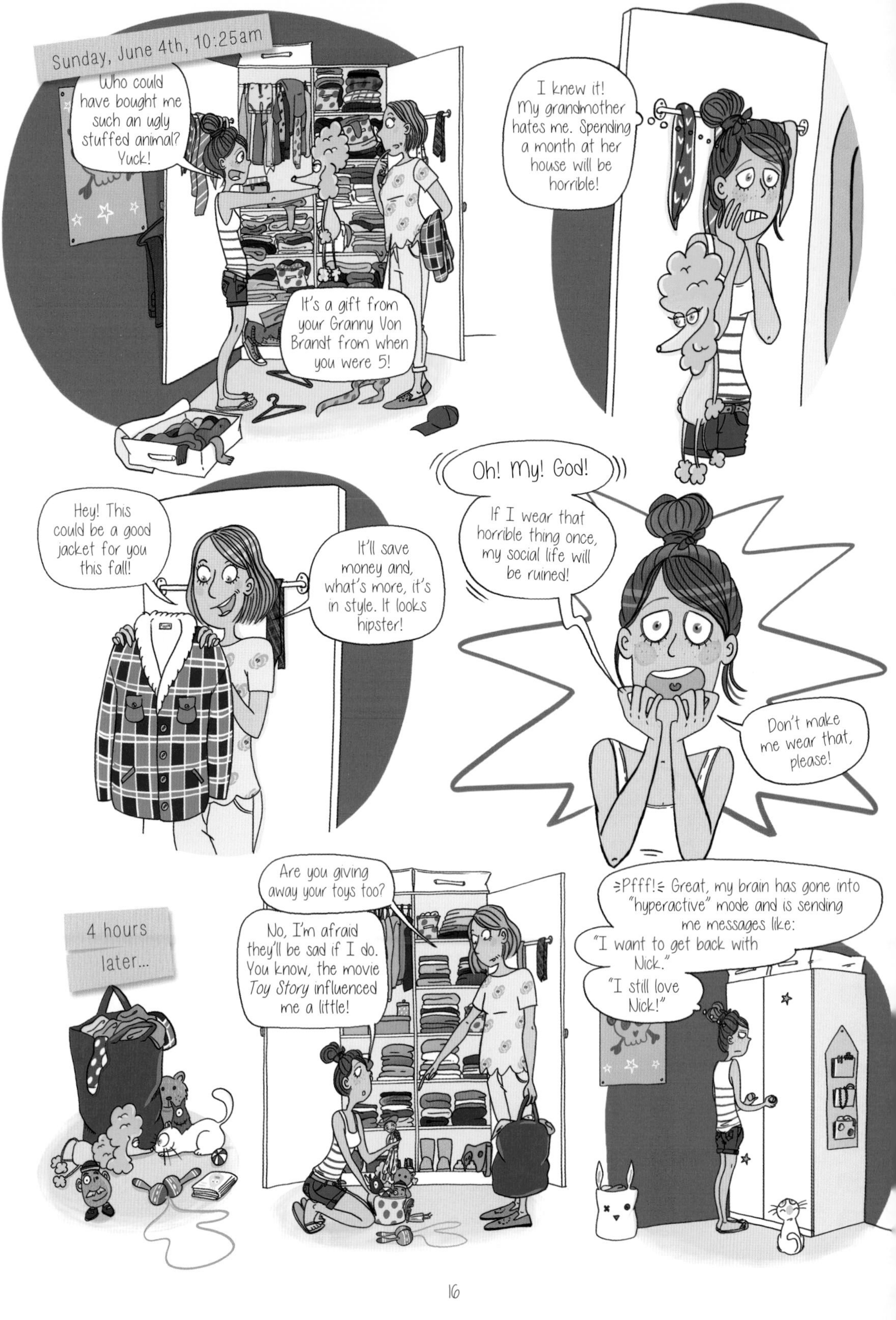
Sunday, June 4th, 10:25am
Who could have bought me such an ugly stuffed animal? Yuck!
It's a gift from your Granny Von Brandt from when you were 5!
I knew it! My grandmother hates me. Spending a month at her house will be horrible!
Hey! This could be a good jacket for you this fall!
It'll save money and, what's more, it's in style. It looks hipster!
Oh! My! God!
If I wear that horrible thing once, my social life will be ruined!
Don't make me wear that, please!
4 hours later...
Are you giving away your toys too?
No, I'm afraid they'll be sad if I do. You know, the movie *Toy Story* influenced me a little!
Pfff! Great, my brain has gone into "hyperactive" mode and is sending me messages like:
"I want to get back with Nick."
"I still love Nick!"

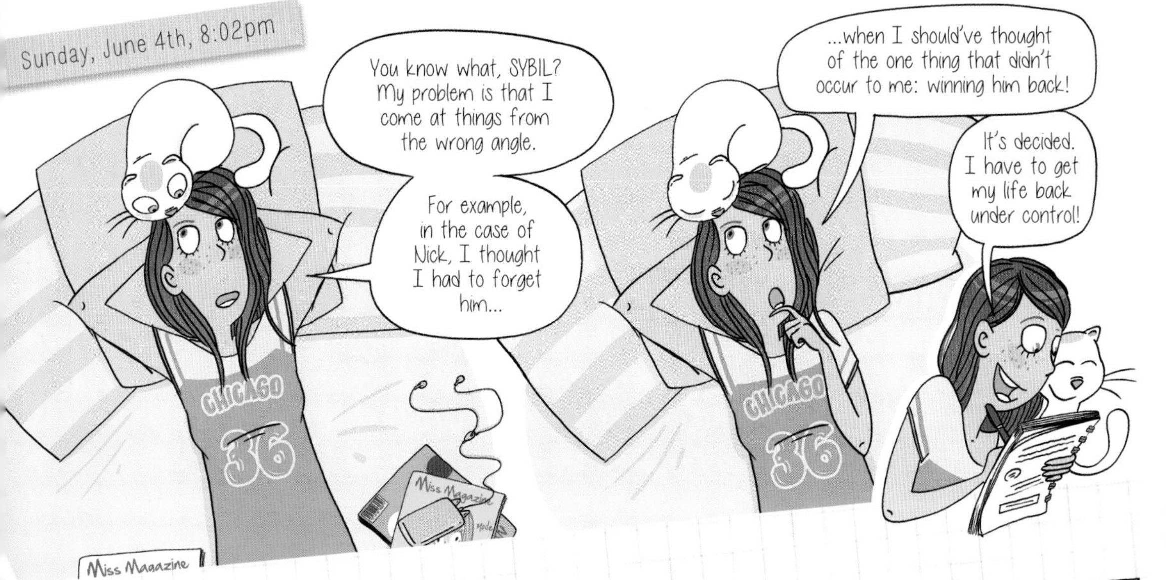
Sunday, June 4th, 8:02pm
You know what, SYBIL? My problem is that I come at things from the wrong angle.
For example, in the case of Nick, I thought I had to forget him...
...when I should've thought of the one thing that didn't occur to me: winning him back!
It's decided. I have to get my life back under control!
CHICAGO
36
Miss Magazine
Miss Magazine

- LIFE PLAN (for the moment):

① Win back Nick (real important).

② Reveal that Frank Blay is a fiend and, thereby, protect my mom from a horrible trip.

③ Pass my finals.

④ Match my mom up with Dennis Belcher (he'd go perfectly with my mom and, what's more, as my step-dad, he could give me the test questions in advance, which would make my passing school a whole lot easier).

⑤ Try to reduce my daily dose of chocolate a little (ever since the vomiting episode at the fair, I don't feel like stuffing my face all that much).

- WAYS TO REACH MY GOALS:

⑥ If technology permits, find a way to clone myself.

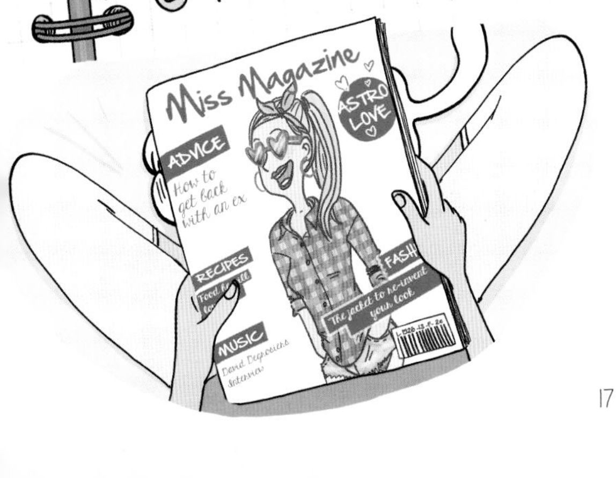
Miss Magazine
ASTRO LOVE
ADVICE
How to get back with an ex
RECIPES
MUSIC
The jacket to re-invent your look

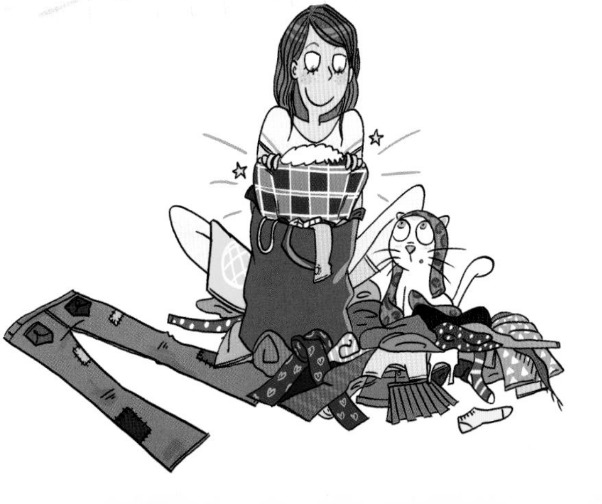

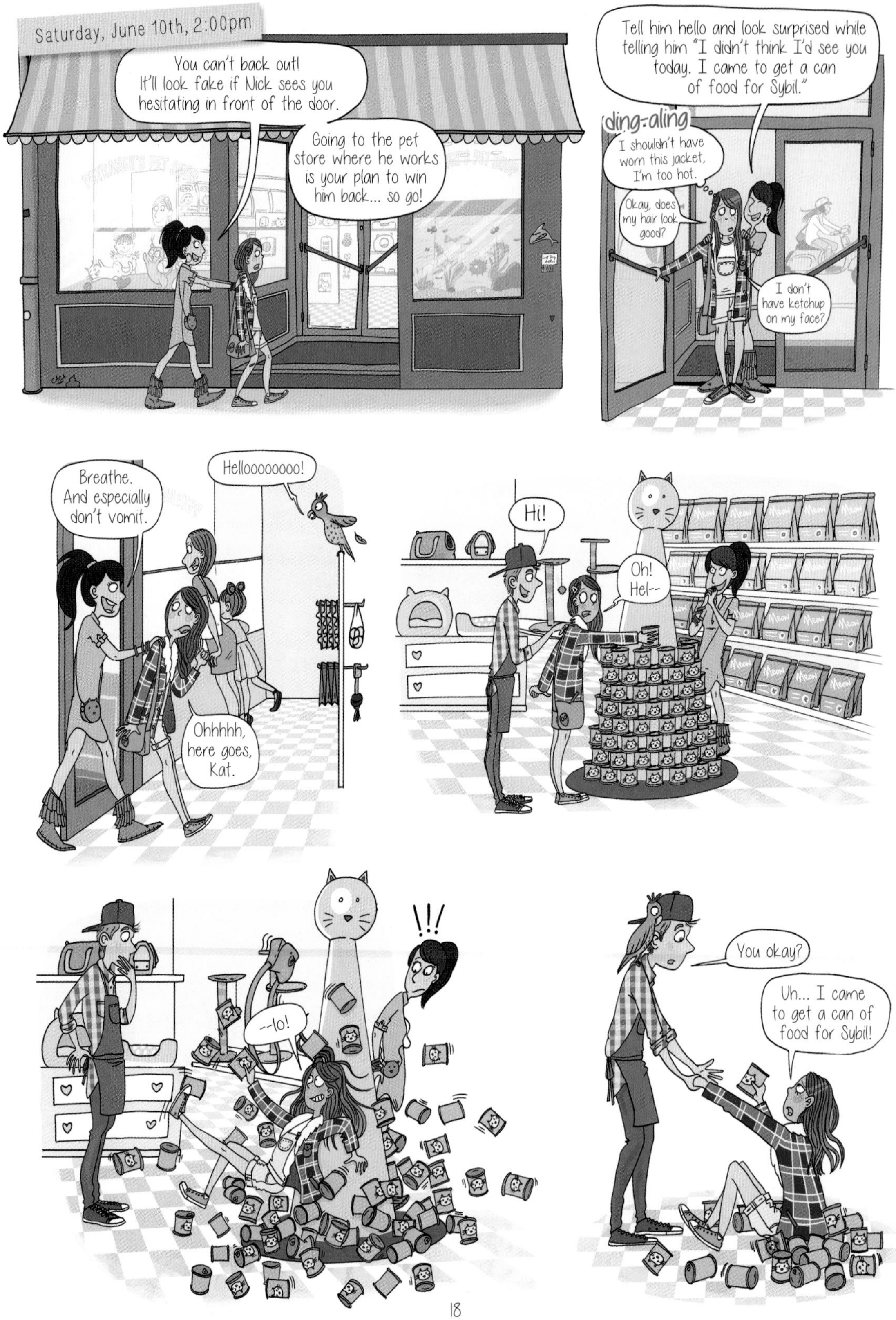

Saturday, June 10th, 2:00pm
You can't back out! It'll look fake if Nick sees you hesitating in front of the door.
Going to the pet store where he works is your plan to win him back... so go!
Tell him hello and look surprised while telling him "I didn't think I'd see you today. I came to get a can of food for Sybil."
ding-aling
I shouldn't have worn this jacket, I'm too hot.
Okay, does my hair look good?
I don't have ketchup on my face?
Breathe. And especially don't vomit.
Hellooooooooo!
Ohhhhh, here goes, Kat.
Hi!
Oh! Hel--
!!!
--lo!
You okay?
Uh... I came to get a can of food for Sybil!

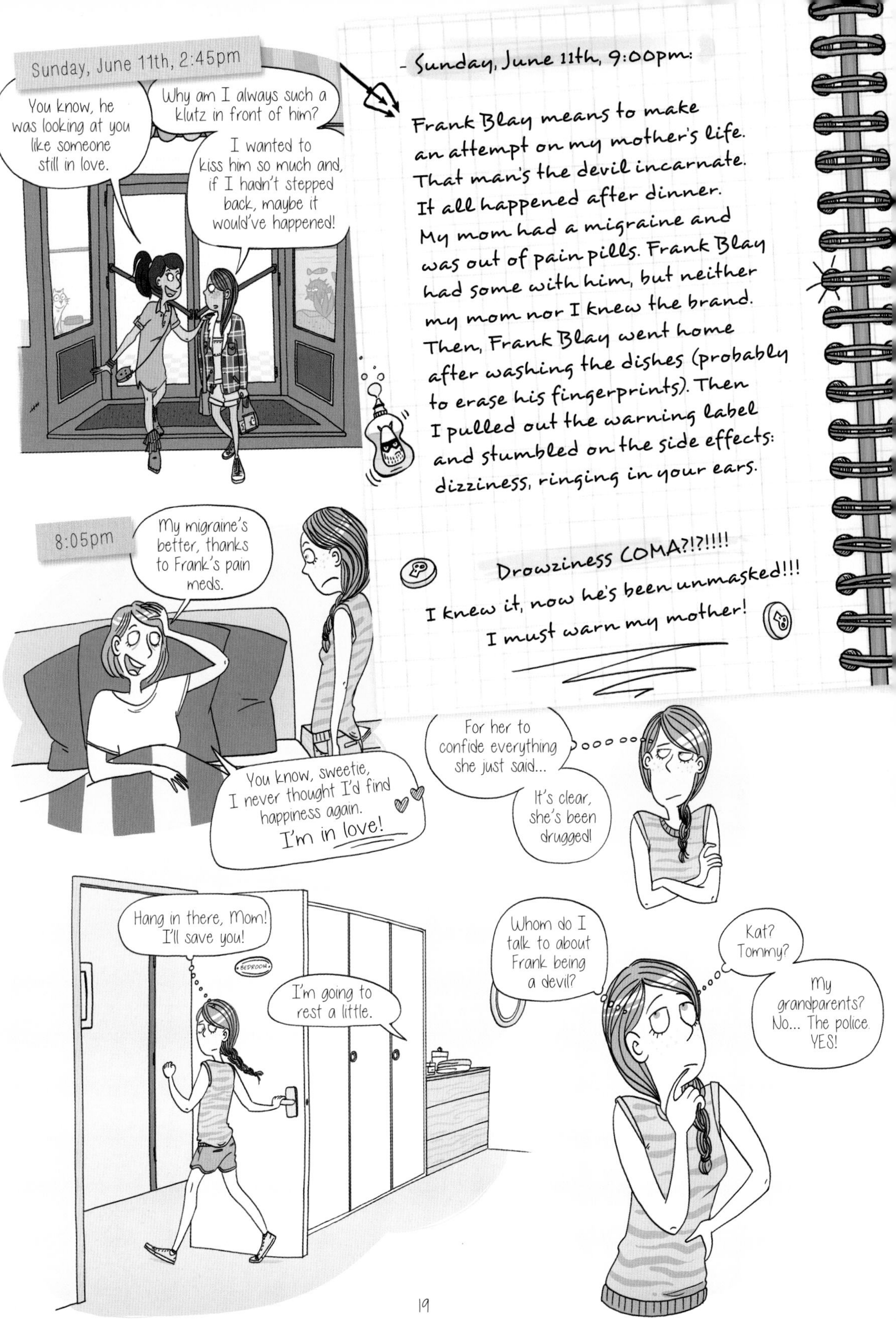
Sunday, June 11th, 2:45pm
You know, he was looking at you like someone still in love.
Why am I always such a klutz in front of him?
I wanted to kiss him so much and, if I hadn't stepped back, maybe it would've happened!
- Sunday, June 11th, 9:00pm:
Frank Blay means to make an attempt on my mother's life. That man's the devil incarnate. It all happened after dinner. My mom had a migraine and was out of pain pills. Frank Blay had some with him, but neither my mom nor I knew the brand. Then, Frank Blay went home after washing the dishes (probably to erase his fingerprints). Then I pulled out the warning label and stumbled on the side effects: dizziness, ringing in your ears.
Drowziness COMA?!?!!!!
I knew it, now he's been unmasked!!!
I must warn my mother!
8:05pm
My migraine's better, thanks to Frank's pain meds.
You know, sweetie, I never thought I'd find happiness again. I'm in love!
For her to confide everything she just said...
It's clear, she's been drugged!
Hang in there, Mom! I'll save you!
BEDROOM
I'm going to rest a little.
Whom do I talk to about Frank being a devil?
Kat? Tommy?
My grandparents? No... The police. YES!

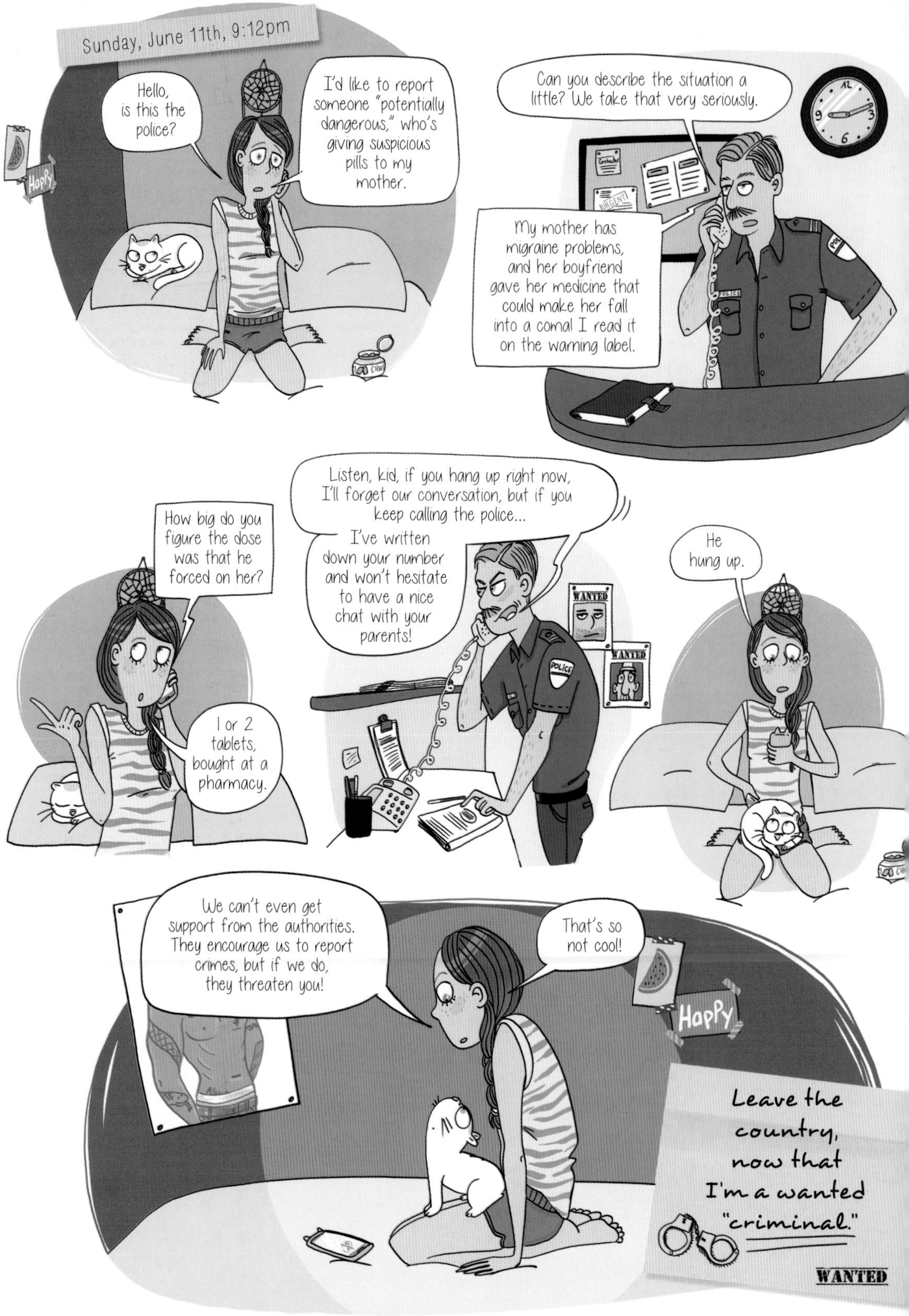
Sunday, June 11th, 9:12pm
Hello, is this the police?
I'd like to report someone "potentially dangerous," who's giving suspicious pills to my mother.
Happy
Can you describe the situation a little? We take that very seriously.
My mother has migraine problems, and her boyfriend gave her medicine that could make her fall into a coma! I read it on the warning label.
Contacts
URGENT
POLICE
How big do you figure the dose was that he forced on her?
1 or 2 tablets, bought at a pharmacy.
Listen, kid, if you hang up right now, I'll forget our conversation, but if you keep calling the police...
I've written down your number and won't hesitate to have a nice chat with your parents!
WANTED
WANTED
POLICE
He hung up.
We can't even get support from the authorities. They encourage us to report crimes, but if we do, they threaten you!
That's so not cool!
Happy
Leave the country, now that I'm a wanted "criminal."
WANTED

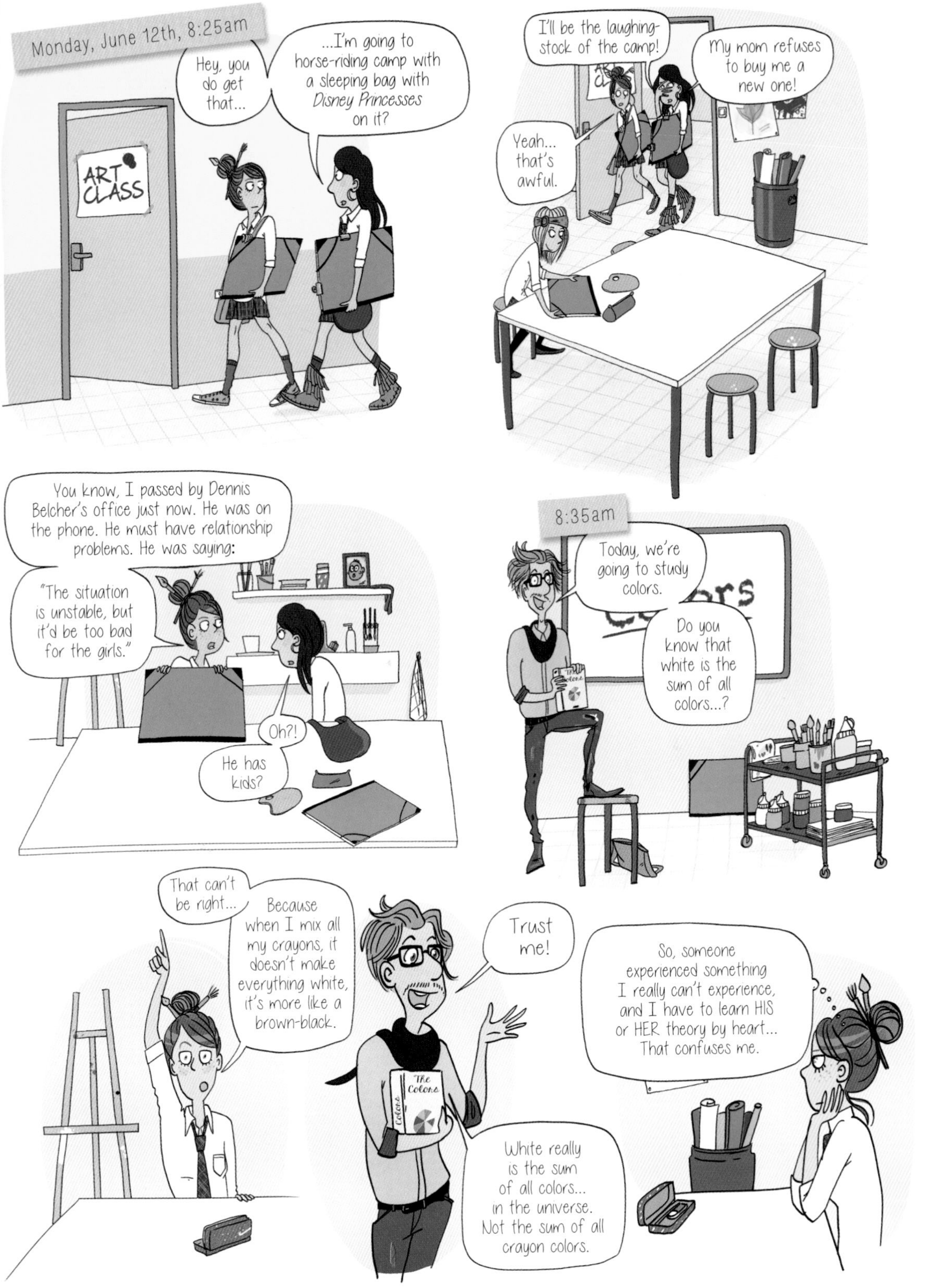
Monday, June 12th, 8:25am
ART CLASS
Hey, you do get that...
...I'm going to horse-riding camp with a sleeping bag with *Disney Princesses* on it?
I'll be the laughing-stock of the camp!
My mom refuses to buy me a new one!
Yeah... that's awful.
You know, I passed by Dennis Belcher's office just now. He was on the phone. He must have relationship problems. He was saying:
"The situation is unstable, but it'd be too bad for the girls."
Oh?!
He has kids?
8:35am
Today, we're going to study colors.
Do you know that white is the sum of all colors...?
That can't be right...
Because when I mix all my crayons, it doesn't make everything white, it's more like a brown-black.
Trust me!
White really is the sum of all colors... in the universe. Not the sum of all crayon colors.
So, someone experienced something I really can't experience, and I have to learn HIS or HER theory by heart... That confuses me.

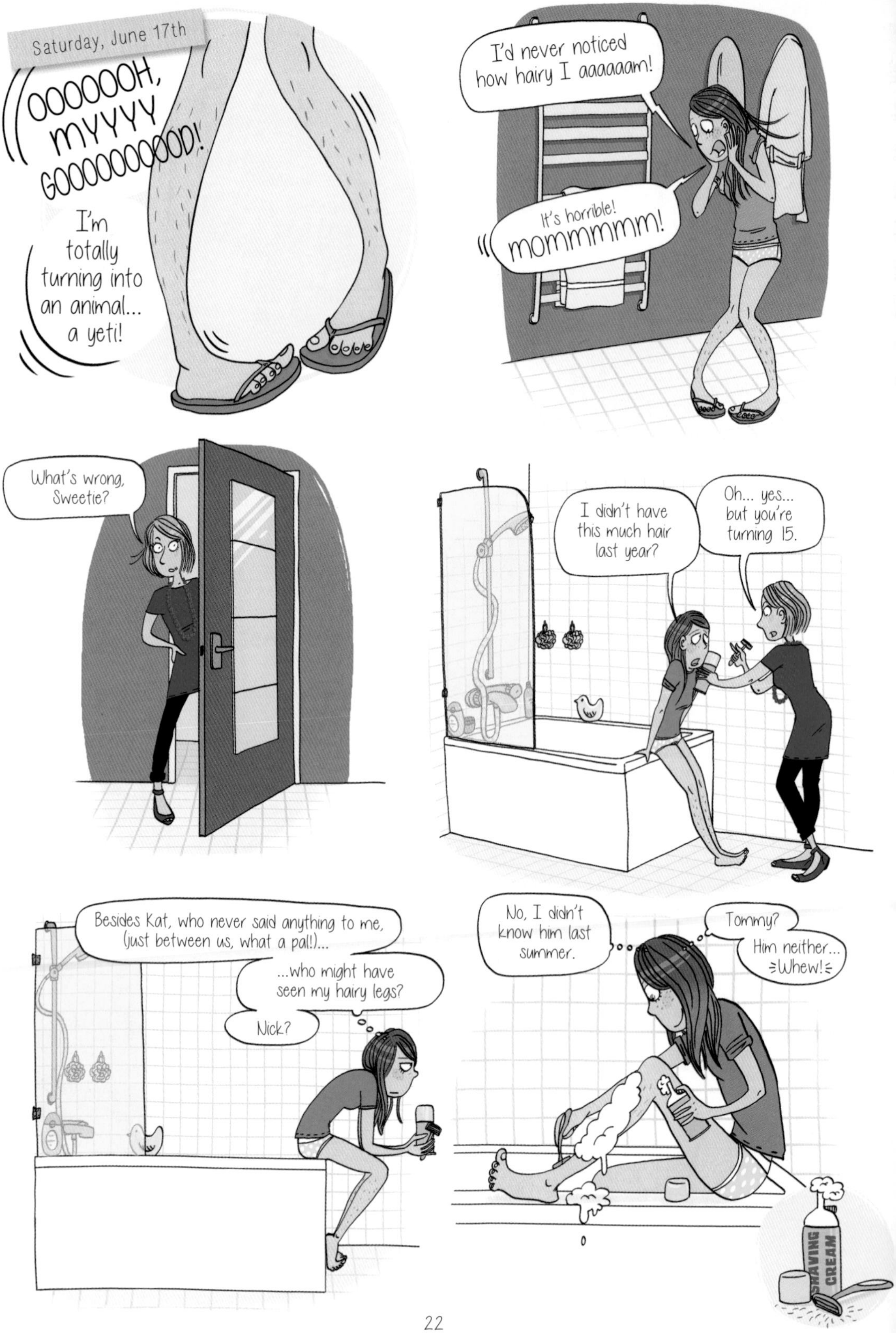
Saturday, June 17th
OOOOOOH, MYYYY GOOOOOOOOOD!
I'm totally turning into an animal... a yeti!
I'd never noticed how hairy I aaaaaam!
It's horrible! MOMMMMM!
What's wrong, Sweetie?
I didn't have this much hair last year?
Oh... yes... but you're turning 15.
Besides Kat, who never said anything to me, (just between us, what a pal!)...
...who might have seen my hairy legs?
Nick?
No, I didn't know him last summer.
Tommy?
Him neither... Whew!
SHAVING CREAM

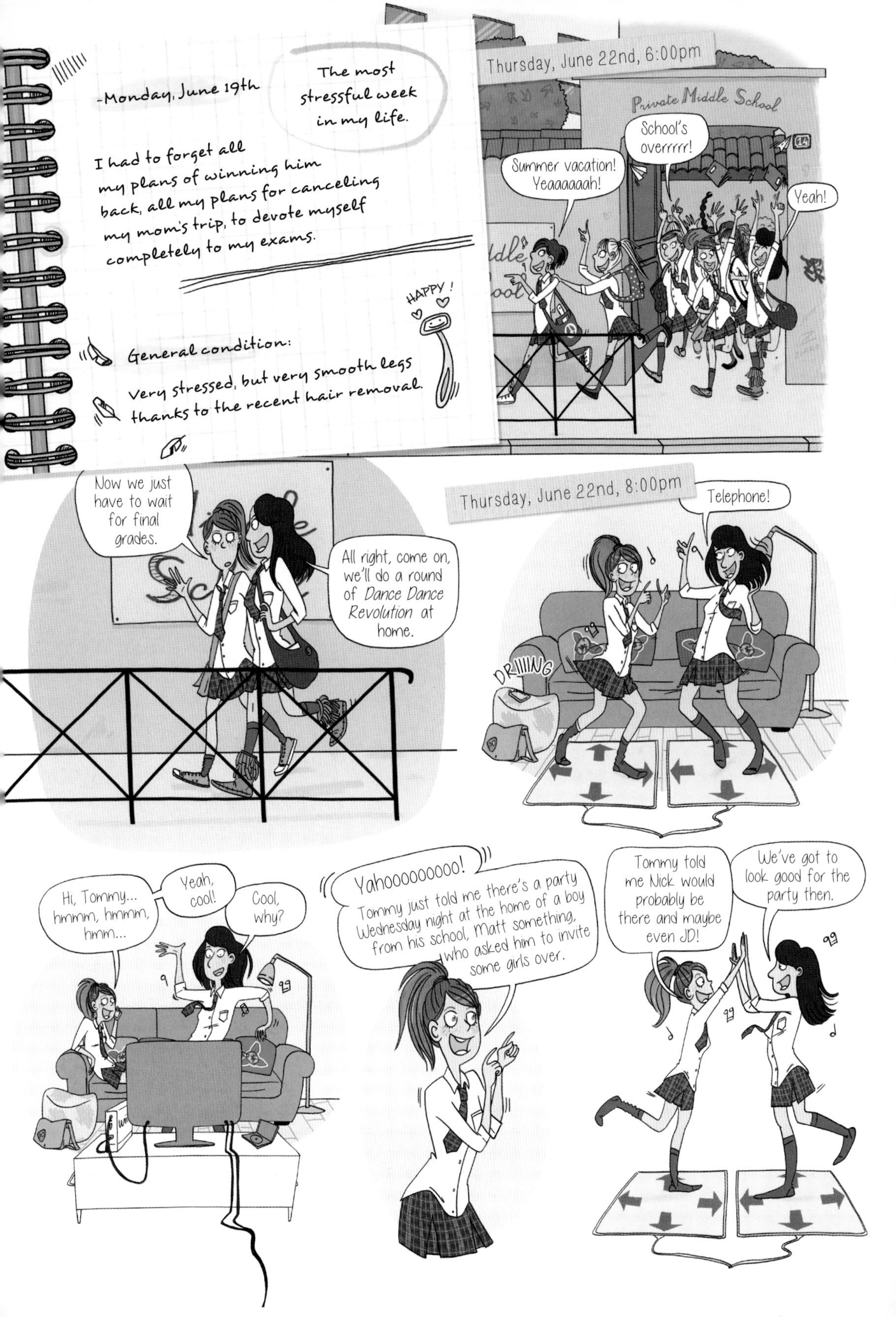

-Monday, June 19th
The most stressful week in my life.
I had to forget all my plans of winning him back, all my plans for canceling my mom's trip, to devote myself completely to my exams.
HAPPY !
General condition:
Very stressed, but very smooth legs thanks to the recent hair removal.
Thursday, June 22nd, 6:00pm
Private Middle School
Summer vacation! Yeaaaaaah!
School's overrrrrr!
Yeah!
Now we just have to wait for final grades.
All right, come on, we'll do a round of *Dance Dance Revolution* at home.
Thursday, June 22nd, 8:00pm
Telephone!
DRIIIING
Hi, Tommy... hmmm, hmmm, hmm...
Yeah, cool!
Cool, why?
Yahoooooooooo!
Tommy just told me there's a party Wednesday night at the home of a boy from his school, Matt something, who asked him to invite some girls over.
Tommy told me Nick would probably be there and maybe even JD!
We've got to look good for the party then.

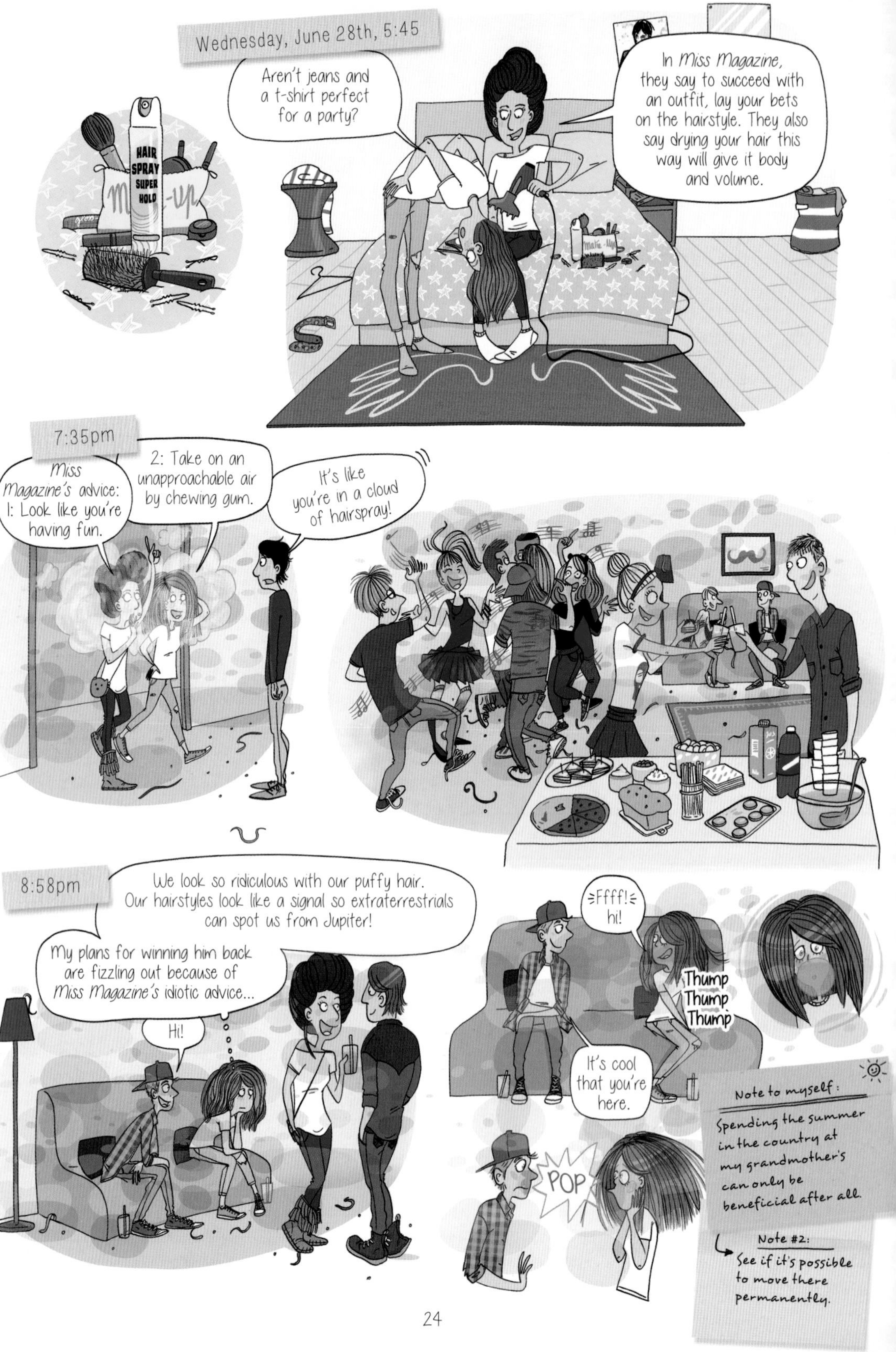
Wednesday, June 28th, 5:45
HAIR SPRAY SUPER HOLD
Aren't jeans and a t-shirt perfect for a party?
In Miss Magazine, they say to succeed with an outfit, lay your bets on the hairstyle. They also say drying your hair this way will give it body and volume.
7:35pm
Miss Magazine's advice: 1: Look like you're having fun.
2: Take on an unapproachable air by chewing gum.
It's like you're in a cloud of hairspray!
8:58pm
We look so ridiculous with our puffy hair. Our hairstyles look like a signal so extraterrestrials can spot us from Jupiter!
My plans for winning him back are fizzling out because of Miss Magazine's idiotic advice...
Hi!
Ffff! hi!
Thump Thump Thump
It's cool that you're here.
POP
Note to myself:
Spending the summer in the country at my grandmother's can only be beneficial after all.
Note #2:
See if it's possible to move there permanently.

WWWWWW - Sunday, July 2nd:

3:05pm:
So, so embarrassed! When I picture my chewing gum coated in saliva sliding down Nick's cheek... Chewing gum as a secret weapon of absolute charm!!! Nick took the chewing gum off his cheek and gave it back to me. Yup. Nick GAVE IT BACK! Every time I think about it, I hit my head against the wall...

Okay, one positive thing is that I asked Nick if he'd seen me at the fair the other day, and he said no. THANK YOU, THANK YOU, THANK YOU... He didn't see me puking into the trash can!

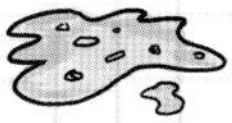

*Dear 11:11...
I'm making a wish

3:07pm:
On the other hand, when we played "spin the bottle" at the party, we sat down in a circle... I secretly prayed that, at the moment when it was Nick's turn or mine, the bottle would point towards us so we could kiss and he'd rediscover his love for me...

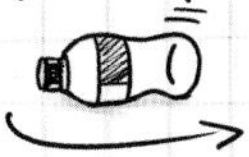

3:08pm:
But nope... it never works out like you'd want!!!
The bottle that Nick spun stopped in front of a super beautiful redhead (whose name is Lauren), and he was forced to kiss her...

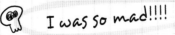

I was so mad!!!!

And I got mad again when Tommy spun the bottle and it stopped... on me and he said in front of everyone: "Hey, this game is stupid! I can't kiss Amy. She's my friend, I pass."

3:30pm: Okay, I have to pack my bag. Tomorrow I'm going on vacation to my grandmother's. I'm so excited (#not).

Note to myself:
I think he was trying
to make up for the
Music Plus episode
in front of Nick.
He's cool!

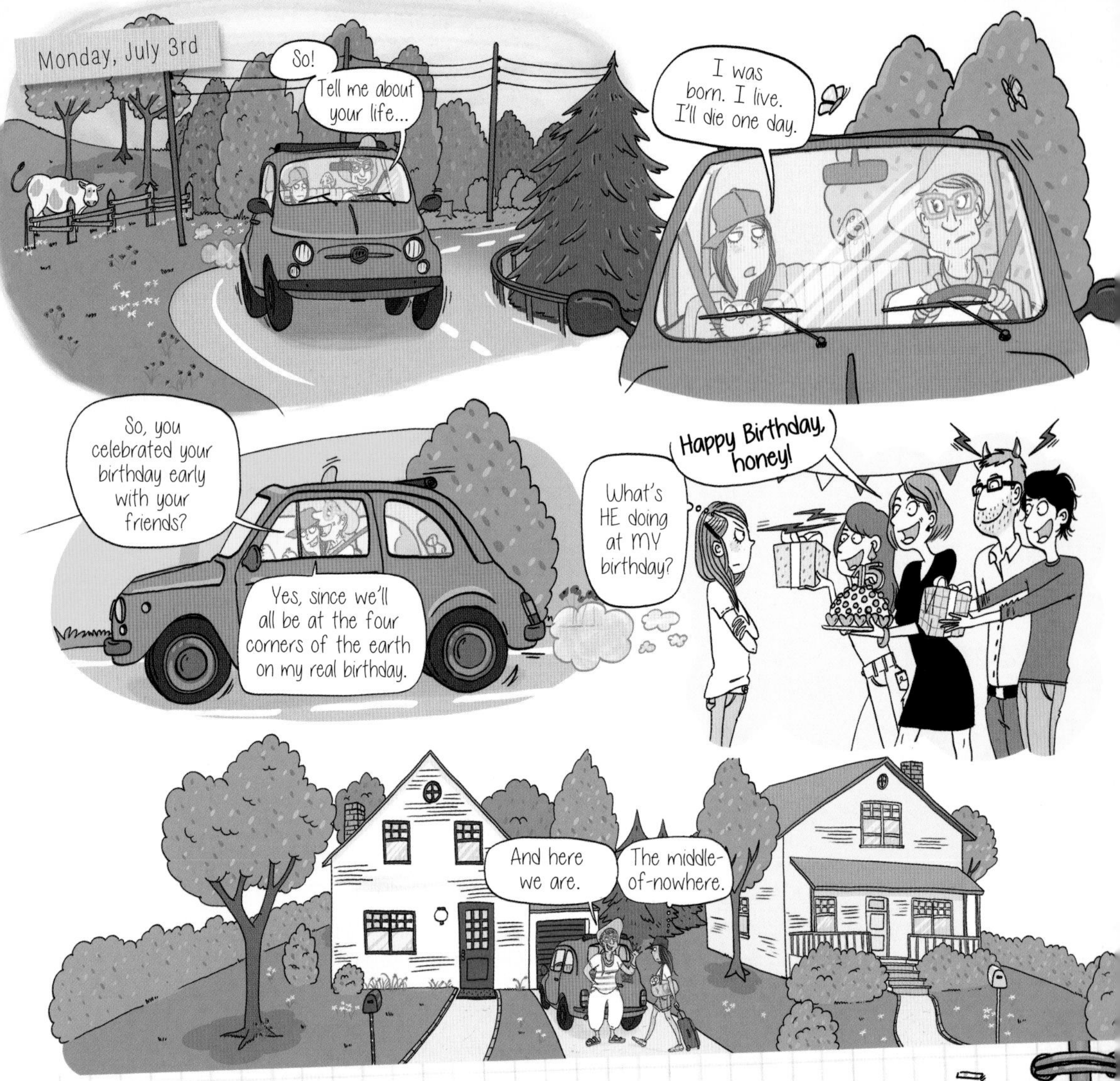
Monday, July 3rd
So!
Tell me about your life...
I was born. I live. I'll die one day.
So, you celebrated your birthday early with your friends?
Yes, since we'll all be at the four corners of the earth on my real birthday.
Happy Birthday, honey!
What's HE doing at MY birthday?
And here we are.
The middle-of-nowhere.

- Tuesday, July 4th, what I did today:
- Read a few magazines.
- Did all the "Special Tests" in Miss Magazine (except for the ones about love).
- Cleaned out Sybil's litterbox.
- Petted Sybil.
- Changed the décor of my bedroom a little to personalize it. I put up a poster of a sexy guy (my grandmother yelped when she saw it).
- Drank some chocolate milk.
- Walked around the house.
- Answered the phone (it was Monique, the neighbor).
- Helped Granny do the dishes (without a dishwasher).
- Listened to the clock ticking.
- Read my email (Tommy wrote to me to say hi).
- Got irritated by the clock's ticking.
- Chewed my fingernails.
- Went to bed.

Fiiiiiinally, one day down.

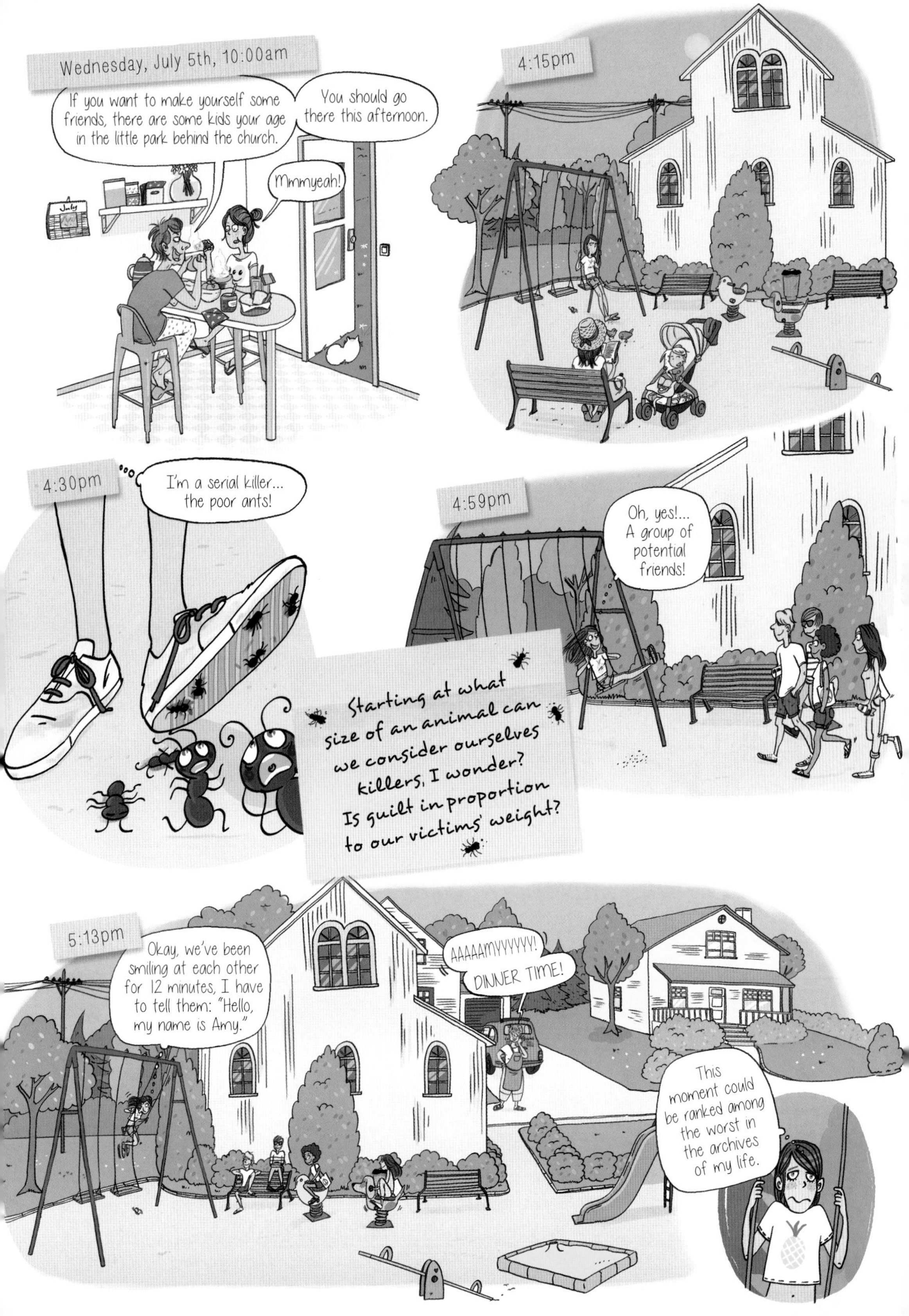
Wednesday, July 5th, 10:00am
If you want to make yourself some friends, there are some kids your age in the little park behind the church.
You should go there this afternoon.
Mmmyeah!
4:15pm
4:30pm
I'm a serial killer... the poor ants!
Starting at what size of an animal can we consider ourselves killers, I wonder? Is guilt in proportion to our victims' weight?
4:59pm
Oh, yes!... A group of potential friends!
5:13pm
Okay, we've been smiling at each other for 12 minutes, I have to tell them: "Hello, my name is Amy."
AAAAAMYYYYYY!
DINNER TIME!
This moment could be ranked among the worst in the archives of my life.

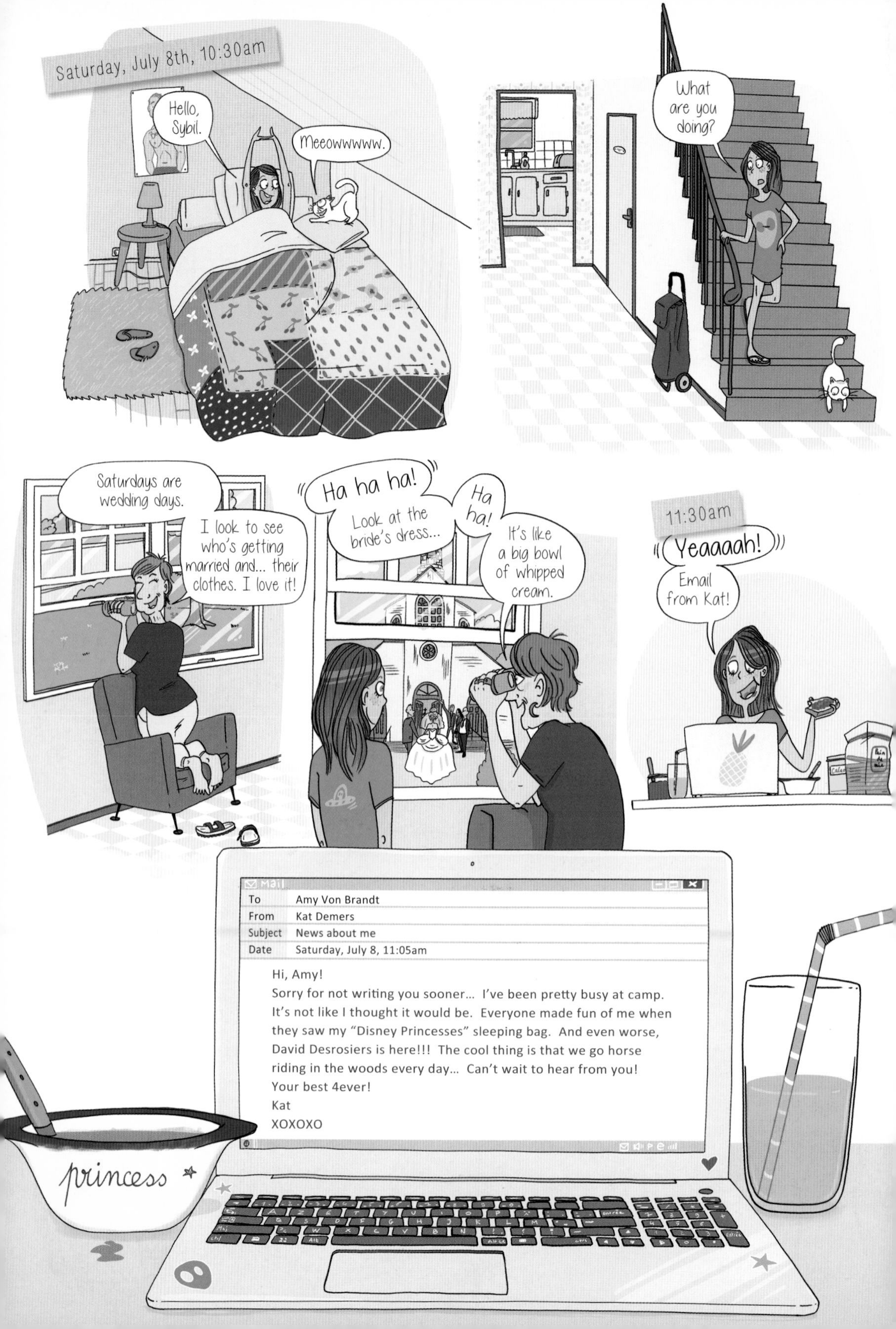
Saturday, July 8th, 10:30am
Hello, Sybil.
Meeowwwww.
What are you doing?
Saturdays are wedding days.
I look to see who's getting married and... their clothes. I love it!
Ha ha ha!
Look at the bride's dress...
Ha ha!
It's like a big bowl of whipped cream.
11:30am
Yeaaaah!
Email from Kat!
Mail
To Amy Von Brandt
From Kat Demers
Subject News about me
Date Saturday, July 8, 11:05am
Hi, Amy!
Sorry for not writing you sooner... I've been pretty busy at camp. It's not like I thought it would be. Everyone made fun of me when they saw my "Disney Princesses" sleeping bag. And even worse, David Desrosiers is here!!! The cool thing is that we go horse riding in the woods every day... Can't wait to hear from you!
Your best 4ever!
Kat
XOXOXO
princess

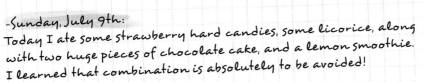

-Sunday, July 9th:
Today I ate some strawberry hard candies, some licorice, along with two huge pieces of chocolate cake, and a lemon smoothie. I learned that combination is absolutely to be avoided!

-Monday, July 10th:
While shopping at the grocery store with my grandmother, I got to the hair conditioner aisle. I sniffed every bottle. There were: scent of hay, lilacs, turf, and I didn't find Nick's scent. My grandmother told me they added pig pheromones to the conditioner. That's why she never buys any of it.
Conclusion: I'm not attracted to Nick's scent, but that of... pigs?!!??!!! **Yuuuuck!**

-Tuesday, July 11th:
Got an email from mom. She's in love with Paris... and... Gross and Double Gross... still in love with Frank Blay. Because of her email, I indulged in a chocolate bar.

Monday, July 17th, 12:00pm

Happy Birthday, honey!

Granny, your crepes are the best in the universe!

So, did you get tons of messages for your birthday?

Yes, and Mom's supposed to call tonight.

3:00pm

Could you go to the hardware store and buy me a new grill brush?

I'd like to make some nice kebabs tonight, and the grill's dirty.

A few minutes later...

It's my birthday, and I'm forced to run errands even though I hate that!

Hardware

Brushes
Waxes
Dyes
Chemicals
Insecticide

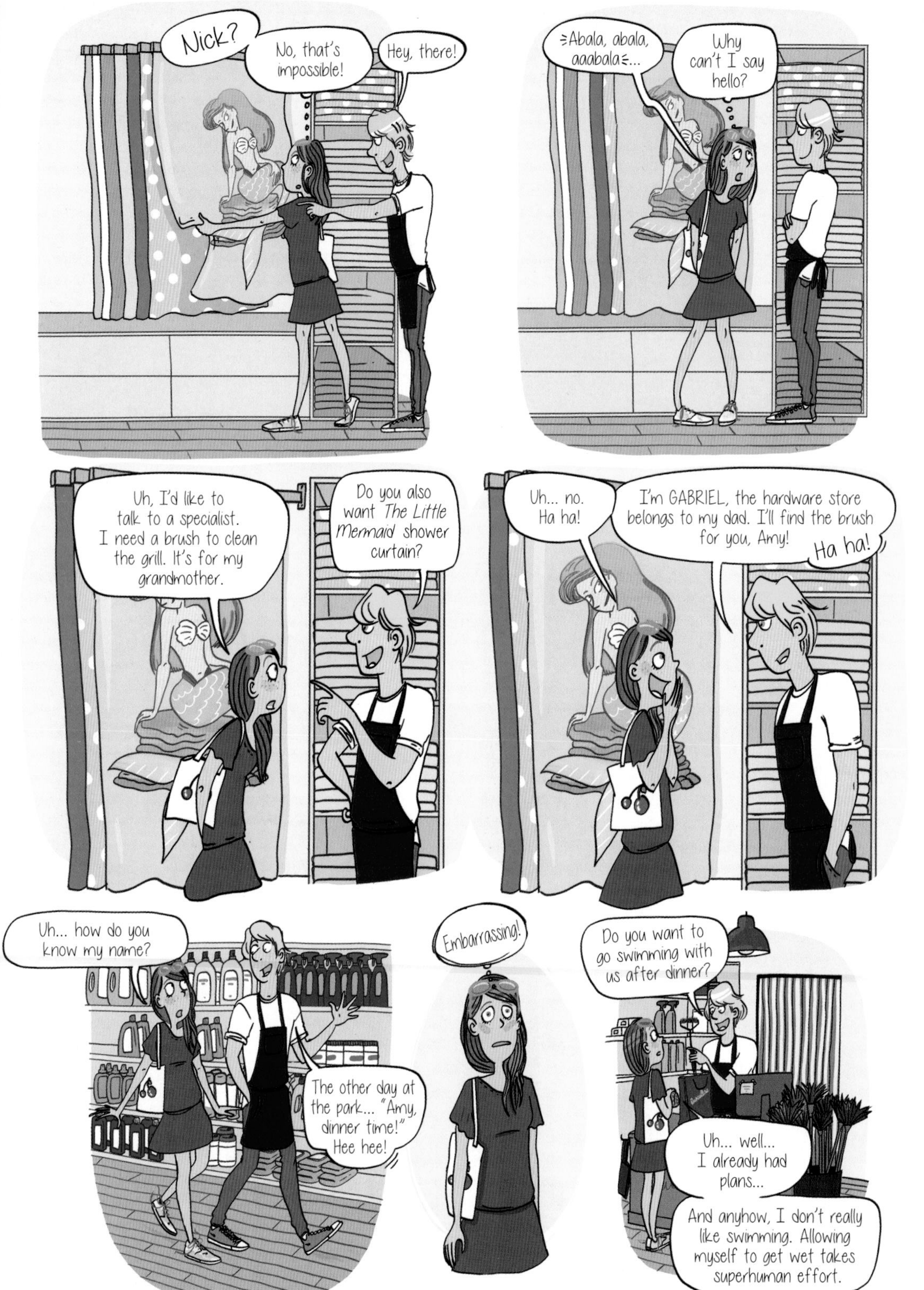
Nick?
No, that's impossible!
Hey, there!
≑Abala, abala, aaabala≑...
Why can't I say hello?
Uh, I'd like to talk to a specialist. I need a brush to clean the grill. It's for my grandmother.
Do you also want *The Little Mermaid* shower curtain?
Uh... no. Ha ha!
I'm GABRIEL, the hardware store belongs to my dad. I'll find the brush for you, Amy!
Ha ha!
Uh... how do you know my name?
The other day at the park... "Amy, dinner time!" Hee hee!
Embarrassing!
Do you want to go swimming with us after dinner?
Uh... well... I already had plans...
And anyhow, I don't really like swimming. Allowing myself to get wet takes superhuman effort.

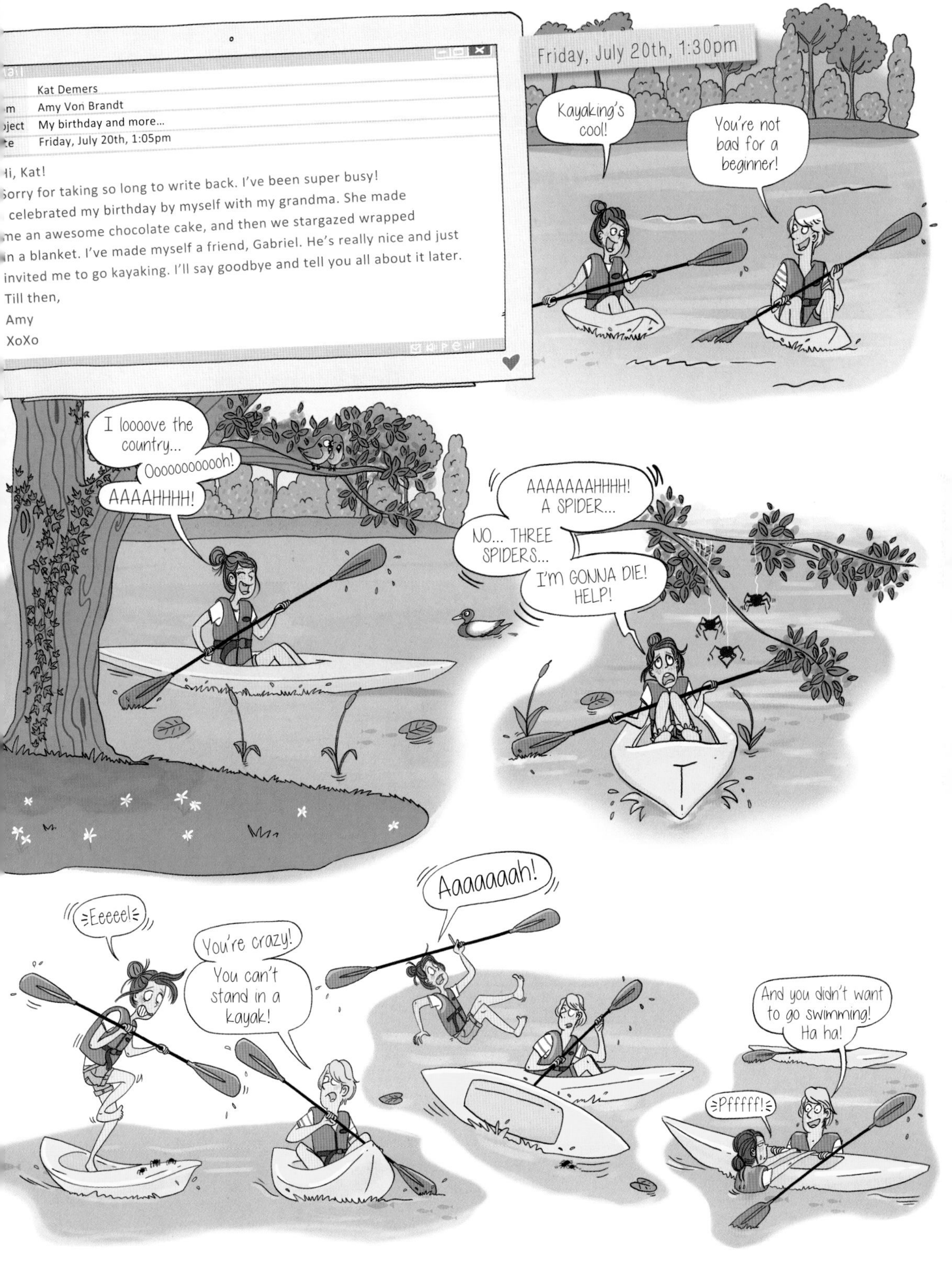
Kat Demers
Amy Von Brandt
My birthday and more...
Friday, July 20th, 1:05pm
Hi, Kat!
Sorry for taking so long to write back. I've been super busy!
I celebrated my birthday by myself with my grandma. She made me an awesome chocolate cake, and then we stargazed wrapped in a blanket. I've made myself a friend, Gabriel. He's really nice and just invited me to go kayaking. I'll say goodbye and tell you all about it later.
Till then,
Amy
XoXo
Friday, July 20th, 1:30pm
Kayaking's cool!
You're not bad for a beginner!
I loooove the country...
Ooooooooooooh!
AAAAHHHH!
AAAAAAAHHHH! A SPIDER...
NO... THREE SPIDERS...
I'M GONNA DIE! HELP!
Eeeee!
You're crazy!
You can't stand in a kayak!
Aaaaaaah!
And you didn't want to go swimming! Ha ha!
Pfffff!

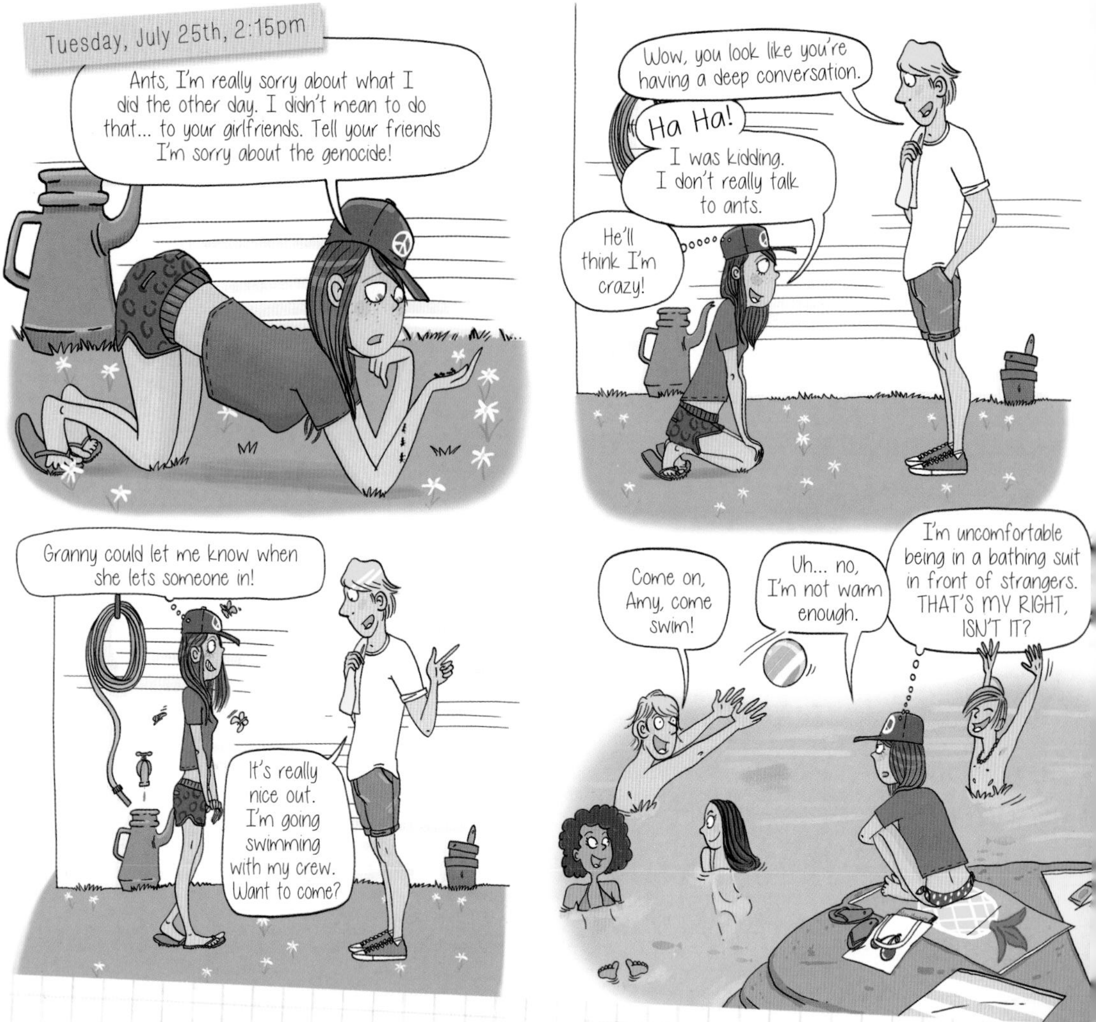
Tuesday, July 25th, 2:15pm
Ants, I'm really sorry about what I did the other day. I didn't mean to do that... to your girlfriends. Tell your friends I'm sorry about the genocide!
Wow, you look like you're having a deep conversation.
Ha Ha!
I was kidding. I don't really talk to ants.
He'll think I'm crazy!
Granny could let me know when she lets someone in!
It's really nice out. I'm going swimming with my crew. Want to come?
Come on, Amy, come swim!
Uh... no, I'm not warm enough.
I'm uncomfortable being in a bathing suit in front of strangers. THAT'S MY RIGHT, ISN'T IT?

-Tuesday, July 25th, 9:00pm

Gabriel is cool. I went back to the lake this afternoon, I put on my bikini, and he told me I shouldn't be uncomfortable being in a bathing suit because he thinks I'm "beautiful." I told him I'd come back in a few days, and he invited me to his cousin's wedding on Saturday.

Note: Find myself a beautiful dress.

Note to myself: Thinking about school before the end of July isn't good for my personal mental balance. Remember that.

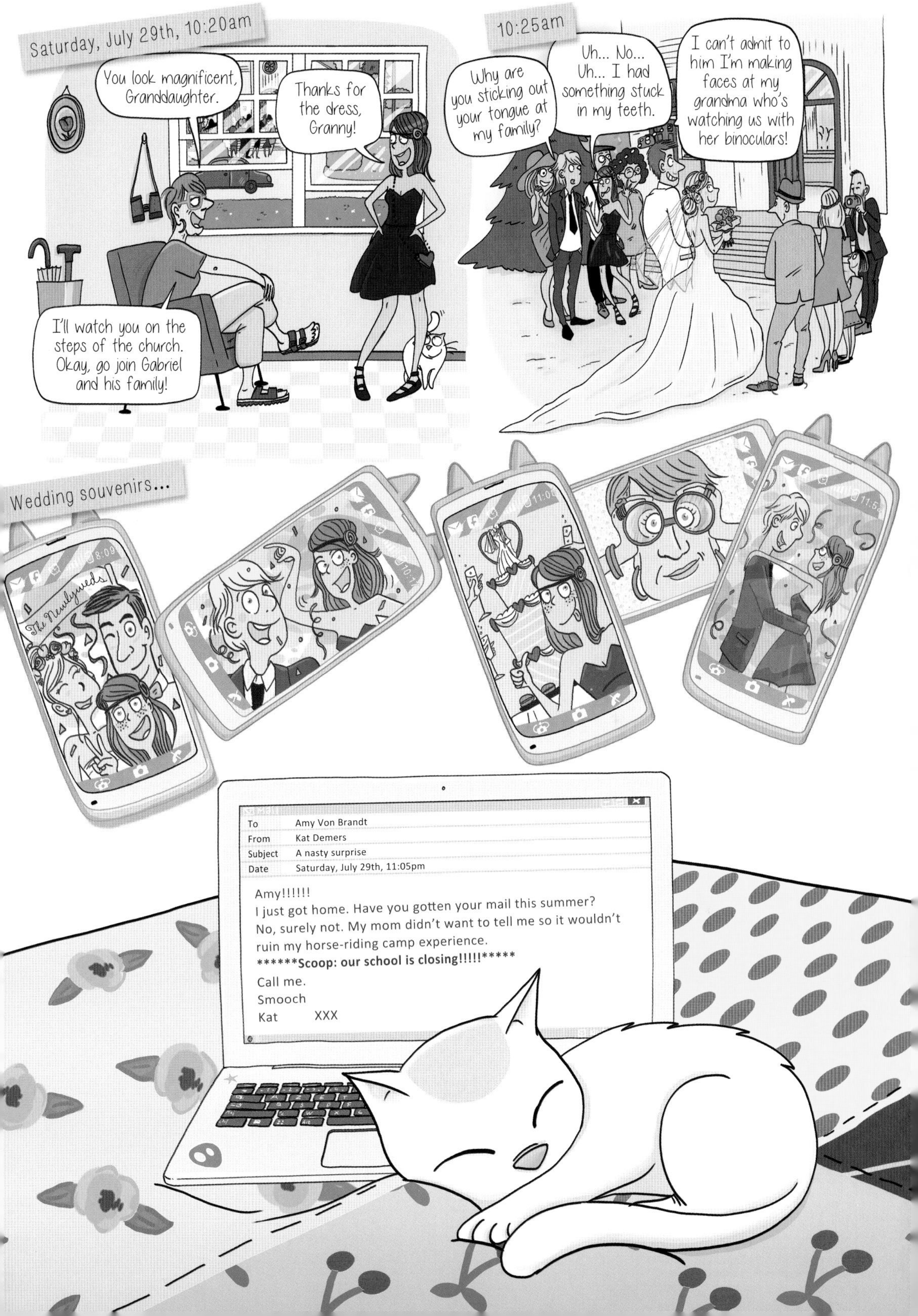
Saturday, July 29th, 10:20am
You look magnificent, Granddaughter.
Thanks for the dress, Granny!
I'll watch you on the steps of the church. Okay, go join Gabriel and his family!
10:25am
Why are you sticking out your tongue at my family?
Uh... No... Uh... I had something stuck in my teeth.
I can't admit to him I'm making faces at my grandma who's watching us with her binoculars!
Wedding souvenirs...
The Newlyweds
To Amy Von Brandt
From Kat Demers
Subject A nasty surprise
Date Saturday, July 29th, 11:05pm
Amy!!!!!!
I just got home. Have you gotten your mail this summer?
No, surely not. My mom didn't want to tell me so it wouldn't ruin my horse-riding camp experience.
******Scoop: our school is closing!!!!!*****
Call me.
Smooch
Kat XXX

AUGUST

The big clean-up

-Tuesday, August 1st

1:05pm:
BREEEEATHE! BREEEEATHE! BREEEEATHE!
Don't panic. Don't panic! Do. Not. Panic. Weirdly, for some time now, I'd felt like my life was on "pause." That I was living another life, parallel to my own, and that after leaving here, I'd find everything like it was before, just as I'd left it.

But, NO! It's like, while I was on "pause," everything happened at an accelerated speed.

1:07pm
Everyone got a letter signed by Dennis Belcher, explaining that the school was experiencing financial difficulties, bla-bla-bla, budget shortfalls, bla-bla-bla, and that the students might be transferred to another private school or placed in the public high school closest to their homes.

1:09pm

80% IN LANGUAGE ARTS

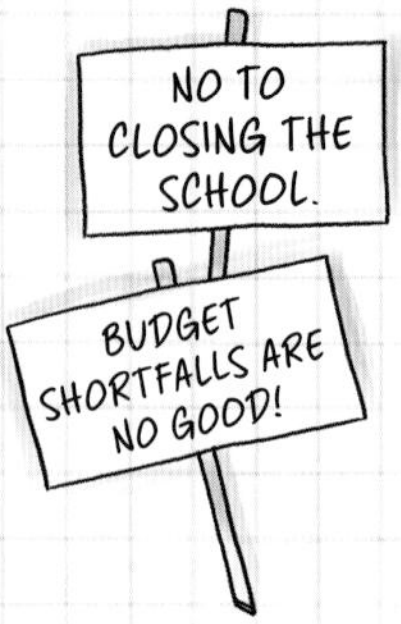
NO TO CLOSING THE SCHOOL.
BUDGET SHORTFALLS ARE NO GOOD!

I'm mad at the girls who protested against school uniforms!
I hold them responsible for the school's closing!

1:10pm
I'm mad at Dennis Belcher, too. He could've done something.

I'M MAD AT THE WHOLE EARTH!

1:12pm
In fact, it's all my fault. The school is closing because of me. Because, let's say, of my paranormal powers... I'd wished that... I'd said the only thing I wished for in the universe was that Nick didn't see me puking. And HE DIDN'T SEE ME puke = paranormal powers.

BREEEEATHE
BREEEEATHE
BREEEETHE

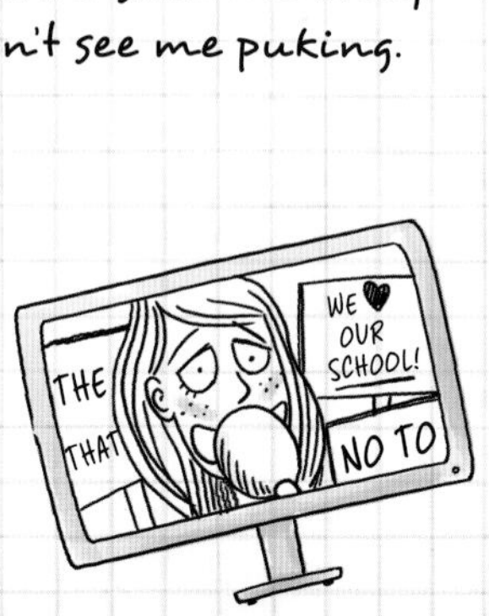
WE ♥ OUR SCHOOL!
THE
THAT
NO TO

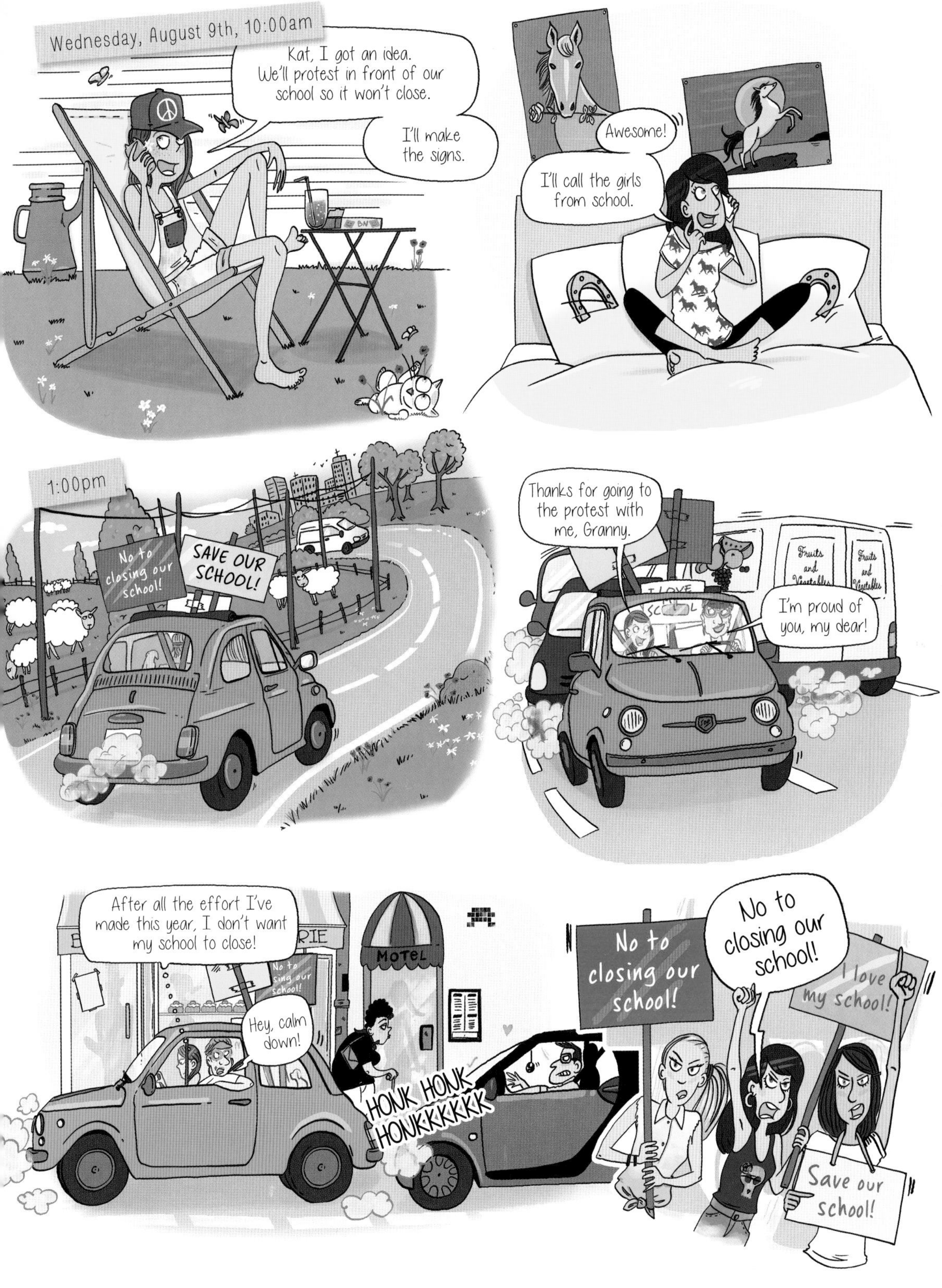
Wednesday, August 9th, 10:00am
Kat, I got an idea. We'll protest in front of our school so it won't close.
I'll make the signs.
Awesome!
I'll call the girls from school.
1:00pm
No to closing our school!
SAVE OUR SCHOOL!
Thanks for going to the protest with me, Granny.
Fruits and Vegetables
Fruits and Vegetables
I'm proud of you, my dear!
After all the effort I've made this year, I don't want my school to close!
MOTEL
Hey, calm down!
HONK HONK HONKKKKKK
No to closing our school!
No to closing our school!
I love my school!
Save our school!

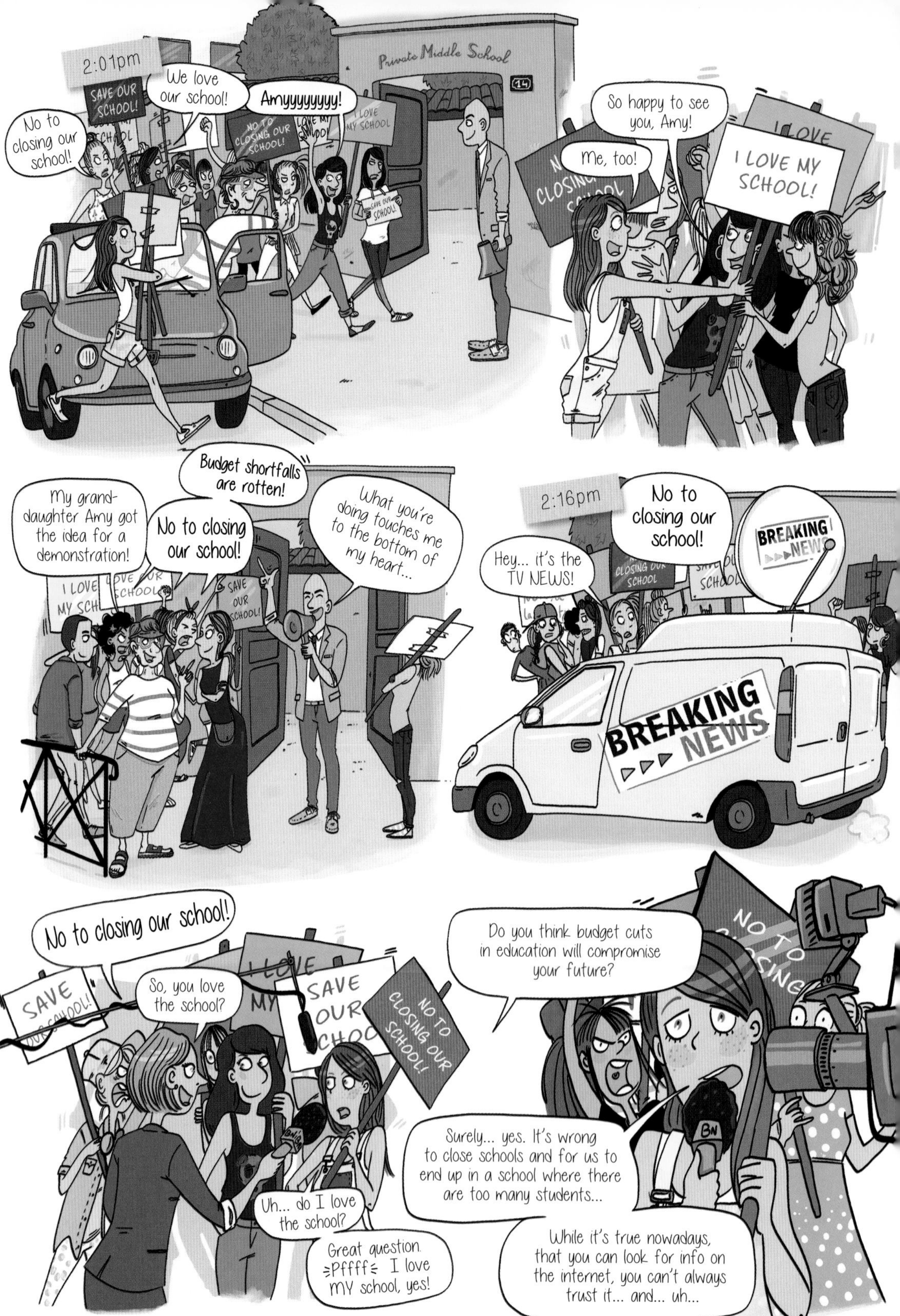
2:01pm
Private Middle School
SAVE OUR SCHOOL!
No to closing our school!
We love our school!
NO TO CLOSING OUR SCHOOL!
Amyyyyyyyy!
I LOVE MY SCHOOL
SAVE OUR SCHOOL!
So happy to see you, Amy!
Me, too!
I LOVE MY SCHOOL!
Budget shortfalls are rotten!
My grand-daughter Amy got the idea for a demonstration!
No to closing our school!
What you're doing touches me to the bottom of my heart...
I LOVE MY SCH
LOVE OUR SCHOOL
SAVE OUR SCHOOL!
2:16pm
No to closing our school!
Hey... it's the TV NEWS!
BREAKING NEWS
BREAKING NEWS
No to closing our school!
SAVE OUR SCHOOL!
I LOVE MY
SAVE OUR SCHOO
NO TO CLOSING OUR SCHOOL!
So, you love the school?
Uh... do I love the school?
Great question. Pffff I love MY school, yes!
Do you think budget cuts in education will compromise your future?
Surely... yes. It's wrong to close schools and for us to end up in a school where there are too many students...
While it's true nowadays, that you can look for info on the internet, you can't always trust it... and... uh...

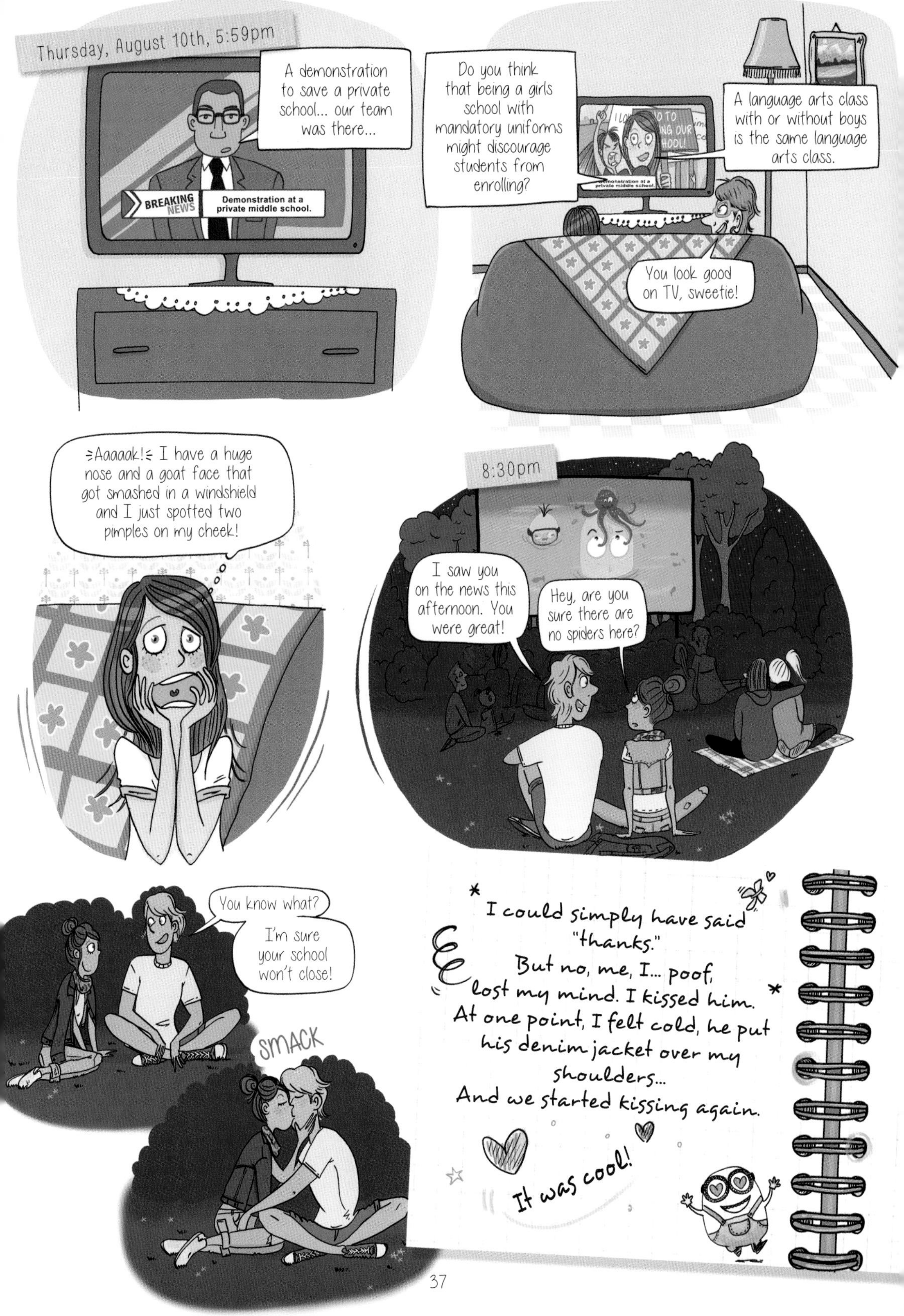

Thursday, August 10th, 5:59pm
A demonstration to save a private school... our team was there...
BREAKING NEWS
Demonstration at a private middle school.
Do you think that being a girls school with mandatory uniforms might discourage students from enrolling?
A language arts class with or without boys is the same language arts class.
You look good on TV, sweetie!
≋Aaaaak!≋ I have a huge nose and a goat face that got smashed in a windshield and I just spotted two pimples on my cheek!
8:30pm
I saw you on the news this afternoon. You were great!
Hey, are you sure there are no spiders here?
You know what?
I'm sure your school won't close!
SMACK
I could simply have said "thanks."
But no, me, I... poof, lost my mind. I kissed him.
At one point, I felt cold, he put his denim jacket over my shoulders...
And we started kissing again.
It was cool!

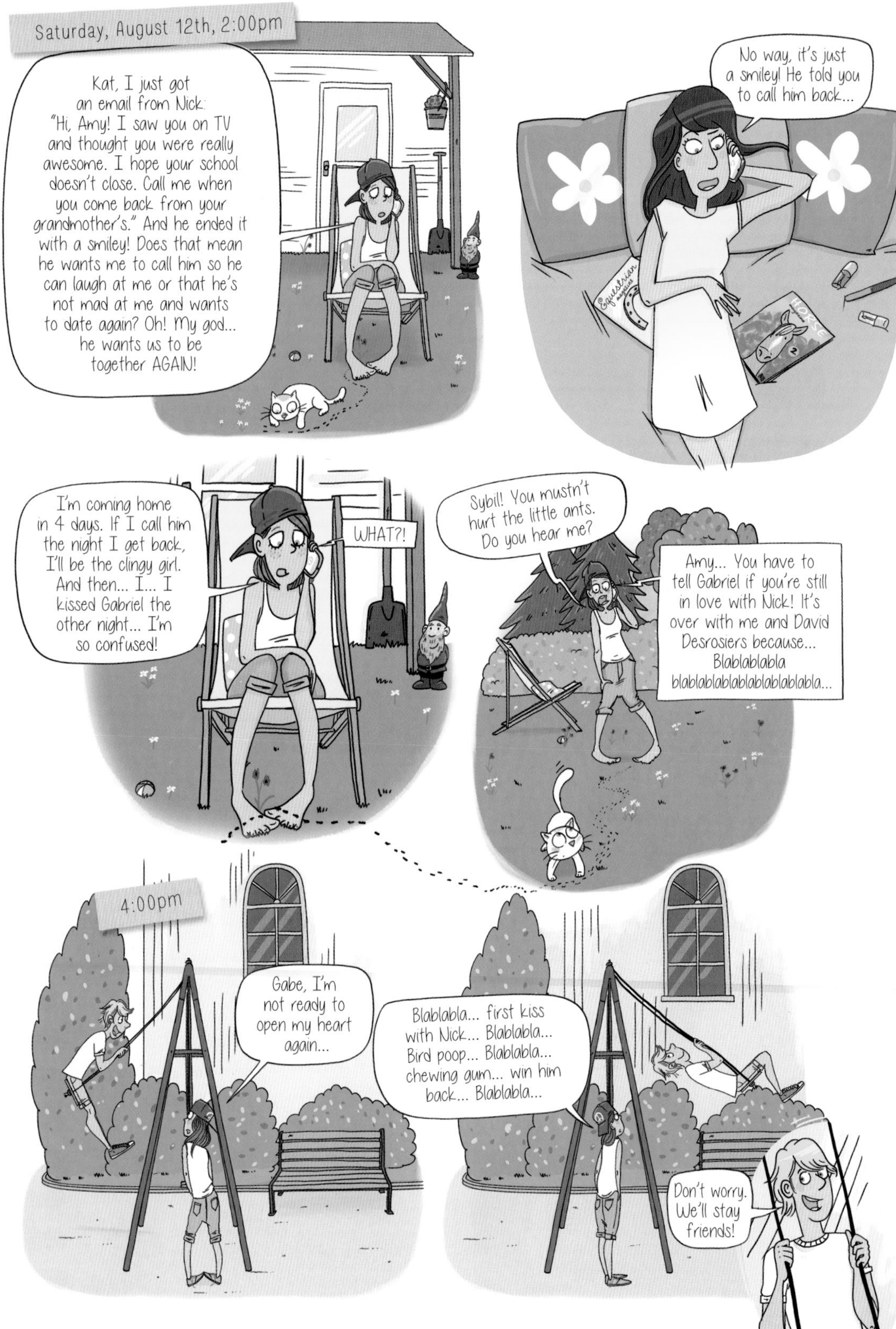

Saturday, August 12th, 2:00pm
Kat, I just got an email from Nick: "Hi, Amy! I saw you on TV and thought you were really awesome. I hope your school doesn't close. Call me when you come back from your grandmother's." And he ended it with a smiley! Does that mean he wants me to call him so he can laugh at me or that he's not mad at me and wants to date again? Oh! My god... he wants us to be together AGAIN!
No way, it's just a smiley! He told you to call him back...
I'm coming home in 4 days. If I call him the night I get back, I'll be the clingy girl. And then... I... I kissed Gabriel the other night... I'm so confused!
WHAT?!
Sybil! You mustn't hurt the little ants. Do you hear me?
Amy... You have to tell Gabriel if you're still in love with Nick! It's over with me and David Desrosiers because... Blablablabla blablablablablablablablabla...
4:00pm
Gabe, I'm not ready to open my heart again...
Blablabla... first kiss with Nick... Blablabla... Bird poop... Blablabla... chewing gum... win him back... Blablabla...
Don't worry. We'll stay friends!

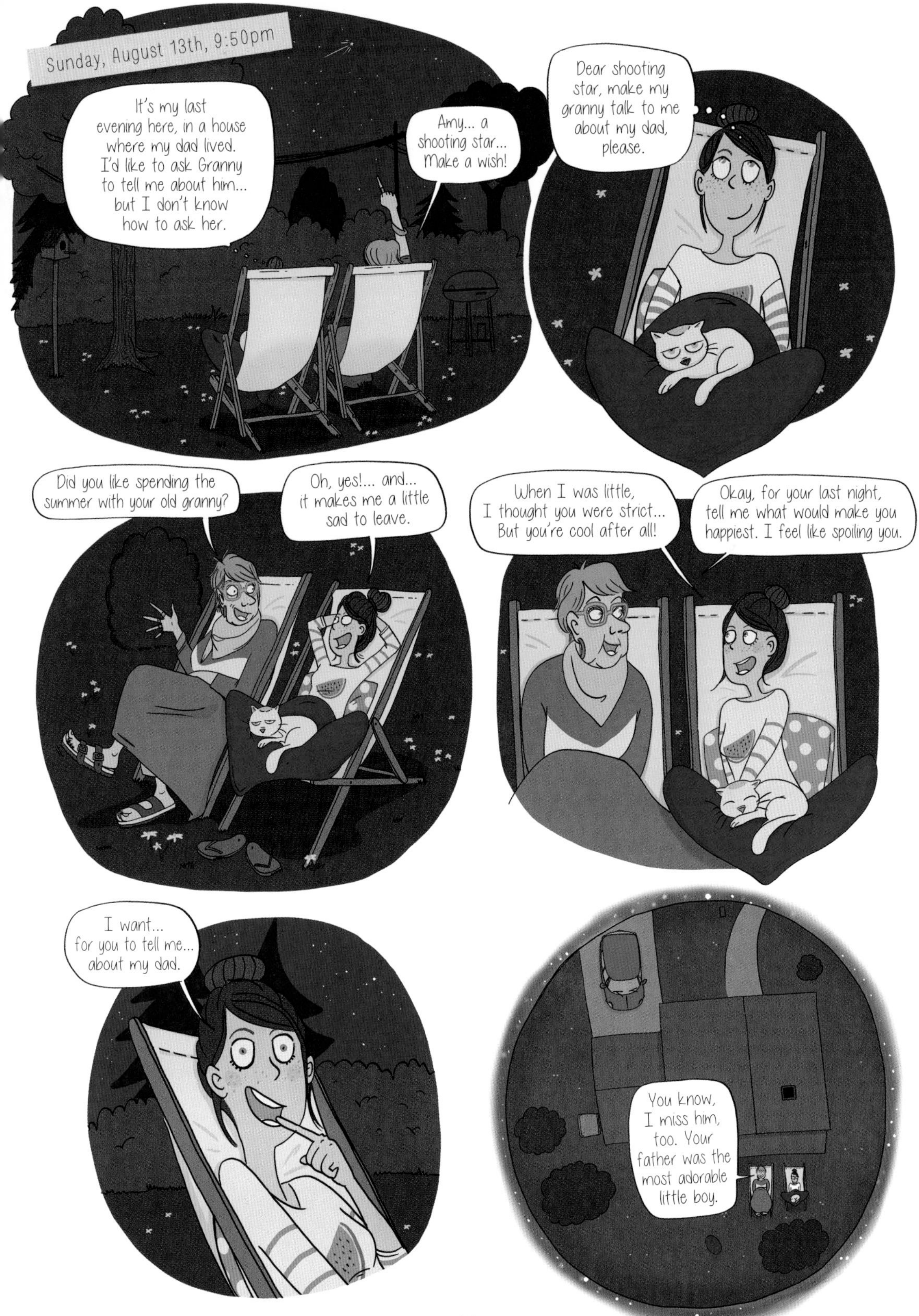
Sunday, August 13th, 9:50pm
It's my last evening here, in a house where my dad lived. I'd like to ask Granny to tell me about him... but I don't know how to ask her.
Amy... a shooting star... Make a wish!
Dear shooting star, make my granny talk to me about my dad, please.
Did you like spending the summer with your old granny?
Oh, yes!... and... it makes me a little sad to leave.
When I was little, I thought you were strict... But you're cool after all!
Okay, for your last night, tell me what would make you happiest. I feel like spoiling you.
I want... for you to tell me... about my dad.
You know, I miss him, too. Your father was the most adorable little boy.

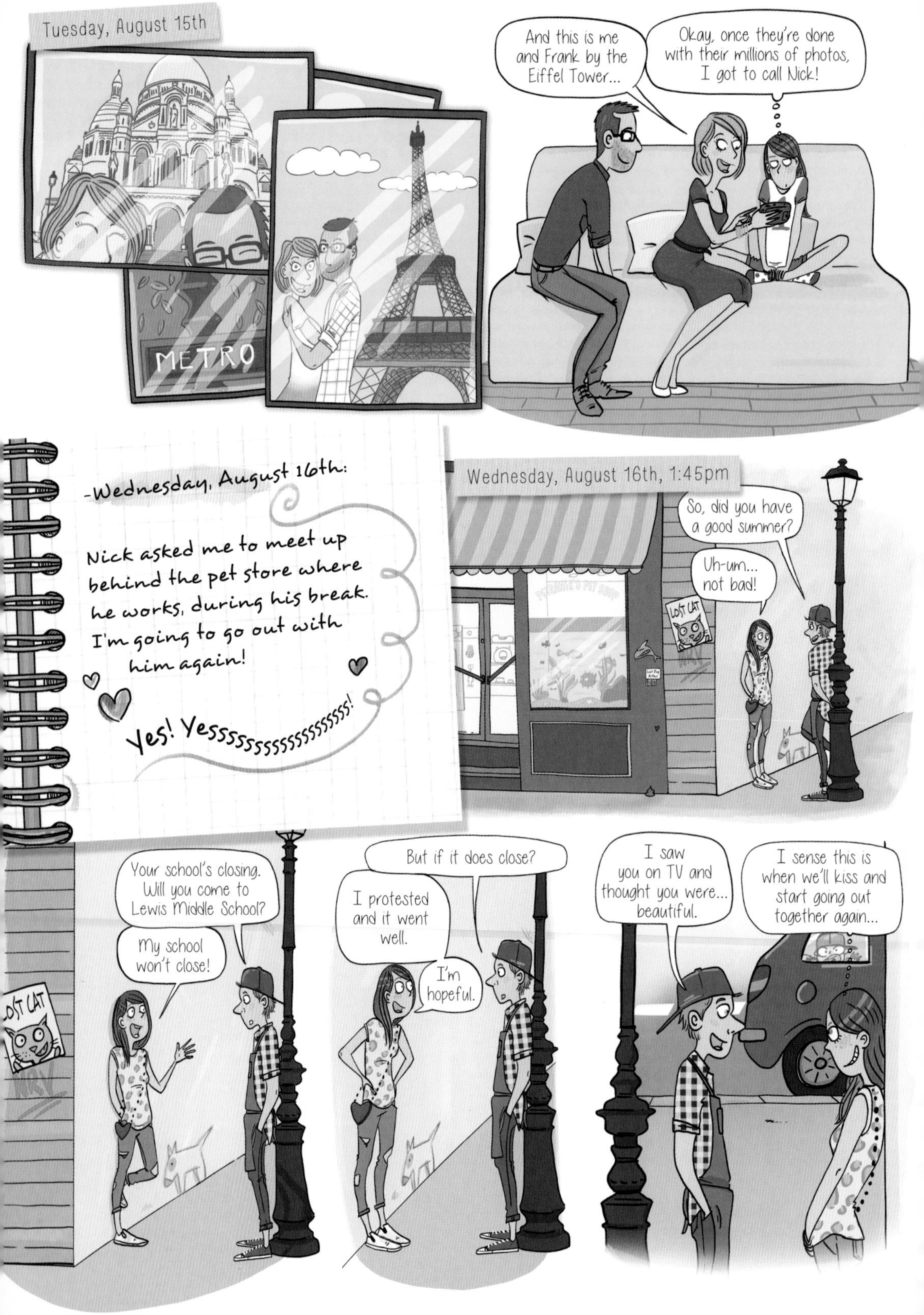
Tuesday, August 15th
METRO
And this is me and Frank by the Eiffel Tower...
Okay, once they're done with their millions of photos, I got to call Nick!
-Wednesday, August 16th:
Nick asked me to meet up behind the pet store where he works, during his break. I'm going to go out with him again!
Yes! Yessssssssssssssss!
Wednesday, August 16th, 1:45pm
So, did you have a good summer?
Uh-um... not bad!
LOST CAT
Your school's closing. Will you come to Lewis Middle School?
My school won't close!
LOST CAT
But if it does close?
I protested and it went well.
I'm hopeful.
I saw you on TV and thought you were... beautiful.
I sense this is when we'll kiss and start going out together again...

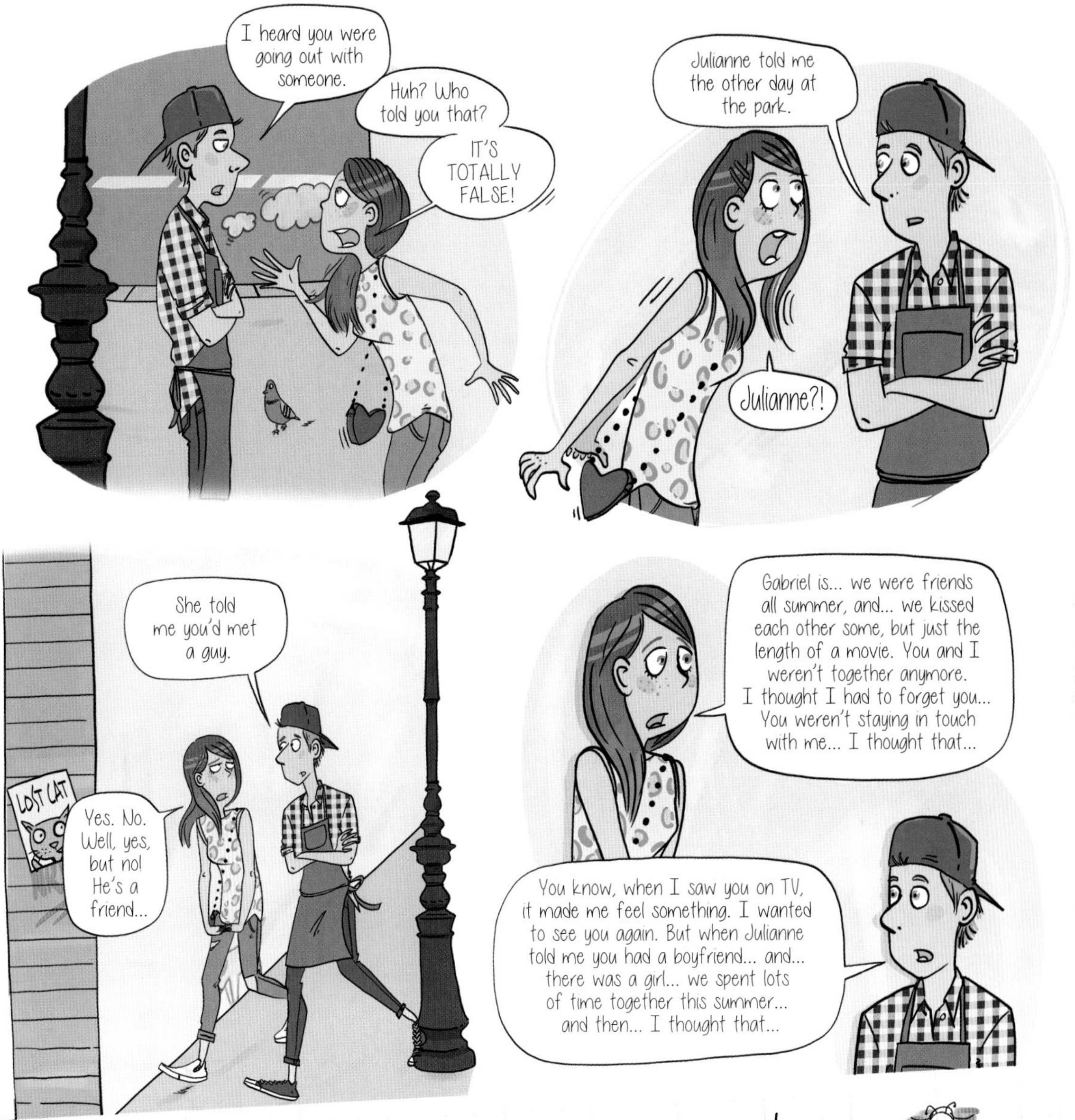
I heard you were going out with someone.
Huh? Who told you that?
IT'S TOTALLY FALSE!
Julianne told me the other day at the park.
Julianne?!
She told me you'd met a guy.
LOST CAT
Yes. No. Well, yes, but no! He's a friend...
Gabriel is... we were friends all summer, and... we kissed each other some, but just the length of a movie. You and I weren't together anymore. I thought I had to forget you... You weren't staying in touch with me... I thought that...
You know, when I saw you on TV, it made me feel something. I wanted to see you again. But when Julianne told me you had a boyfriend... and... there was a girl... we spent lots of time together this summer... and then... I thought that...

I ran to Kat's to tell her that, if her sister were an ant, I'd smash her without hesitation! Kat and I cornered Julianne against a wall. She admitted she'd listened in on our conversation on the phone. And she did it to defend me when she saw Nick in the park talking with a girl. She ruined my chance to go out with Nick again!

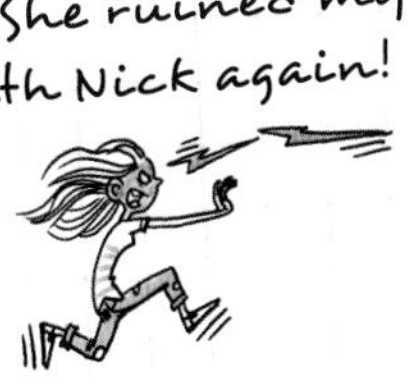

Public service announcement to the whole wide world:

HIS SMILEY REALLY DID MEAN HE WANTED TO GET BACK WITH ME!

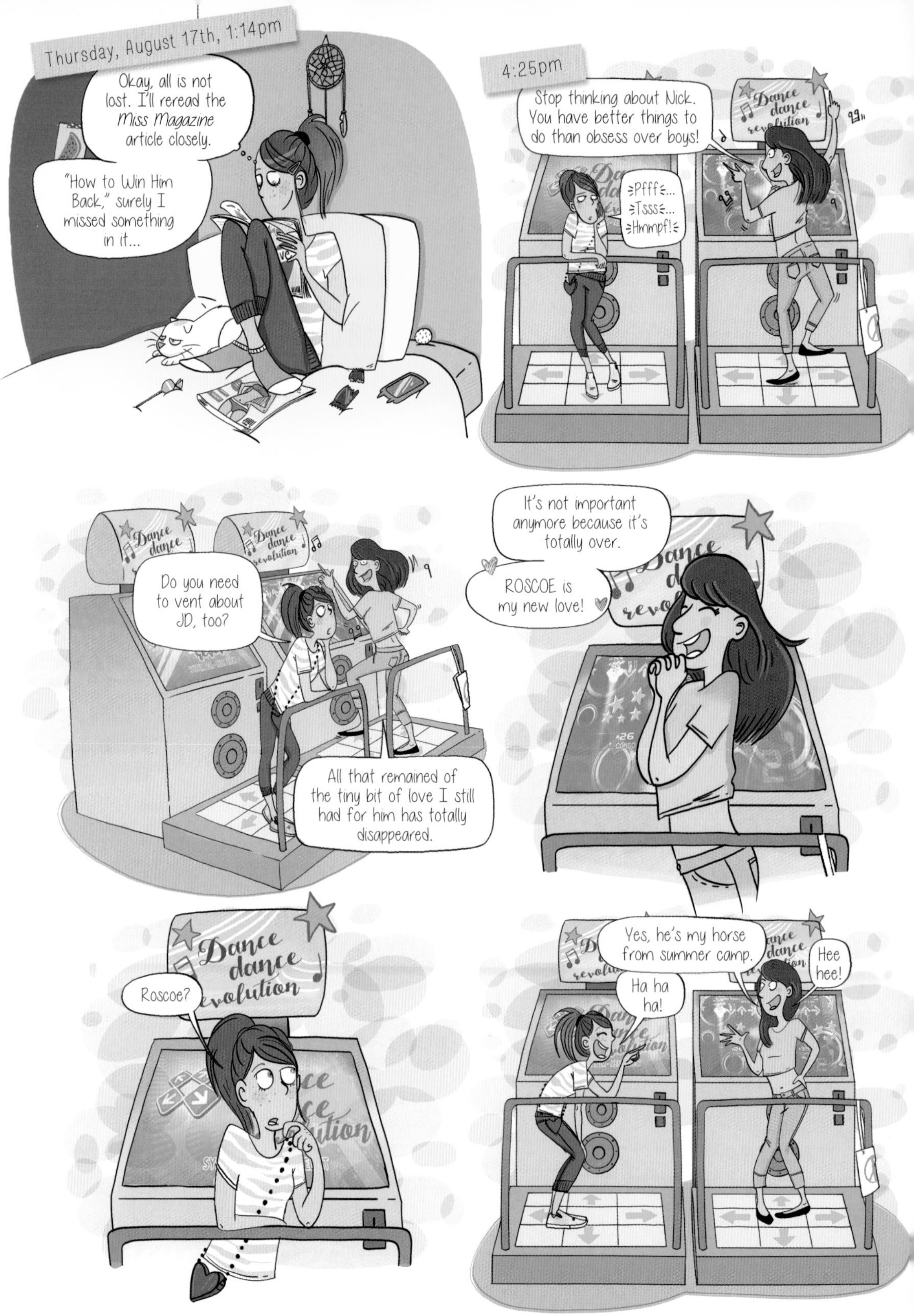
Thursday, August 17th, 1:14pm
Okay, all is not lost. I'll reread the *Miss Magazine* article closely.
"How to Win Him Back," surely I missed something in it...
4:25pm
Stop thinking about Nick. You have better things to do than obsess over boys!
Pfff...
Tsss...
Hmmpf!
Dance dance revolution
Do you need to vent about JD, too?
All that remained of the tiny bit of love I still had for him has totally disappeared.
It's not important anymore because it's totally over.
ROSCOE is my new love!
Roscoe?
Yes, he's my horse from summer camp.
Ha ha ha!
Hee hee!

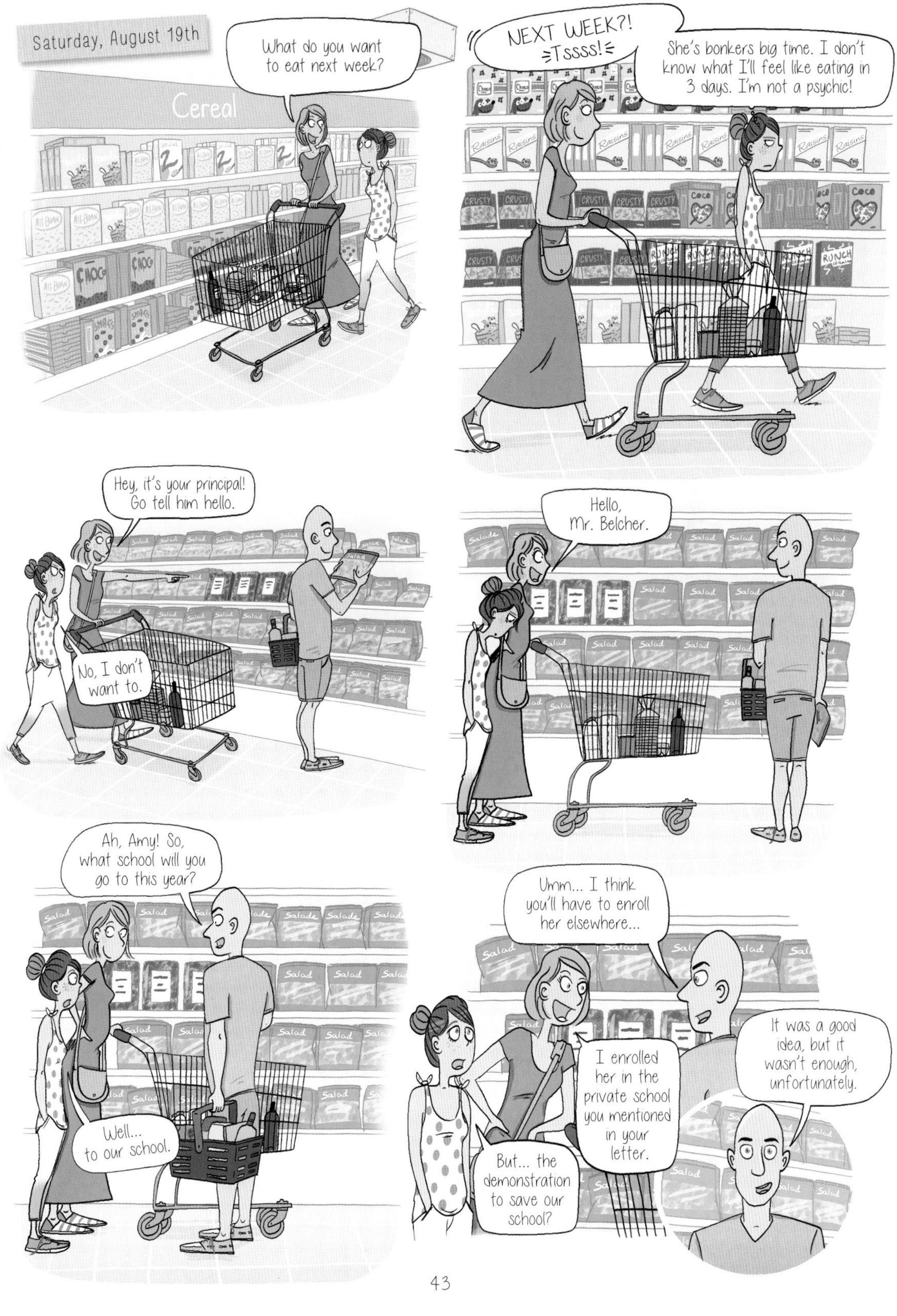
Saturday, August 19th
What do you want to eat next week?
Cereal
NEXT WEEK?! Tssss!
She's bonkers big time. I don't know what I'll feel like eating in 3 days. I'm not a psychic!
Hey, it's your principal! Go tell him hello.
No, I don't want to.
Hello, Mr. Belcher.
Ah, Amy! So, what school will you go to this year?
Well... to our school.
Umm... I think you'll have to enroll her elsewhere...
I enrolled her in the private school you mentioned in your letter.
But... the demonstration to save our school?
It was a good idea, but it wasn't enough, unfortunately.

SEPTEMBER
The tide turns

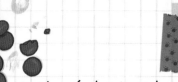

-Friday, September 1st:

10:34am:
When I awoke, I saw the picture my mom took of Tommy, Kat, and me before our party at the beginning of summer and, ironically, I tell myself I'm all right with my situation. (Dear 11:11, shooting star, or God, this isn't a wish, heh heh!) While looking at the photo, I reflect and conclude that several things remain the same. Kat's continuing horse-riding because she loves horses. Tommy will continue to read about them. My mom still thinks my room isn't clean enough for her liking, and for my part, I'll always love chocolate... In short, the world will continue to spin. But deep down, I have the distinct impression everything's going to change.

THE BIG BOOK OF DREAMS

3:05pm:
I asked my mom to cancel my enrollment in the private school. Kat and I have decided to go to the local public school. My mom answered that, considering that my grades aren't very good, I needed supervision and would find that in private schools. I said it was a mistake to believe there was more supervision in a private school, than there would be some in public schools too. So there!

♡ It's sooooo beautiful!

3:07pm:
She answered: "My decision is made, period!"
I shouted: "You were wrong to enroll me without talking to me! It's MY life, I'm the one who decides!"

3:08pm:
She answered (her shouting, too): "GO TO YOUR ROOM!"
WHY IN REAL LIFE DO I ALWAYS END UP GETTING INTO A SHOUTING MATCH WITH MY MOM??!!(my only ally is Sybil).

9:30pm:
Yessssssssssssssss! My mom has changed her mind. She's going to let me go to the school of my choice! When I asked her what made her change her opinion, she answered: "Frank!" Okay, so the serial killer's cool after all! (But I wonder, however, just what is his diabolical plan?)
My life's going to change. But for now, it's impossible to predict if it'll change for the better!

My new technique for eating less chocolate. I only eat chocolate chips in cookies...

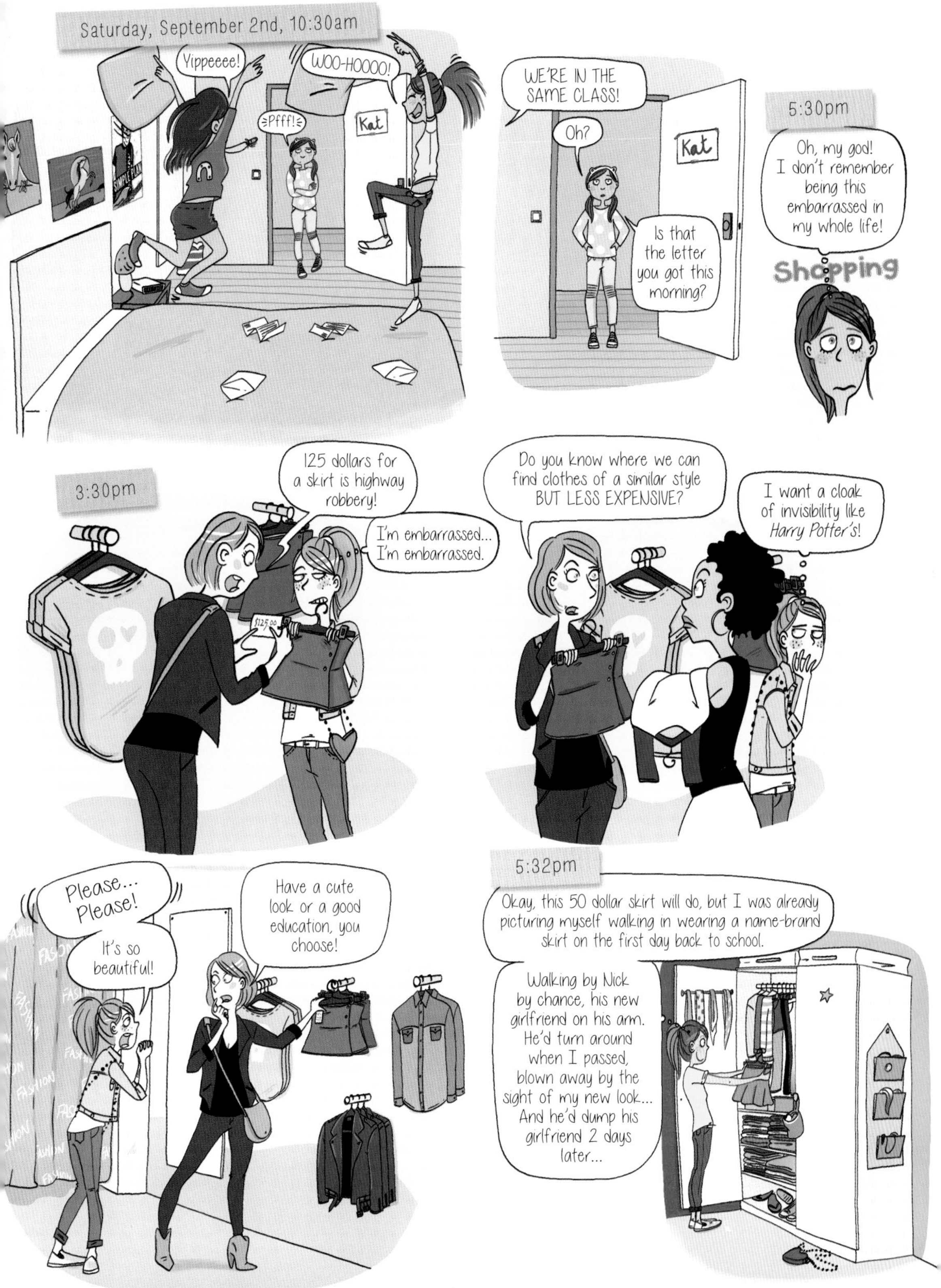

Saturday, September 2nd, 10:30am
Yippeeee!
WOO-HOOOO!
Pfff!
Kat
WE'RE IN THE SAME CLASS!
Oh?
Kat
Is that the letter you got this morning?
5:30pm
Oh, my god! I don't remember being this embarrassed in my whole life!
Shopping
3:30pm
125 dollars for a skirt is highway robbery!
$125.00
I'm embarrassed... I'm embarrassed.
Do you know where we can find clothes of a similar style BUT LESS EXPENSIVE?
I want a cloak of invisibility like *Harry Potter's*!
Please... Please!
It's so beautiful!
Have a cute look or a good education, you choose!
5:32pm
Okay, this 50 dollar skirt will do, but I was already picturing myself walking in wearing a name-brand skirt on the first day back to school.
Walking by Nick by chance, his new girlfriend on his arm. He'd turn around when I passed, blown away by the sight of my new look... And he'd dump his girlfriend 2 days later...

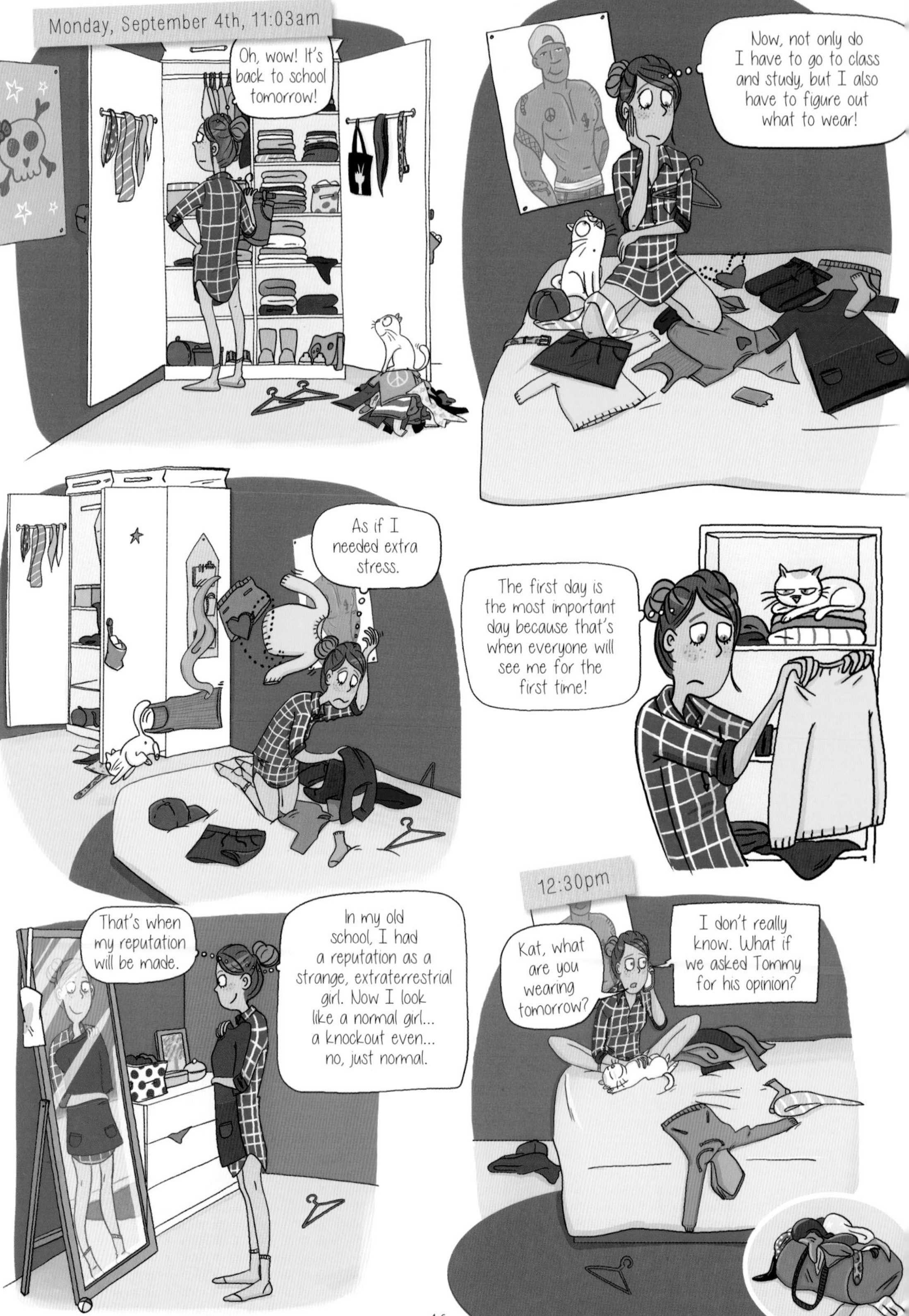
Monday, September 4th, 11:03am
Oh, wow! It's back to school tomorrow!
Now, not only do I have to go to class and study, but I also have to figure out what to wear!
As if I needed extra stress.
The first day is the most important day because that's when everyone will see me for the first time!
That's when my reputation will be made.
In my old school, I had a reputation as a strange, extraterrestrial girl. Now I look like a normal girl... a knockout even... no, just normal.
12:30pm
Kat, what are you wearing tomorrow?
I don't really know. What if we asked Tommy for his opinion?

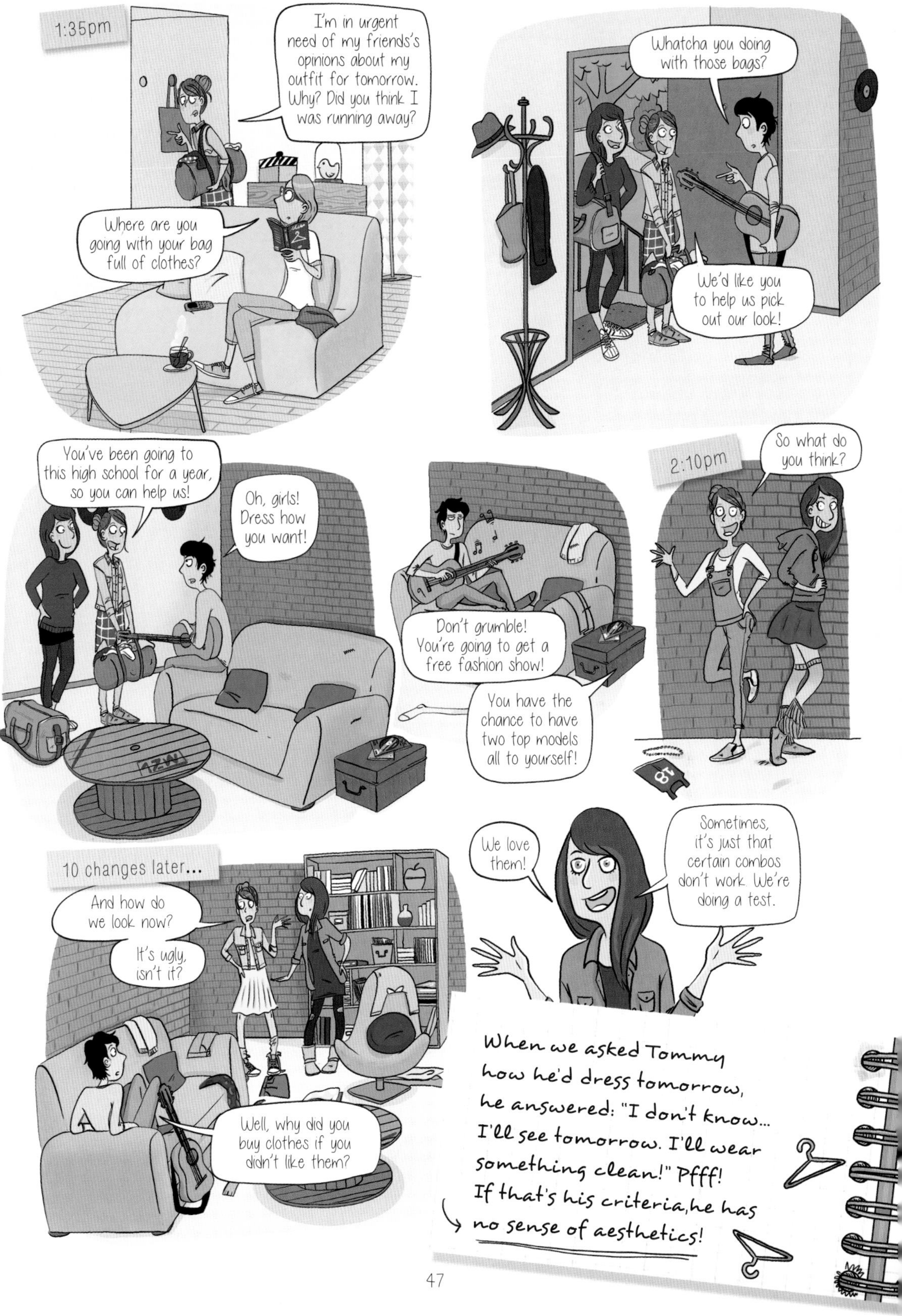
1:35pm
I'm in urgent need of my friends's opinions about my outfit for tomorrow. Why? Did you think I was running away?
Where are you going with your bag full of clothes?
Whatcha you doing with those bags?
We'd like you to help us pick out our look!
You've been going to this high school for a year, so you can help us!
Oh, girls! Dress how you want!
Don't grumble! You're going to get a free fashion show!
You have the chance to have two top models all to yourself!
2:10pm
So what do you think?
10 changes later...
And how do we look now?
It's ugly, isn't it?
Well, why did you buy clothes if you didn't like them?
We love them!
Sometimes, it's just that certain combos don't work. We're doing a test.
When we asked Tommy how he'd dress tomorrow, he answered: "I don't know... I'll see tomorrow. I'll wear something clean!" Pfff! If that's his criteria, he has no sense of aesthetics!

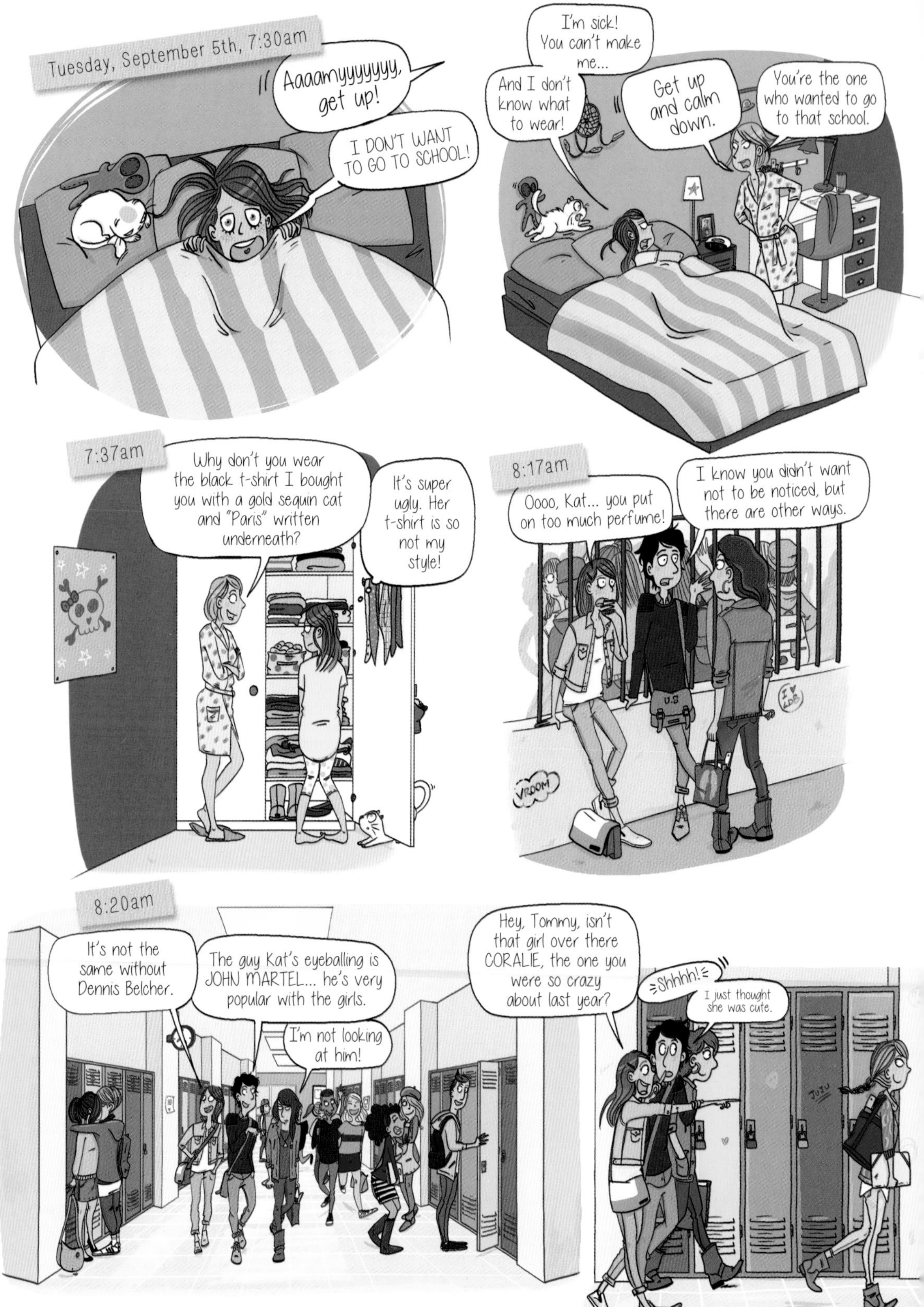
Tuesday, September 5th, 7:30am
Aaaamyyyyyy, get up!
I DON'T WANT TO GO TO SCHOOL!
I'm sick! You can't make me...
And I don't know what to wear!
Get up and calm down.
You're the one who wanted to go to that school.
7:37am
Why don't you wear the black t-shirt I bought you with a gold sequin cat and "Paris" written underneath?
It's super ugly. Her t-shirt is so not my style!
8:17am
Oooo, Kat... you put on too much perfume!
I know you didn't want not to be noticed, but there are other ways.
VROOM
8:20am
It's not the same without Dennis Belcher.
The guy Kat's eyeballing is JOHN MARTEL... he's very popular with the girls.
I'm not looking at him!
Hey, Tommy, isn't that girl over there CORALIE, the one you were so crazy about last year?
Shhhh!
I just thought she was cute.

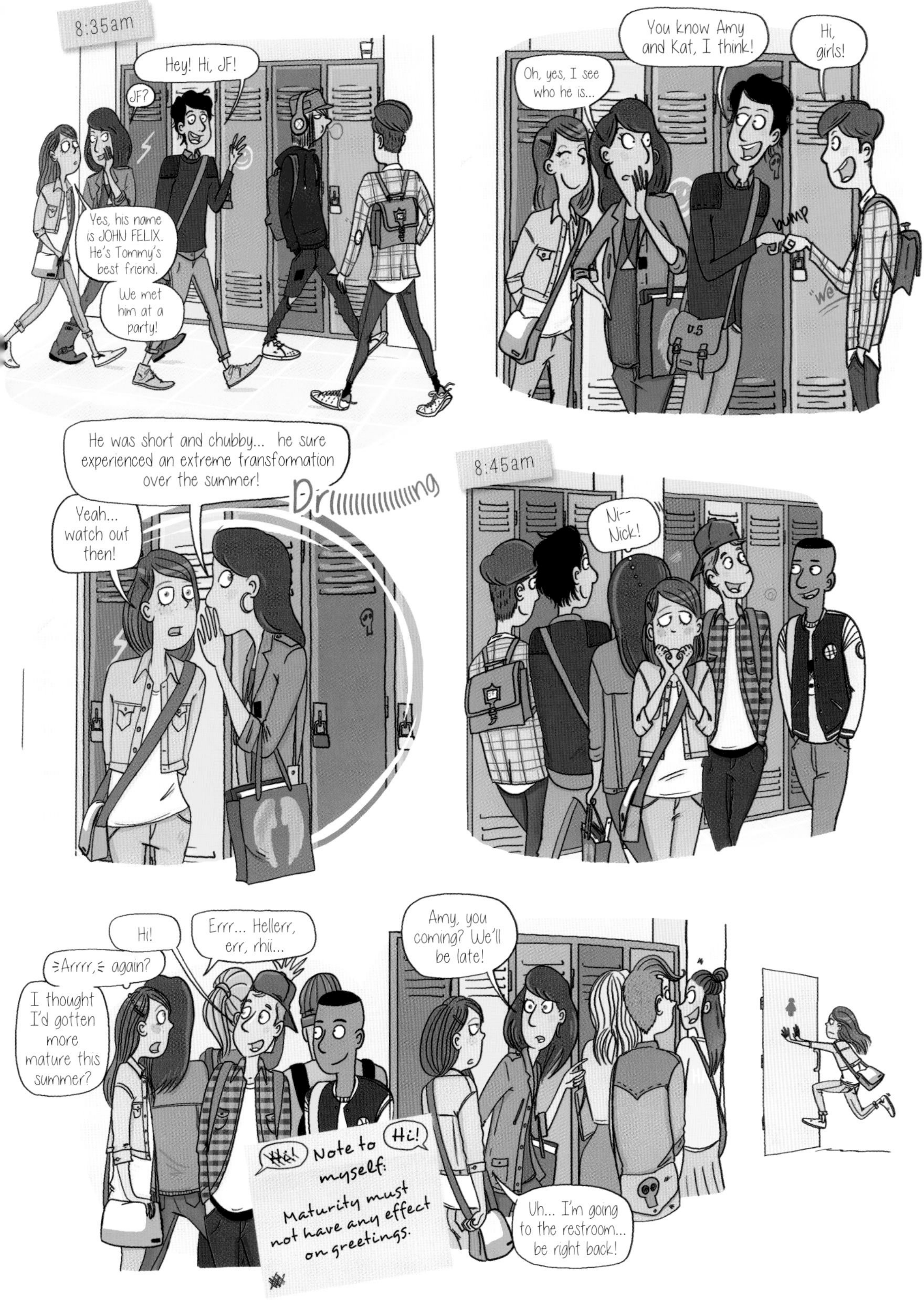
8:35am
Hey! Hi, JF!
JF?
Yes, his name is JOHN FELIX. He's Tommy's best friend.
We met him at a party!
You know Amy and Kat, I think!
Hi, girls!
Oh, yes, I see who he is...
bump
He was short and chubby... he sure experienced an extreme transformation over the summer!
Yeah... watch out then!
Driiiiiiiiiiiiiiing
8:45am
Ni-- Nick!
Hi!
Errr... Hellerr, err, rhii...
≡Arrrr,≡ again?
I thought I'd gotten more mature this summer?
Hi!
Note to myself: Maturity must not have any effect on greetings.
Amy, you coming? We'll be late!
Uh... I'm going to the restroom... be right back!

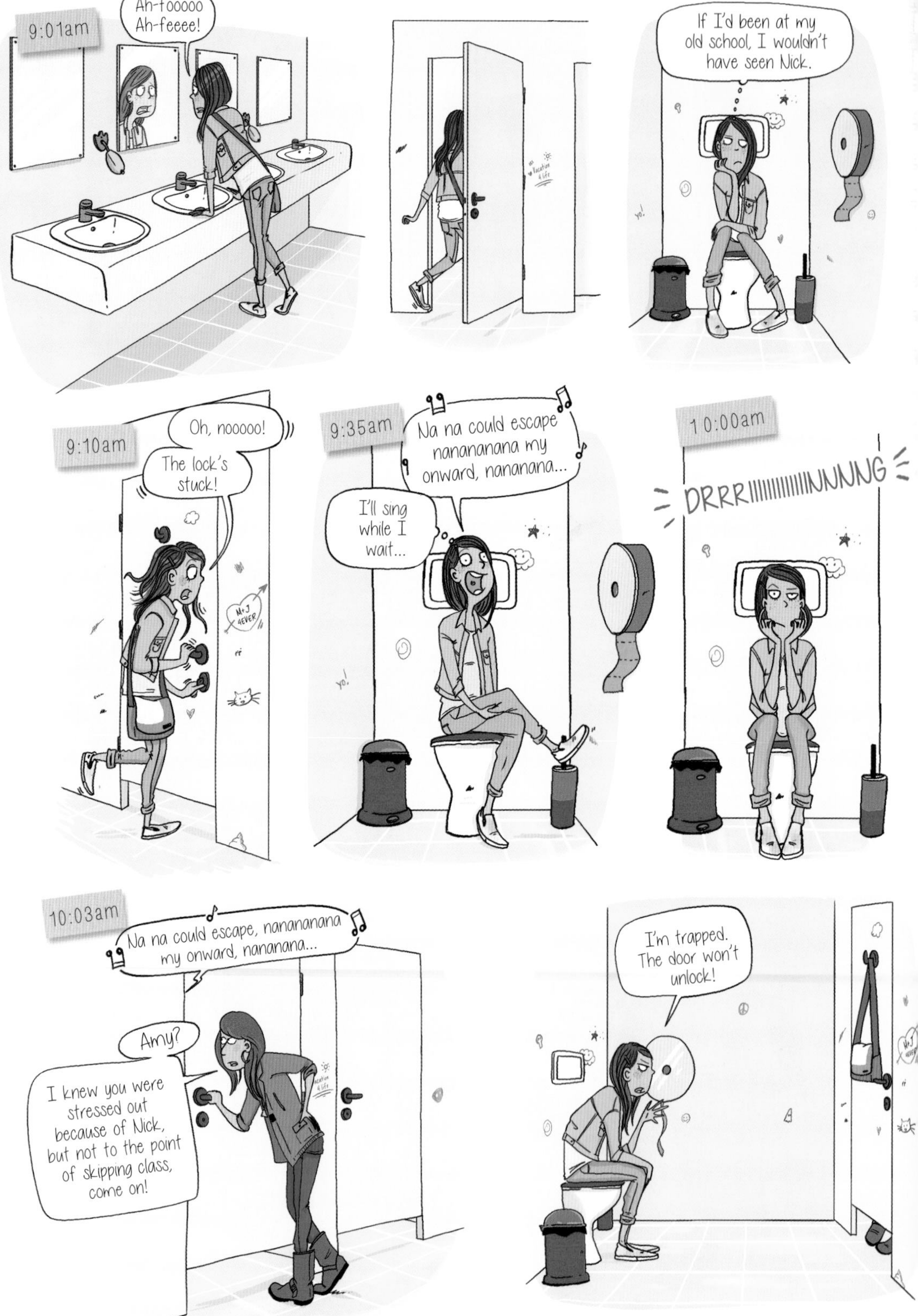
9:01am
Ah-fooooo Ah-feeee!
If I'd been at my old school, I wouldn't have seen Nick.
9:10am
Oh, nooooo!
The lock's stuck!
M+J 4EVER
9:35am
Na na could escape nanananana my onward, nanananana...
I'll sing while I wait...
10:00am
DRRRIIIIIIIIIIIIINNNNG
10:03am
Na na could escape, nanananana my onward, nanananana...
Amy?
I knew you were stressed out because of Nick, but not to the point of skipping class, come on!
I'm trapped. The door won't unlock!

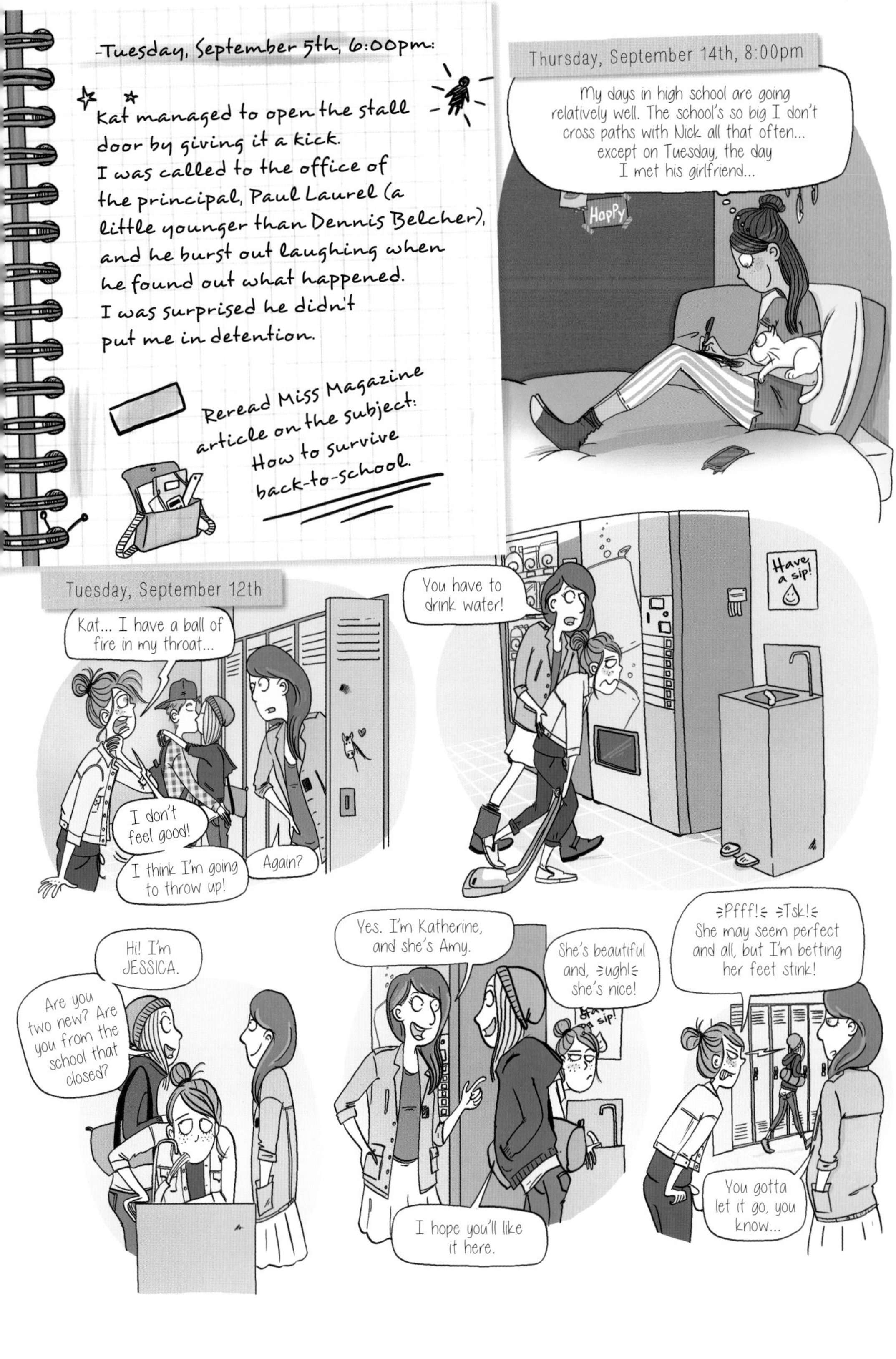
-Tuesday, September 5th, 6:00pm:
Kat managed to open the stall door by giving it a kick.
I was called to the office of the principal, Paul Laurel (a little younger than Dennis Belcher), and he burst out laughing when he found out what happened.
I was surprised he didn't put me in detention.
Reread Miss Magazine article on the subject: How to survive back-to-school.
Thursday, September 14th, 8:00pm
My days in high school are going relatively well. The school's so big I don't cross paths with Nick all that often... except on Tuesday, the day I met his girlfriend...
HaPPy
Tuesday, September 12th
Kat... I have a ball of fire in my throat...
I don't feel good!
I think I'm going to throw up!
Again?
You have to drink water!
Have a sip!
Hi! I'm JESSICA.
Are you two new? Are you from the school that closed?
Yes. I'm Katherine, and she's Amy.
I hope you'll like it here.
She's beautiful and, ≶ugh!≶ she's nice!
≶Pfff!≶ ≶Tsk!≶
She may seem perfect and all, but I'm betting her feet stink!
You gotta let it go, you know...

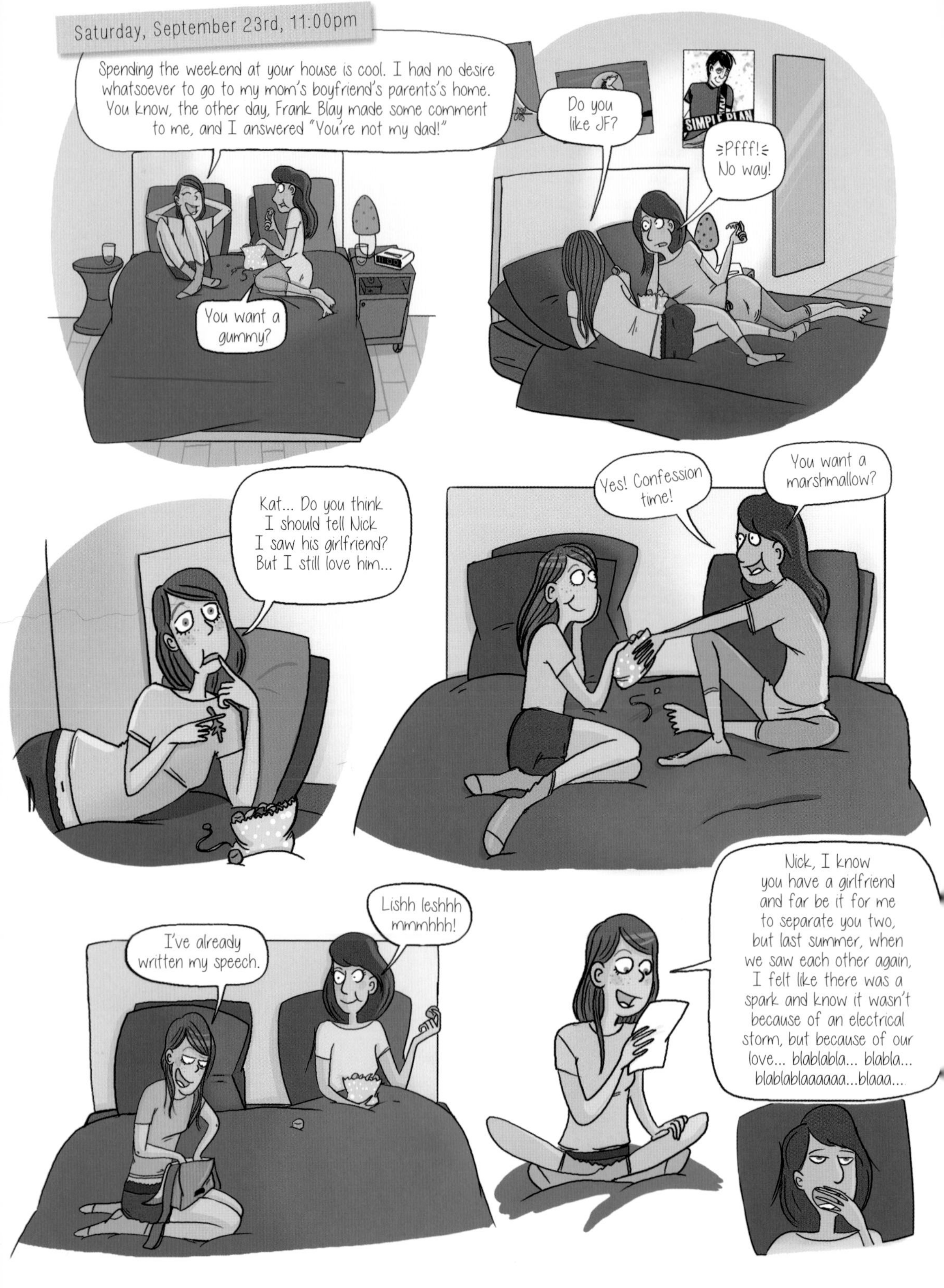
Saturday, September 23rd, 11:00pm
Spending the weekend at your house is cool. I had no desire whatsoever to go to my mom's boyfriend's parents's home. You know, the other day, Frank Blay made some comment to me, and I answered "You're not my dad!"
You want a gummy?
Do you like JF?
SIMPLE PLAN
Pfff! No way!
Kat... Do you think I should tell Nick I saw his girlfriend? But I still love him...
Yes! Confession time!
You want a marshmallow?
I've already written my speech.
Lishh leshhh mmmhhh!
Nick, I know you have a girlfriend and far be it for me to separate you two, but last summer, when we saw each other again, I felt like there was a spark and know it wasn't because of an electrical storm, but because of our love... blablabla... blabla... blablablaaaaaa...blaaa...

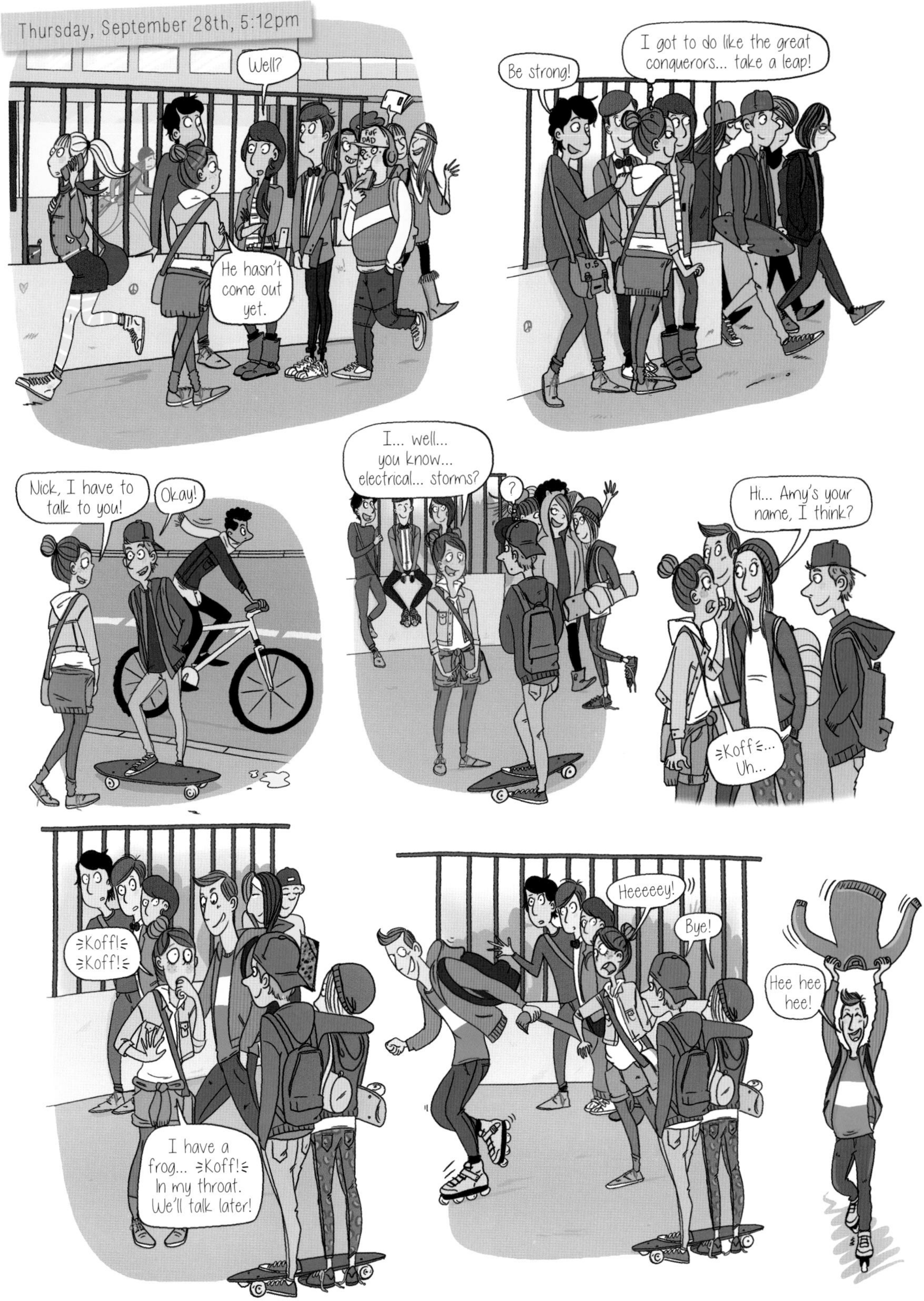

Thursday, September 28th, 5:12pm
Well?
He hasn't come out yet.
FUF DAD
Be strong!
I got to do like the great conquerors... take a leap!
U.S
Nick, I have to talk to you!
Okay!
I... well... you know... electrical... storms?
?
Hi... Amy's your name, I think?
Koff... Uh...
Koff! Koff!
I have a frog... Koff! In my throat. We'll talk later!
Heeeeey!
Bye!
Hee hee hee!

OCTOBER
Disoriented

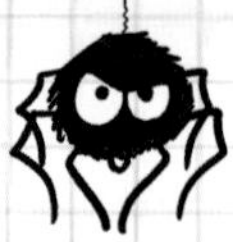

-Monday, October 2nd:

6:05pm:
Great! Not only have I lost all hope of winning Nick back, I'm also the victim of a robber. My life is so weird! Kat was appalled to find out I was the victim of a theft.

I knew my blue sweater was one of my favorites, but before it was stolen, I didn't realize it was my absolute favorite.

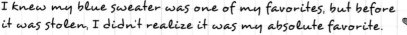

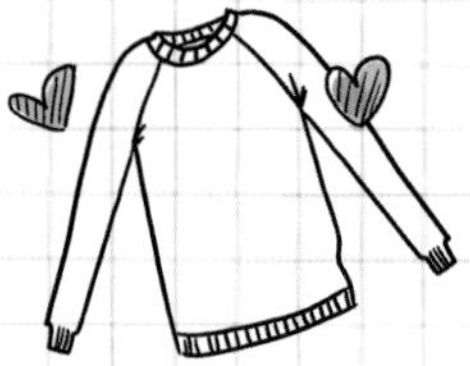

→ Advantage of extortion: Losing something makes us realize its value (and notice we're philosophical and intellectual by making such discoveries).

-Wednesday, October 4th:

YOU Tube
Rome,
Hong Kong
Italy
Egypt

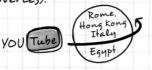

Change schools!
Change schools!
Change schools!
Change schools!

Mr. Letterman, our history teacher, told us about Jacques Cartier. I raised my hand and said: "He's a kind of loser to go looking for India and find Canada. And he was so sure of himself that he called the inhabitants of Canada Indians? What a moron!"
The teacher answered: "Sometimes you don't find what you're looking for, but discover something just as interesting, if not more so!"

CROSS OFF FROM THE LIST OF POTENTIAL CAREERS: HISTORIAN

School really is lots of work and brain energy.

Missing nut!

-Friday, October 6th, 11:10am:

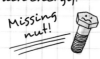

Ahhh! Teacher workshop days, so no school. I got to sleep in till 10:00am, a decent time. It does me good! I think my body has overexerted itself lately: studying, getting used to a new school, creating a decent look, robbery... This is a well-deserved day of rest!

102°F

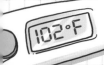

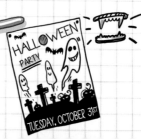

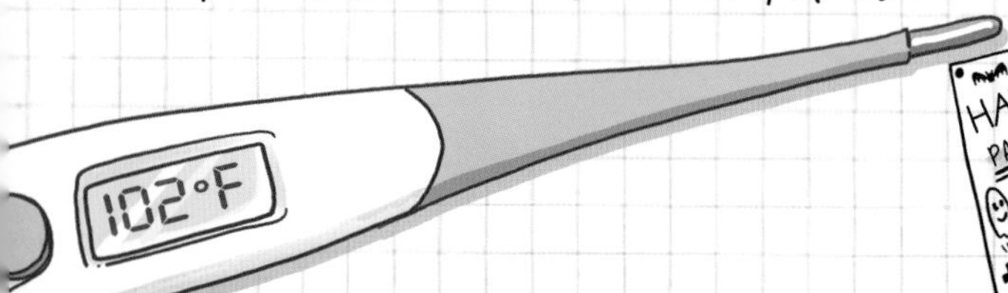

HALLOWEEN
PARTY
TUESDAY, OCTOBER 31ST

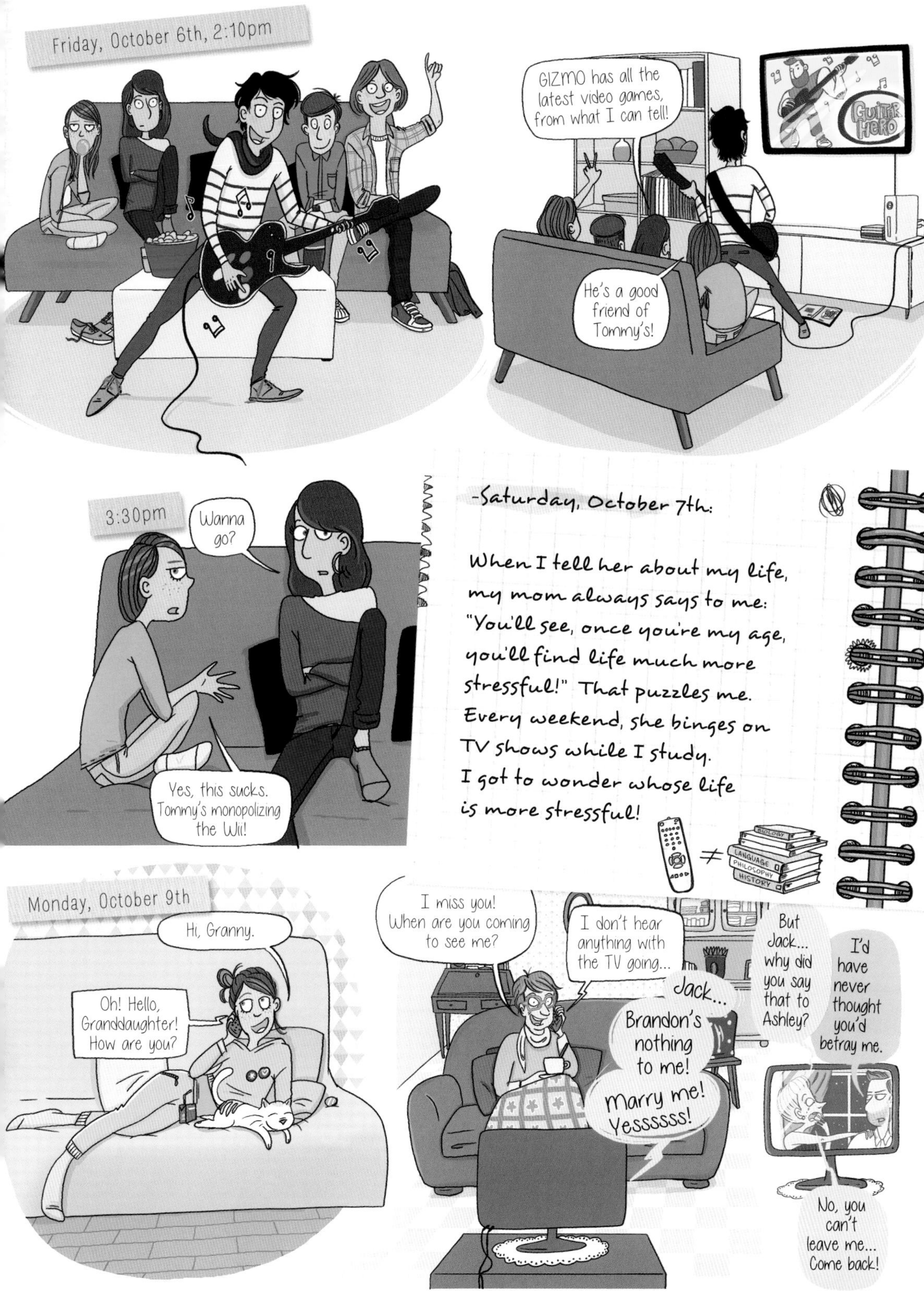

Friday, October 6th, 2:10pm
GIZMO has all the latest video games, from what I can tell!
GUITAR HERO
He's a good friend of Tommy's!
3:30pm
Wanna go?
Yes, this sucks. Tommy's monopolizing the Wii!
-Saturday, October 7th:
When I tell her about my life, my mom always says to me: "You'll see, once you're my age, you'll find life much more stressful!" That puzzles me. Every weekend, she binges on TV shows while I study. I got to wonder whose life is more stressful!
≠
BIOLOGY
LANGUAGE
PHILOSOPHY
HISTORY
Monday, October 9th
Hi, Granny.
Oh! Hello, Granddaughter! How are you?
I miss you! When are you coming to see me?
I don't hear anything with the TV going...
Jack...
Brandon's nothing to me!
Marry me! Yessssss!
But Jack... why did you say that to Ashley?
I'd have never thought you'd betray me.
No, you can't leave me... Come back!

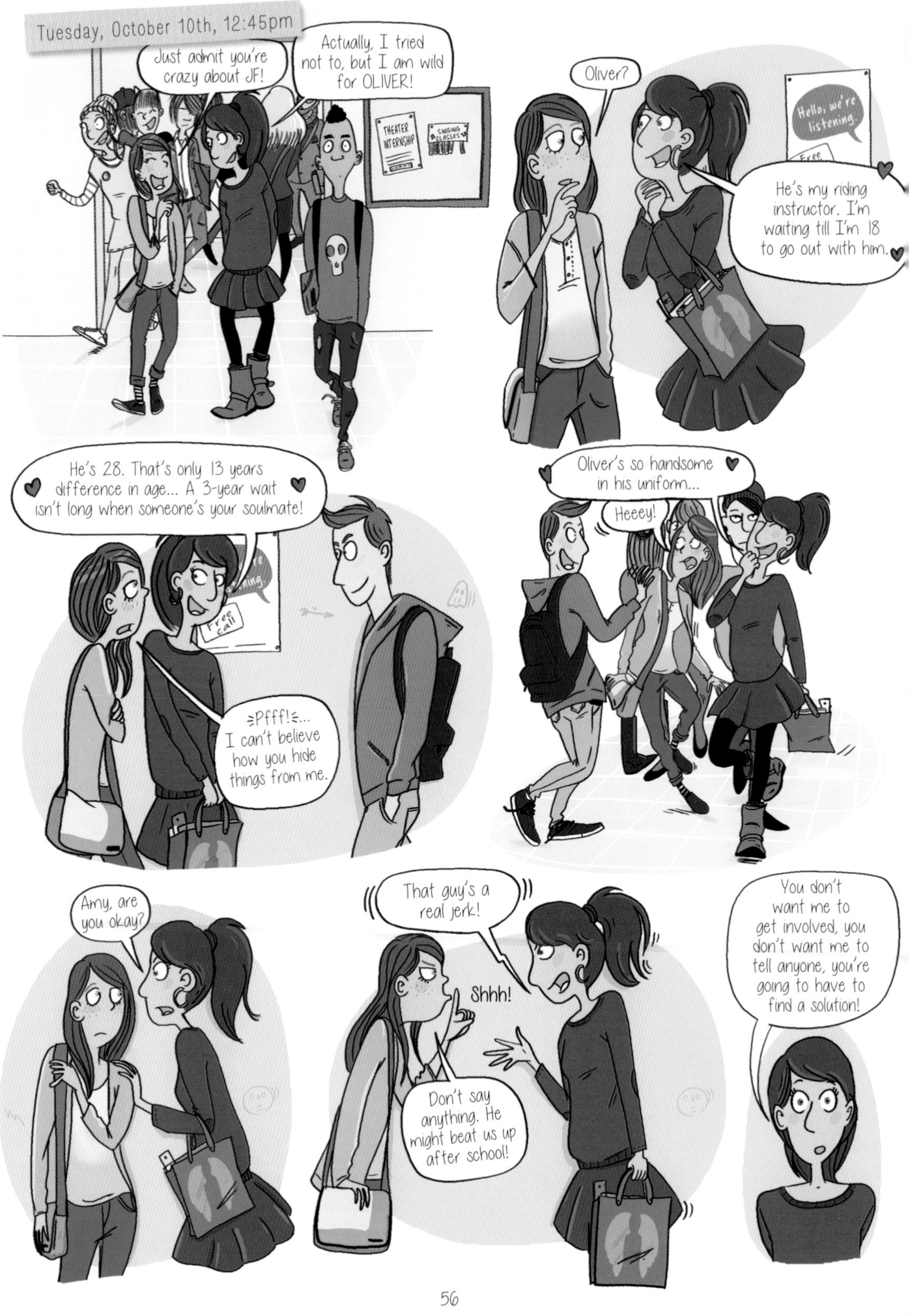
Tuesday, October 10th, 12:45pm
Just admit you're crazy about JF!
Actually, I tried not to, but I am wild for OLIVER!
THEATER INTERNSHIP
SINGING CLASSES
Oliver?
He's my riding instructor. I'm waiting till I'm 18 to go out with him.
Hello, we're listening.
He's 28. That's only 13 years difference in age... A 3-year wait isn't long when someone's your soulmate!
Pfff!... I can't believe how you hide things from me.
Free call
Oliver's so handsome in his uniform...
Heeey!
Amy, are you okay?
That guy's a real jerk!
Shhh!
Don't say anything. He might beat us up after school!
You don't want me to get involved, you don't want me to tell anyone, you're going to have to find a solution!

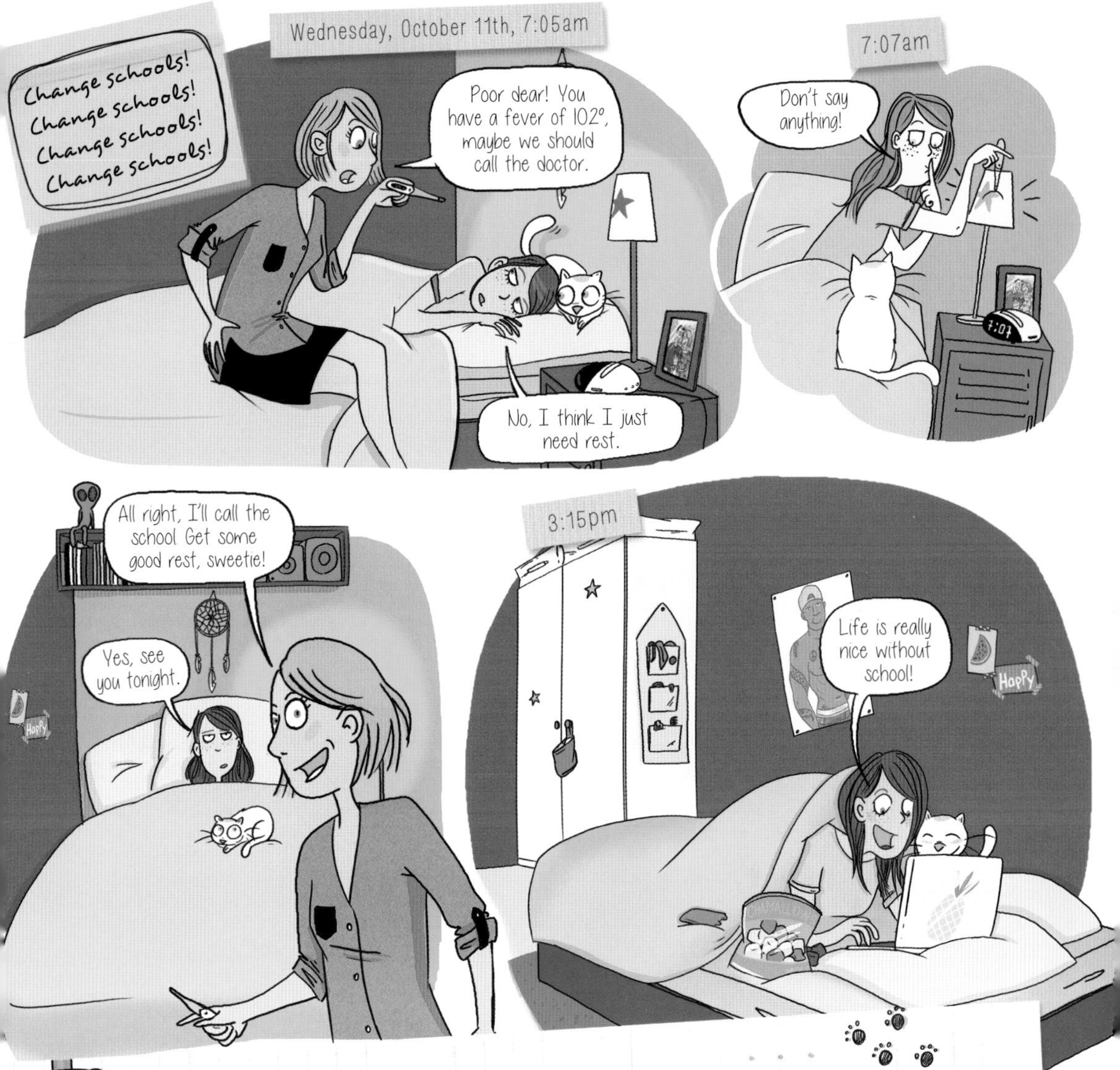
Wednesday, October 11th, 7:05am
Change schools!
Change schools!
Change schools!
Change schools!
Poor dear! You have a fever of 102°, maybe we should call the doctor.
No, I think I just need rest.
7:07am
Don't say anything!
7:07
All right, I'll call the school. Get some good rest, sweetie!
Yes, see you tonight.
Happy
3:15pm
Life is really nice without school!
Happy

-Wednesday, October 11th, 7:15pm:

Kat came by to bring me my homework. She asked me what I had. I told her a very rare, still undiscovered illness. Tommy came to play the guitar for me, and I visited Rome, the Vatican. Thanks to a family from Hong Kong, I visited the Leaning Tower of Pisa. I also met ☆Celine Dion,☆ I saw the pyramids of Egypt... everything thanks to YouTube.

Who needs school when you can teach yourself thanks to the Web?

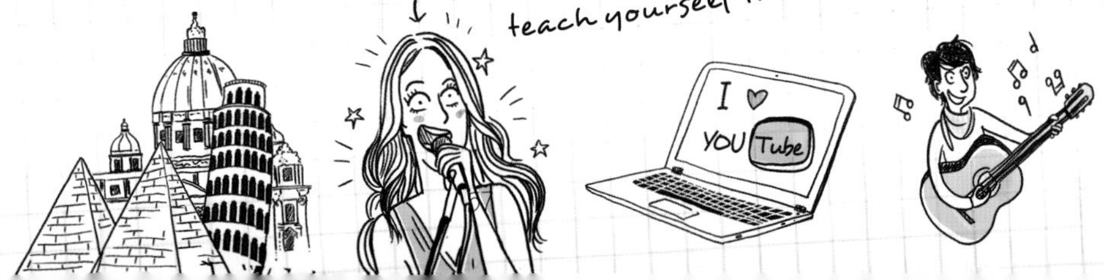
I ♥
YOU Tube

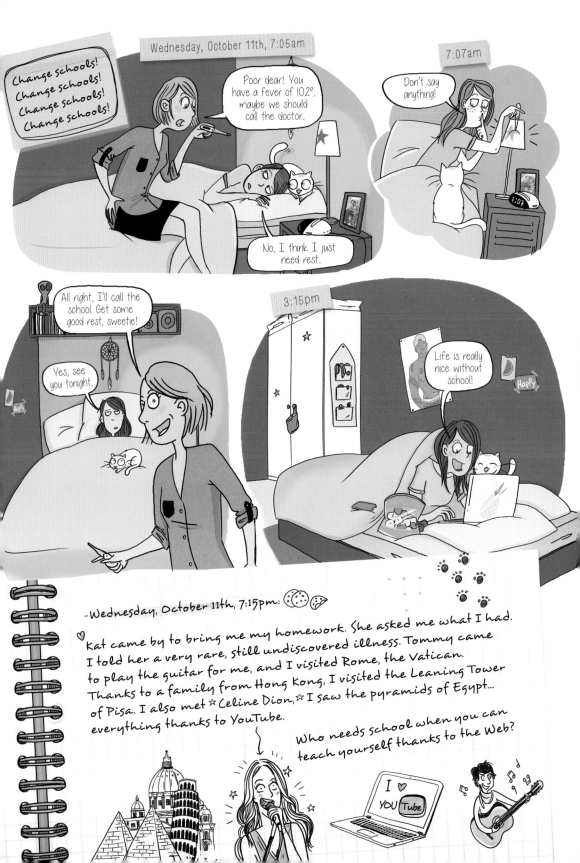

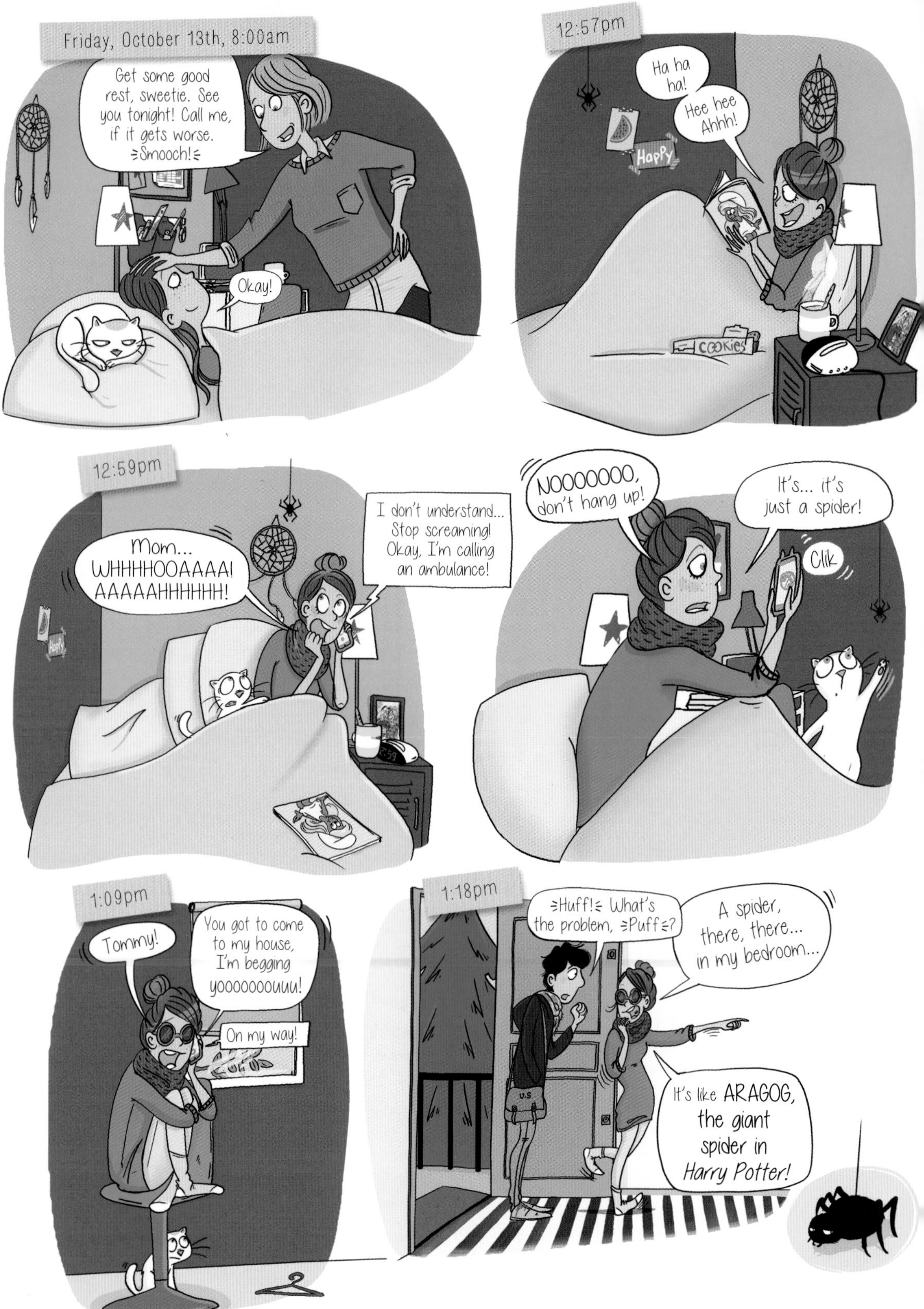
Friday, October 13th, 8:00am
Get some good rest, sweetie. See you tonight! Call me, if it gets worse. ⋟Smooch!⋞
Okay!
12:57pm
Ha ha ha!
Hee hee Ahhh!
HaPPy
COOKIES
12:59pm
Mom... WHHHHOOAAAA! AAAAAHHHHHH!
I don't understand... Stop screaming! Okay, I'm calling an ambulance!
NOOOOOOO, don't hang up!
It's... it's just a spider!
Clik
1:09pm
Tommy!
You got to come to my house, I'm begging yoooooouuu!
On my way!
1:18pm
⋟Huff!⋞ What's the problem, ⋟Puff⋞?
A spider, there, there... in my bedroom...
It's like ARAGOG, the giant spider in *Harry Potter!*

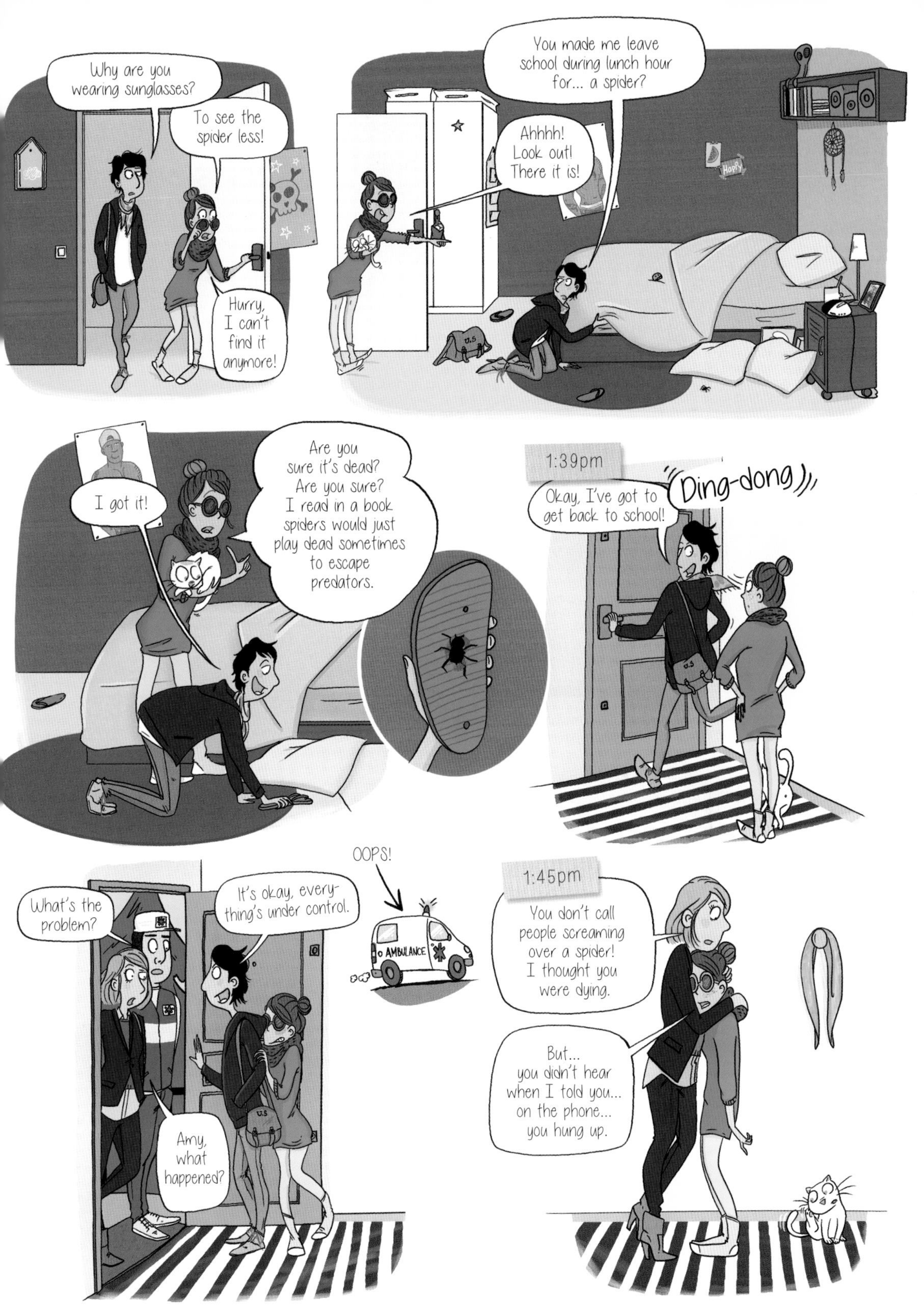
Why are you wearing sunglasses?
To see the spider less!
Hurry, I can't find it anymore!
You made me leave school during lunch hour for... a spider?
Ahhhh! Look out! There it is!
Happy
I got it!
Are you sure it's dead? Are you sure? I read in a book spiders would just play dead sometimes to escape predators.
1:39pm
Okay, I've got to get back to school!
Ding-dong
What's the problem?
It's okay, every-thing's under control.
OOPS!
AMBULANCE
Amy, what happened?
1:45pm
You don't call people screaming over a spider! I thought you were dying.
But... you didn't hear when I told you... on the phone... you hung up.

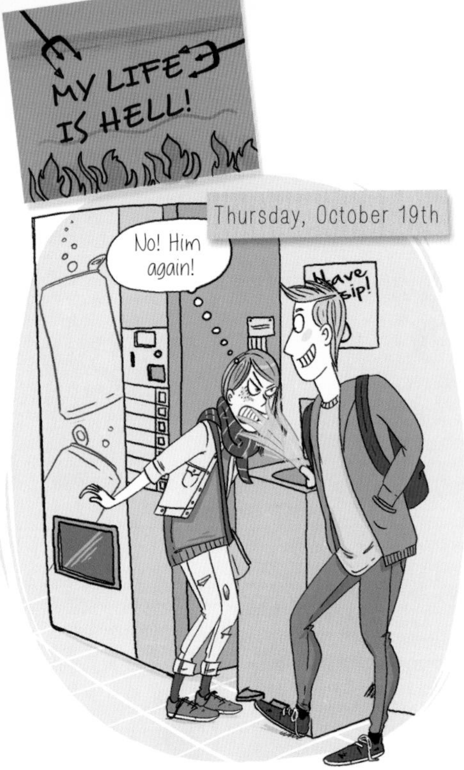
MY LIFE IS HELL!
Thursday, October 19th
No! Him again!

Advantages of my new school:

- Kat, Tommy, JF ← My best friends
- Cool teachers (except for the coaches and science teachers).
- Good grades A+
- Closer to home, so I can get up later. Zzzzzzzzzzz

Disadvantages of my new school:

- Wracking my brains every morning to get dressed.
- My clothes getting stolen and being intimidated.
- Nick and his girlfriend.
- Defective restroom doors (once).

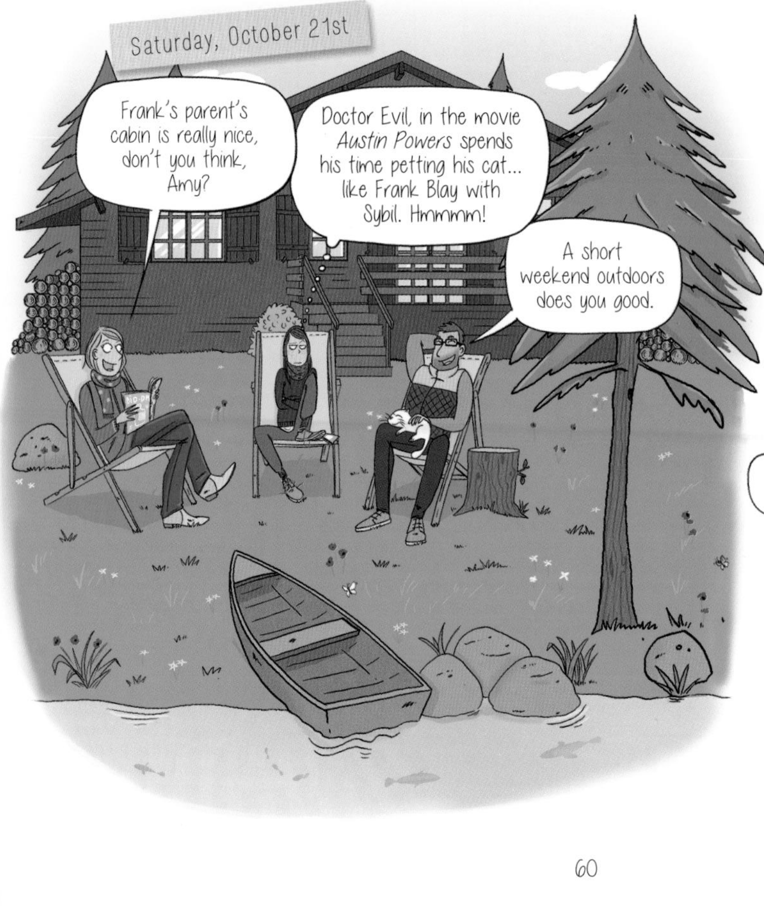
Saturday, October 21st
Frank's parent's cabin is really nice, don't you think, Amy?
Doctor Evil, in the movie *Austin Powers* spends his time petting his cat... like Frank Blay with Sybil. Hmmmm!
A short weekend outdoors does you good.

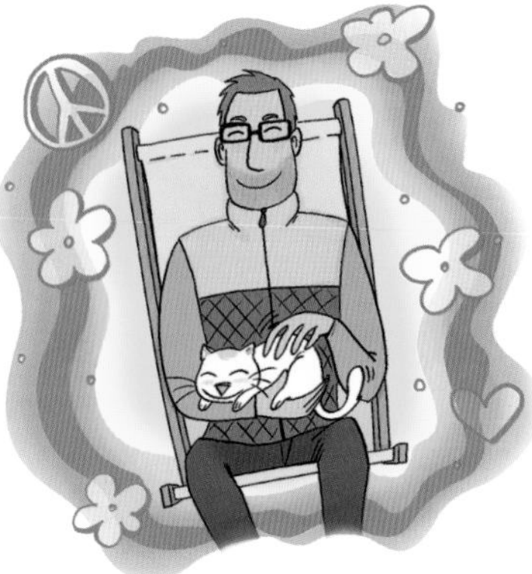

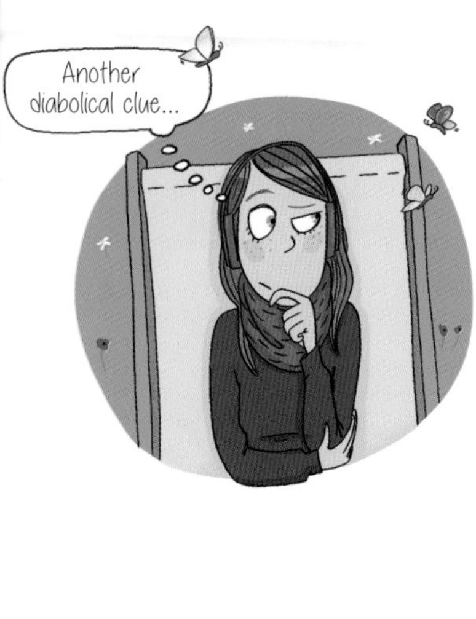
Another diabolical clue...

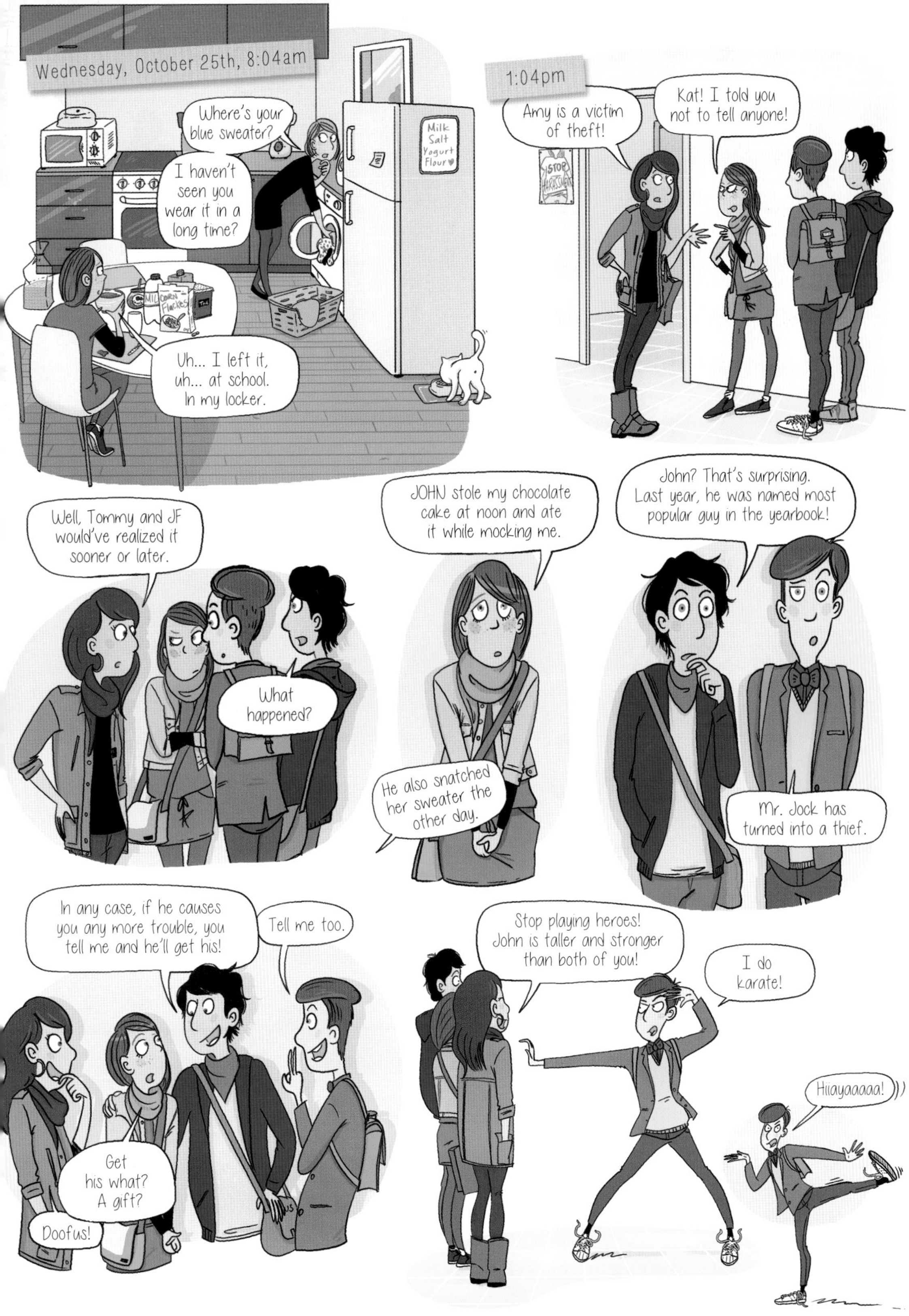
Wednesday, October 25th, 8:04am
Where's your blue sweater?
I haven't seen you wear it in a long time?
Uh... I left it, uh... at school. In my locker.
Milk Salt Yogurt Flour
1:04pm
Amy is a victim of theft!
Kat! I told you not to tell anyone!
Well, Tommy and JF would've realized it sooner or later.
What happened?
JOHN stole my chocolate cake at noon and ate it while mocking me.
He also snatched her sweater the other day.
John? That's surprising. Last year, he was named most popular guy in the yearbook!
Mr. Jock has turned into a thief.
In any case, if he causes you any more trouble, you tell me and he'll get his!
Tell me too.
Get his what? A gift?
Doofus!
Stop playing heroes! John is taller and stronger than both of you!
I do karate!
Hiiayaaaaa!

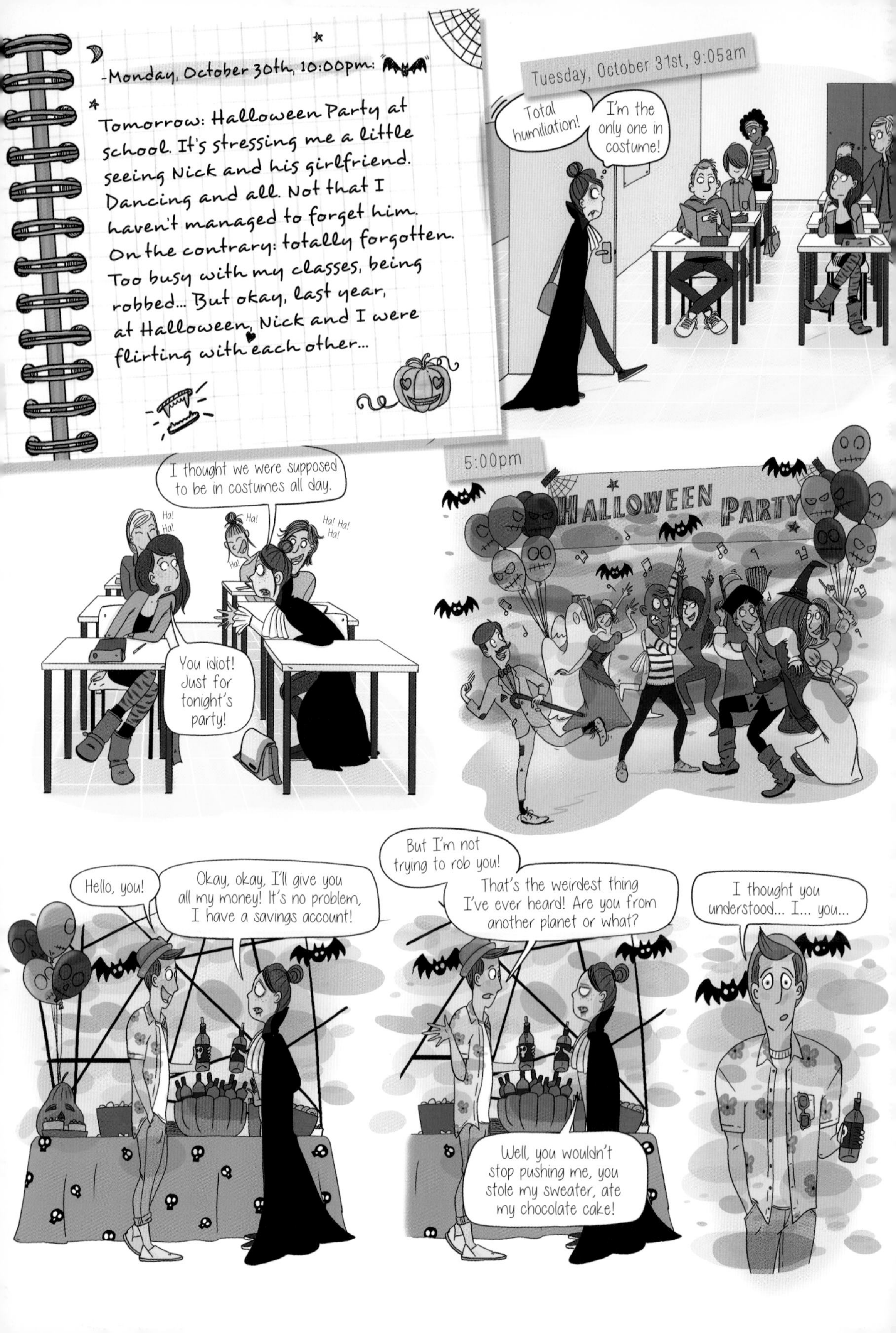
-Monday, October 30th, 10:00pm:
Tomorrow: Halloween Party at school. It's stressing me a little seeing Nick and his girlfriend. Dancing and all. Not that I haven't managed to forget him. On the contrary: totally forgotten. Too busy with my classes, being robbed... But okay, last year, at Halloween, Nick and I were flirting with each other...
Tuesday, October 31st, 9:05am
Total humiliation!
I'm the only one in costume!
I thought we were supposed to be in costumes all day.
Ha! Ha!
Ha!
Ha! Ha! Ha!
Ha!
You idiot! Just for tonight's party!
5:00pm
HALLOWEEN PARTY
Hello, you!
Okay, okay, I'll give you all my money! It's no problem, I have a savings account!
But I'm not trying to rob you!
That's the weirdest thing I've ever heard! Are you from another planet or what?
Well, you wouldn't stop pushing me, you stole my sweater, ate my chocolate cake!
I thought you understood... I... you...

NOVEMBER

Batten Down the Hatches!

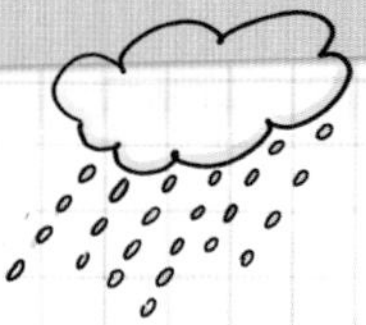

- Saturday, November 4th:

1:05pm:
It's raining, raining, raining, raining, raining...

Ever since Tuesday's party, I've been having trouble concentrating. I can't stop going over everything that's happened since the beginning of the school year.

1:07pm:
Tommy told me yesterday he's convinced John LIKES ME!!!
I said to him: "How could I know that theft = love?" And then he said it wasn't stealing, it was just to be noticed, and he added: "Guys aren't like girls, they don't express themselves the same way!"

Pffffffffffffffffffffffff!

1:10pm:
I don't like that John at all!
→ And I want my sweater back.

4:02pm:
Okay, I have to do my homework. I'll call Kat...

6:30pm:
Kat came over to the house to do our homework together in the kitchen. Instead of working, however, we listened to disco dance music. Frank Blay arrived (it annoys me that he has keys to MY house!). So, he gave us a disco ball with electric lights (something he'd used for his office party that had been left in his car). He plugged in the disco ball in the living room and we danced like crazy!

When my mom got home, she started dancing with us.

It was so fun! Frank Blay's kind of cool after all!

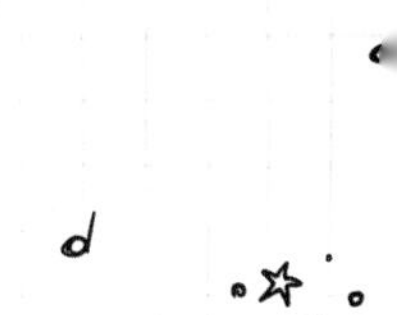

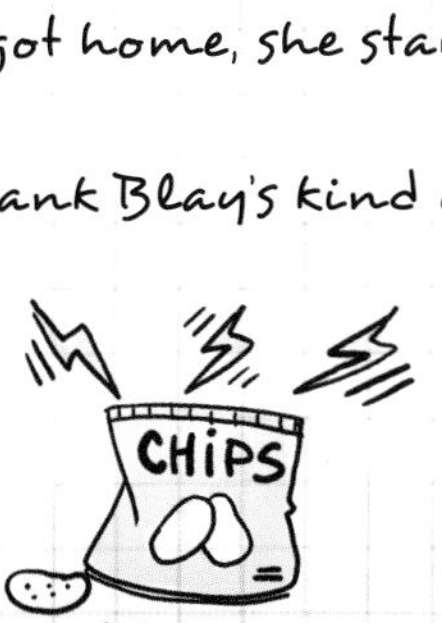
CHIPS

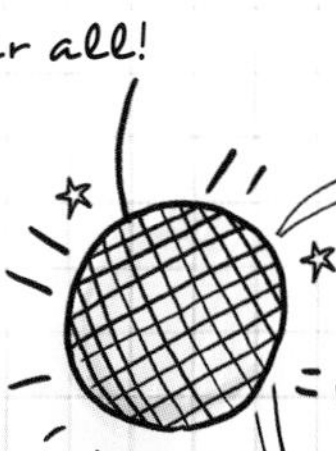

Note: He gave me the disco ball, which I put in my bedroom.

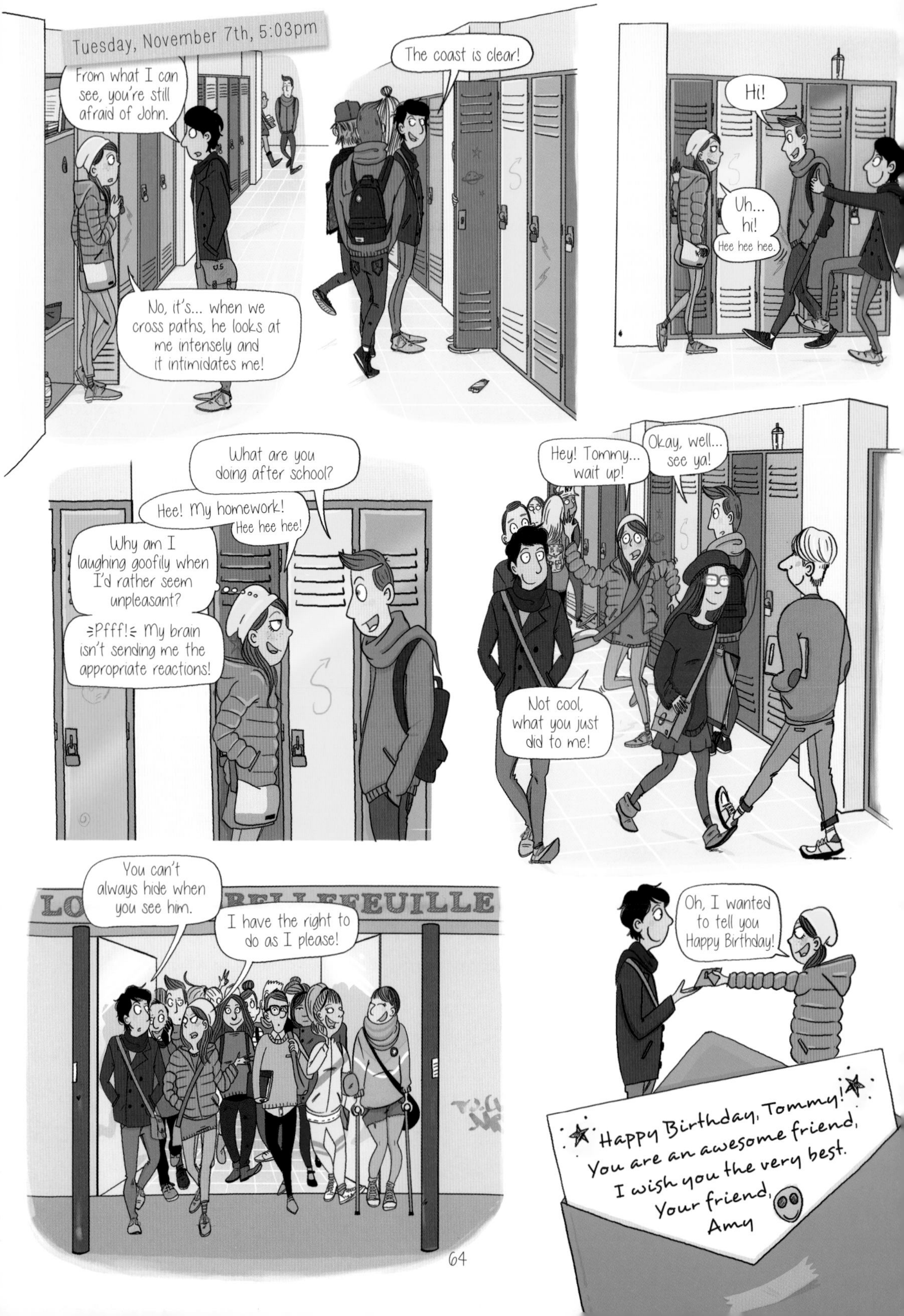

Tuesday, November 7th, 5:03pm
From what I can see, you're still afraid of John.
No, it's... when we cross paths, he looks at me intensely and it intimidates me!
The coast is clear!
Hi!
Uh... hi!
Hee hee hee.
What are you doing after school?
Hee! My homework!
Hee hee hee!
Why am I laughing goofily when I'd rather seem unpleasant?
Pfff! My brain isn't sending me the appropriate reactions!
Hey! Tommy... wait up!
Okay, well... see ya!
Not cool, what you just did to me!
You can't always hide when you see him.
I have the right to do as I please!
Oh, I wanted to tell you Happy Birthday!
Happy Birthday, Tommy!
You are an awesome friend,
I wish you the very best.
Your friend,
Amy

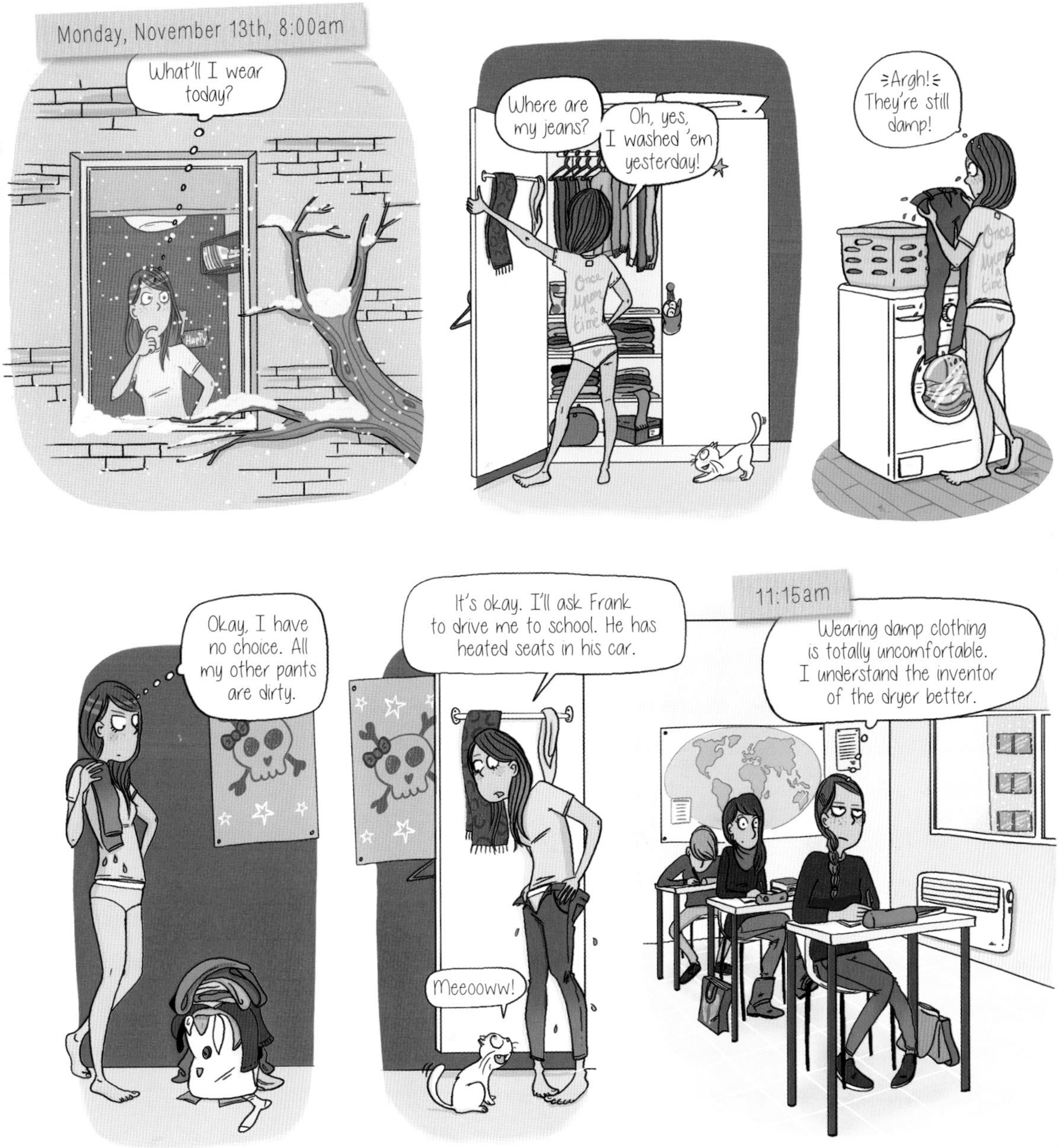
Monday, November 13th, 8:00am
What'll I wear today?
Happy
Where are my jeans?
Oh, yes, I washed 'em yesterday!
Once upon a time
Argh! They're still damp!
Okay, I have no choice. All my other pants are dirty.
It's okay. I'll ask Frank to drive me to school. He has heated seats in his car.
Meeooww!
11:15am
Wearing damp clothing is totally uncomfortable. I understand the inventor of the dryer better.

Future career to envision: **inventor**

I could invent something both practical and awesome (I don't know what yet, I'm waiting for divine inspiration).

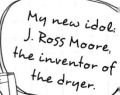

My new idol: J. Ross Moore, the inventor of the dryer.

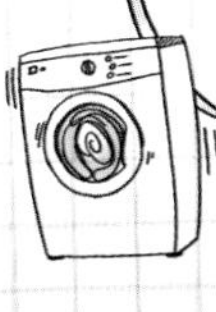

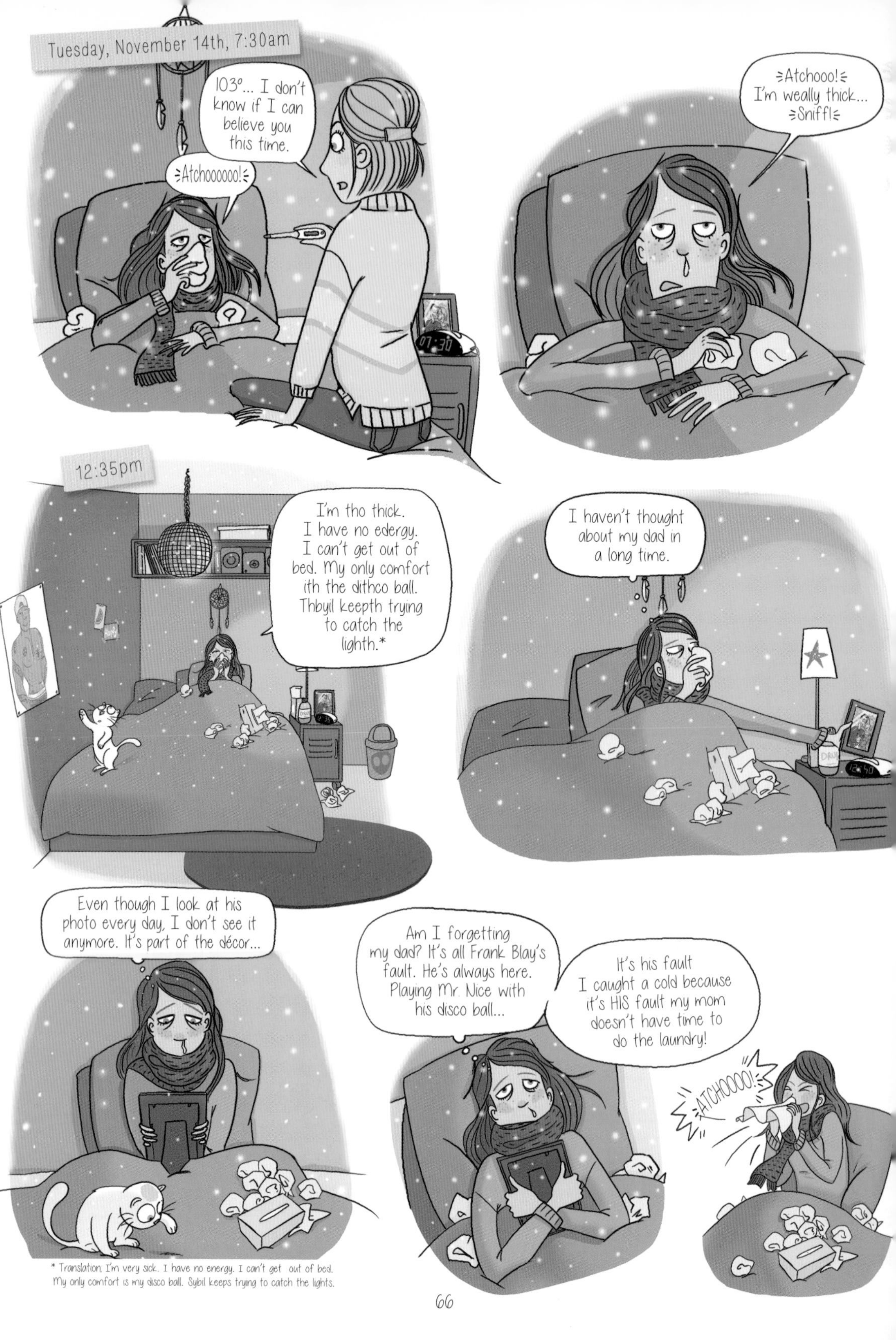

Tuesday, November 14th, 7:30am
103°... I don't know if I can believe you this time.
Atchoooooo!
Atchooo! I'm weally thick... Sniff!
12:35pm
I'm tho thick. I have no edergy. I can't get out of bed. My only comfort ith the dithco ball. Thbyil keepth trying to catch the lighth.*
I haven't thought about my dad in a long time.
Even though I look at his photo every day, I don't see it anymore. It's part of the décor...
Am I forgetting my dad? It's all Frank Blay's fault. He's always here. Playing Mr. Nice with his disco ball...
It's his fault I caught a cold because it's HIS fault my mom doesn't have time to do the laundry!
ATCHOOOO!

* Translation: I'm very sick. I have no energy. I can't get out of bed. My only comfort is my disco ball. Sybil keeps trying to catch the lights.

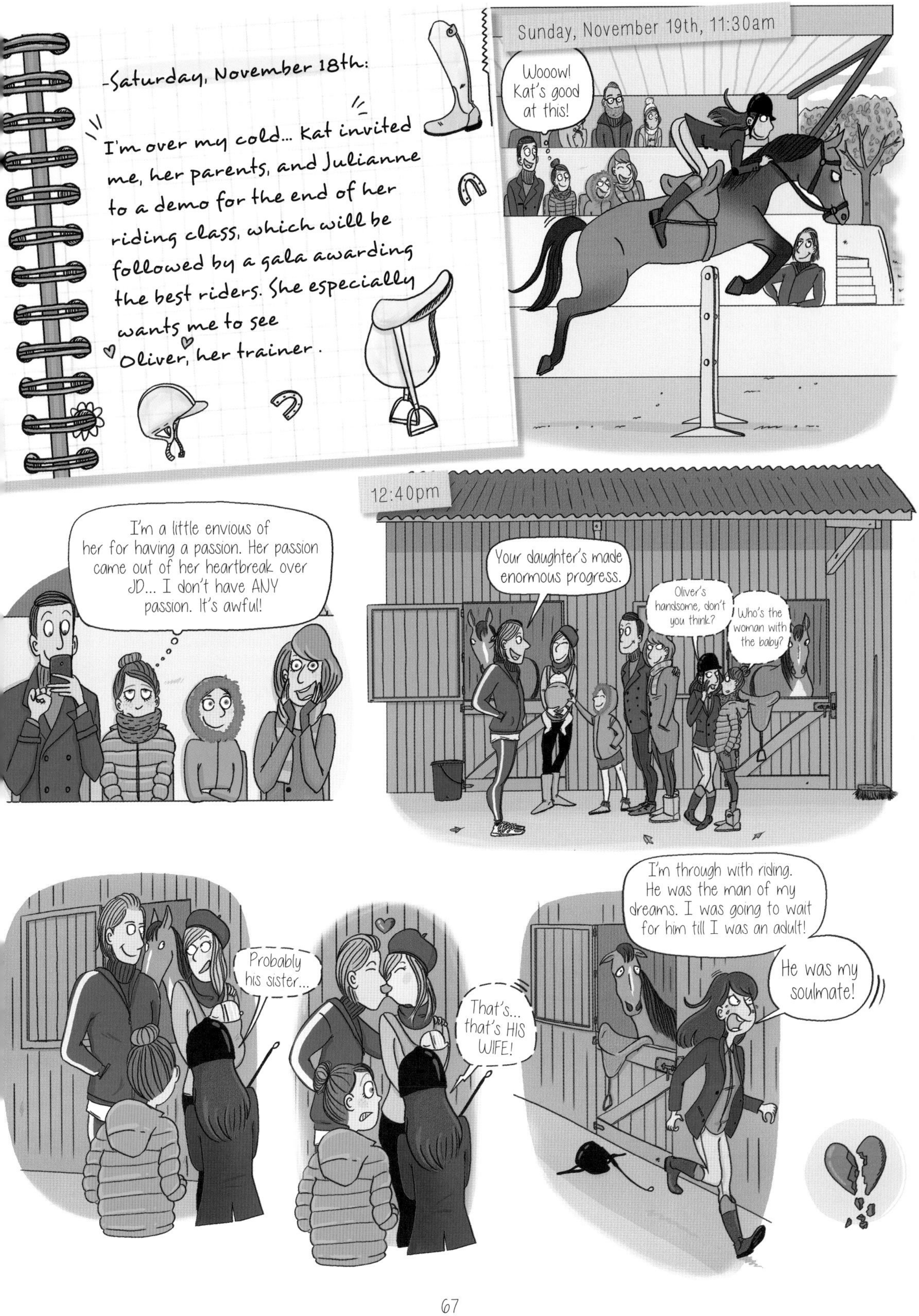

-Saturday, November 18th:
I'm over my cold... Kat invited me, her parents, and Julianne to a demo for the end of her riding class, which will be followed by a gala awarding the best riders. She especially wants me to see Oliver, her trainer.
Sunday, November 19th, 11:30am
Wooow! Kat's good at this!
I'm a little envious of her for having a passion. Her passion came out of her heartbreak over JD... I don't have ANY passion. It's awful!
12:40pm
Your daughter's made enormous progress.
Oliver's handsome, don't you think?
Who's the woman with the baby?
Probably his sister...
That's... that's HIS WIFE!
I'm through with riding. He was the man of my dreams. I was going to wait for him till I was an adult!
He was my soulmate!

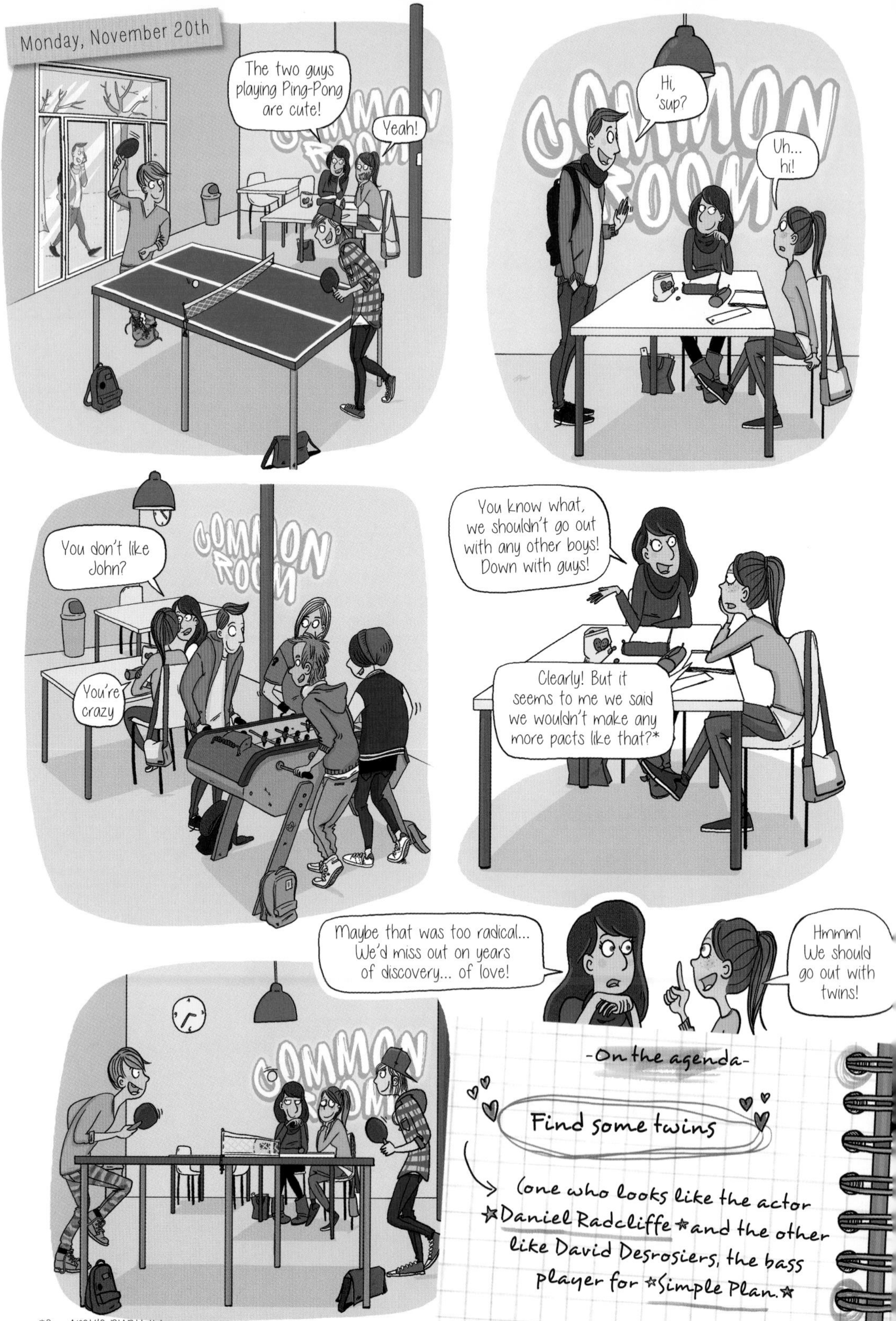

Monday, November 20th
The two guys playing Ping-Pong are cute!
Yeah!
COMMON ROOM
Hi, 'sup?
Uh... hi!
COMMON ROOM
You don't like John?
You're crazy
COMMON ROOM
You know what, we shouldn't go out with any other boys! Down with guys!
Clearly! But it seems to me we said we wouldn't make any more pacts like that?*
Maybe that was too radical... We'd miss out on years of discovery... of love!
Hmmm! We should go out with twins!
COMMON ROOM
-On the agenda-
Find some twins
(one who looks like the actor ☆Daniel Radcliffe☆ and the other like David Desrosiers, the bass player for ☆Simple Plan.☆

*See AMY'S DIARY #1.

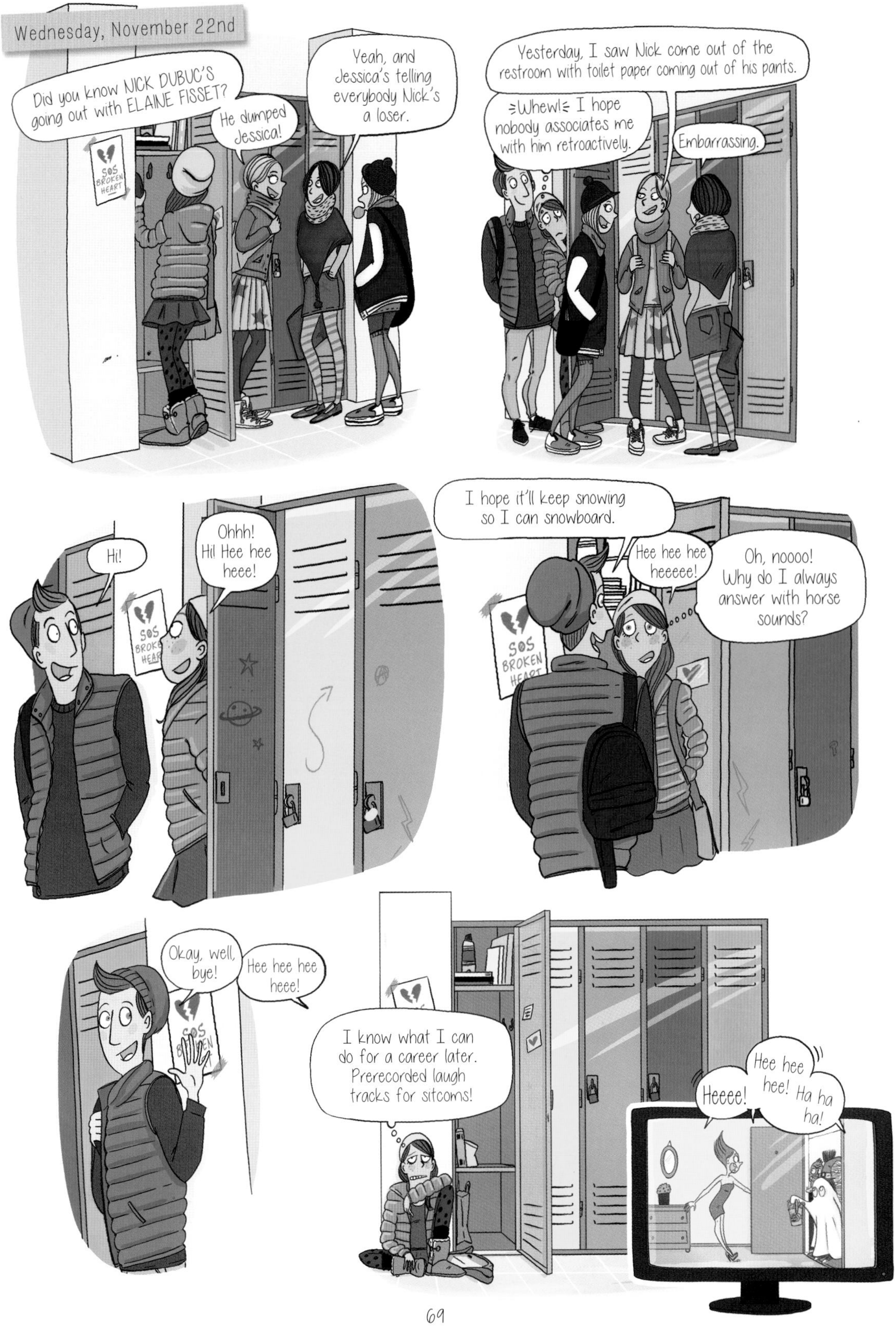
Wednesday, November 22nd
Did you know NICK DUBUC'S going out with ELAINE FISSET?
He dumped Jessica!
Yeah, and Jessica's telling everybody Nick's a loser.
Yesterday, I saw Nick come out of the restroom with toilet paper coming out of his pants.
Whew! I hope nobody associates me with him retroactively.
Embarrassing.
SOS BROKEN HEART
Hi!
Ohhh! Hi! Hee hee heee!
I hope it'll keep snowing so I can snowboard.
Hee hee hee heeeee!
Oh, noooo! Why do I always answer with horse sounds?
Okay, well, bye!
Hee hee hee heee!
I know what I can do for a career later. Prerecorded laugh tracks for sitcoms!
Heeee!
Hee hee hee! Ha ha ha!

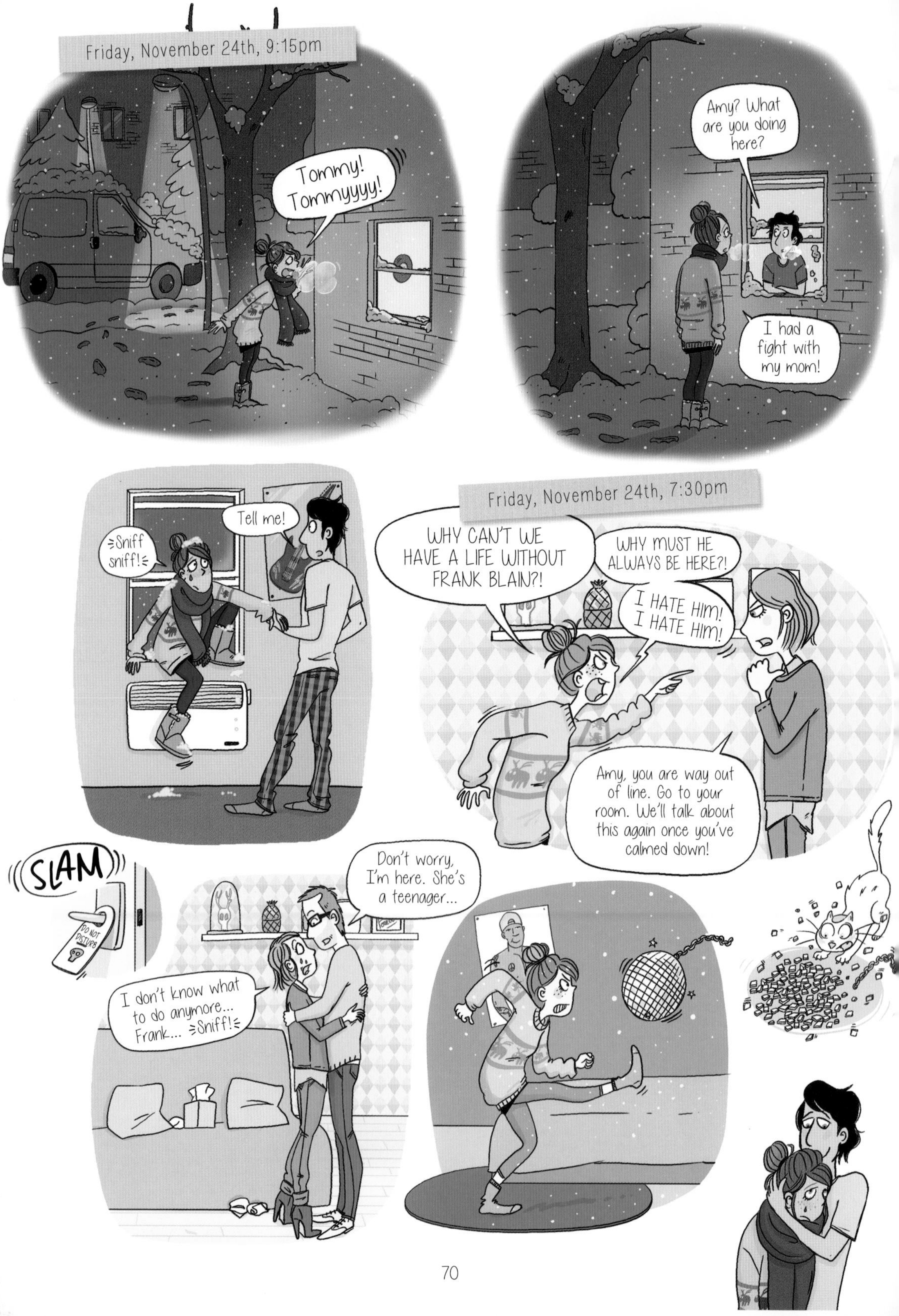

Friday, November 24th, 9:15pm
Tommy! Tommyyyy!
Amy? What are you doing here?
I had a fight with my mom!
Sniff sniff!
Tell me!
Friday, November 24th, 7:30pm
WHY CAN'T WE HAVE A LIFE WITHOUT FRANK BLAIN?!
WHY MUST HE ALWAYS BE HERE?!
I HATE HIM! I HATE HIM!
Amy, you are way out of line. Go to your room. We'll talk about this again once you've calmed down!
SLAM
DO NOT DISTURB
Don't worry, I'm here. She's a teenager...
I don't know what to do anymore... Frank... Sniff!

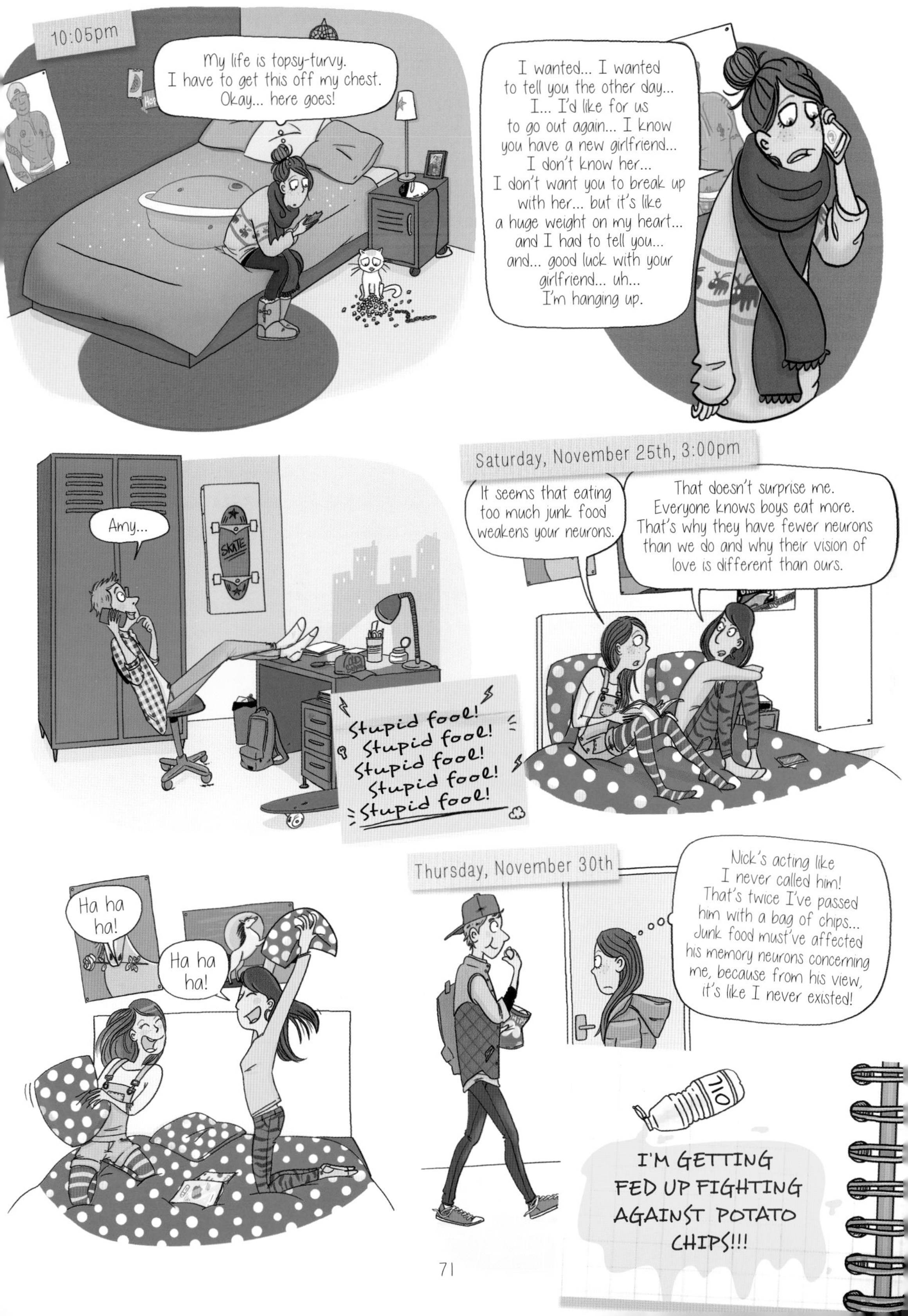
10:05pm
My life is topsy-turvy. I have to get this off my chest. Okay... here goes!
Hop
I wanted... I wanted to tell you the other day... I... I'd like for us to go out again... I know you have a new girlfriend... I don't know her... I don't want you to break up with her... but it's like a huge weight on my heart... and I had to tell you... and... good luck with your girlfriend... uh... I'm hanging up.
Amy...
SKATE
Stupid fool! Stupid fool! Stupid fool! Stupid fool! Stupid fool!
Saturday, November 25th, 3:00pm
It seems that eating too much junk food weakens your neurons.
That doesn't surprise me. Everyone knows boys eat more. That's why they have fewer neurons than we do and why their vision of love is different than ours.
Ha ha ha!
Ha ha ha!
Thursday, November 30th
Nick's acting like I never called him! That's twice I've passed him with a bag of chips... Junk food must've affected his memory neurons concerning me, because from his view, it's like I never existed!
OIL
I'M GETTING FED UP FIGHTING AGAINST POTATO CHIPS!!!

DECEMBER
Back to Basics

-Saturday, December 2nd:

10:15am:

I had a discussion with my mom a few days ago, following our blowout. She came to my bedroom and told me: "We can't go on like this anymore... I don't really understand what's going on lately. We're not on the same wavelength anymore... before we had good times together, it seems to me..."

In fact, this is yet more irrefutable proof of my mom's bad memory!

Ever since my dad's death, she's been little more than a nervous wreck dragging around in sweats when she was at home. I was worried about her. I especially remember wanting to do anything to try to console her so that, once she was better, we could have some good times together!

And then, once she did start doing a little better, she met Frank Blay and HE's the one enjoying her good mood!

I told her that, to me, it was like she was in a cult... The cult of love!

She asked me to apologize to Frank...
Yeah, I'll do it! And she asked me to invite him to the high school poetry slam... Grrrrrr!

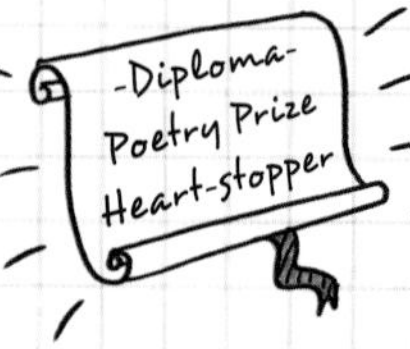
-Diploma-
Poetry Prize
Heart-stopper

8:35pm:

There's no snow any longer, it melted. The Christmas decorations look a little sad on the tree branches without leaves!

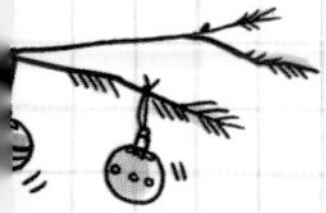

This afternoon, my mom caught Tommy and me having fun (we were pretending to fight on my bed). She thought we were dating, that we were kissing! Whatever... The result, I'm no longer allowed to have guy friends in my bedroom, if the door is closed. Pfffff!

My mom's a total nutjob!

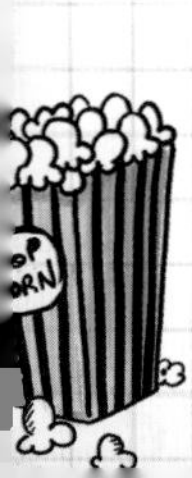

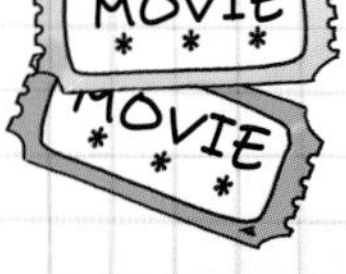
MOVIE
MOVIE

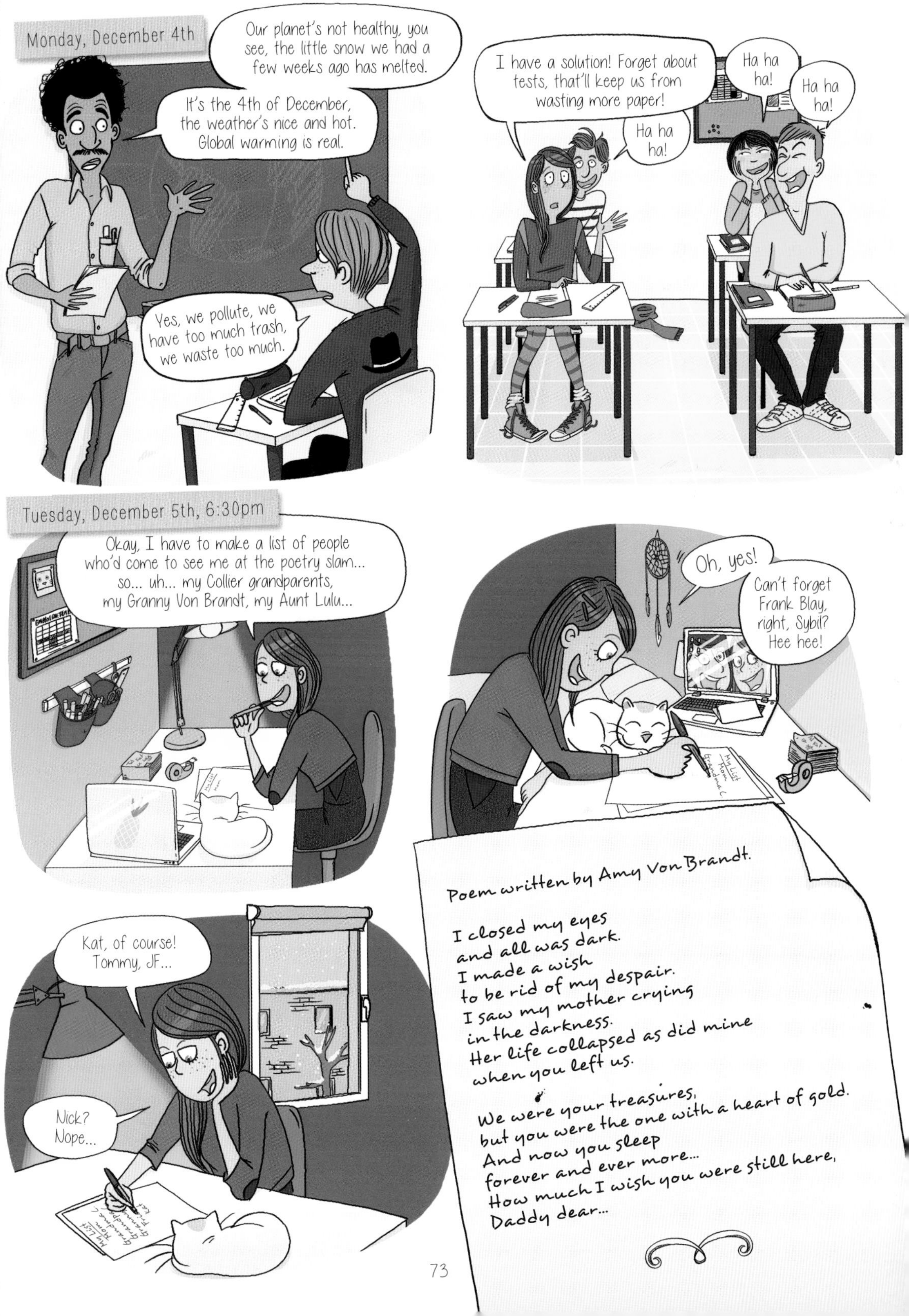
Monday, December 4th
Our planet's not healthy, you see, the little snow we had a few weeks ago has melted.
It's the 4th of December, the weather's nice and hot. Global warming is real.
Yes, we pollute, we have too much trash, we waste too much.
I have a solution! Forget about tests, that'll keep us from wasting more paper!
Ha ha ha!
Ha ha ha!
Ha ha ha!
Tuesday, December 5th, 6:30pm
Okay, I have to make a list of people who'd come to see me at the poetry slam... so... uh... my Collier grandparents, my Granny Von Brandt, my Aunt Lulu...
Oh, yes!
Can't forget Frank Blay, right, Sybil? Hee hee!
Kat, of course! Tommy, JF...
Nick? Nope...
Poem written by Amy Von Brandt.
I closed my eyes
and all was dark.
I made a wish
to be rid of my despair.
I saw my mother crying
in the darkness.
Her life collapsed as did mine
when you left us.
We were your treasures,
but you were the one with a heart of gold.
And now you sleep
forever and ever more...
How much I wish you were still here,
Daddy dear...

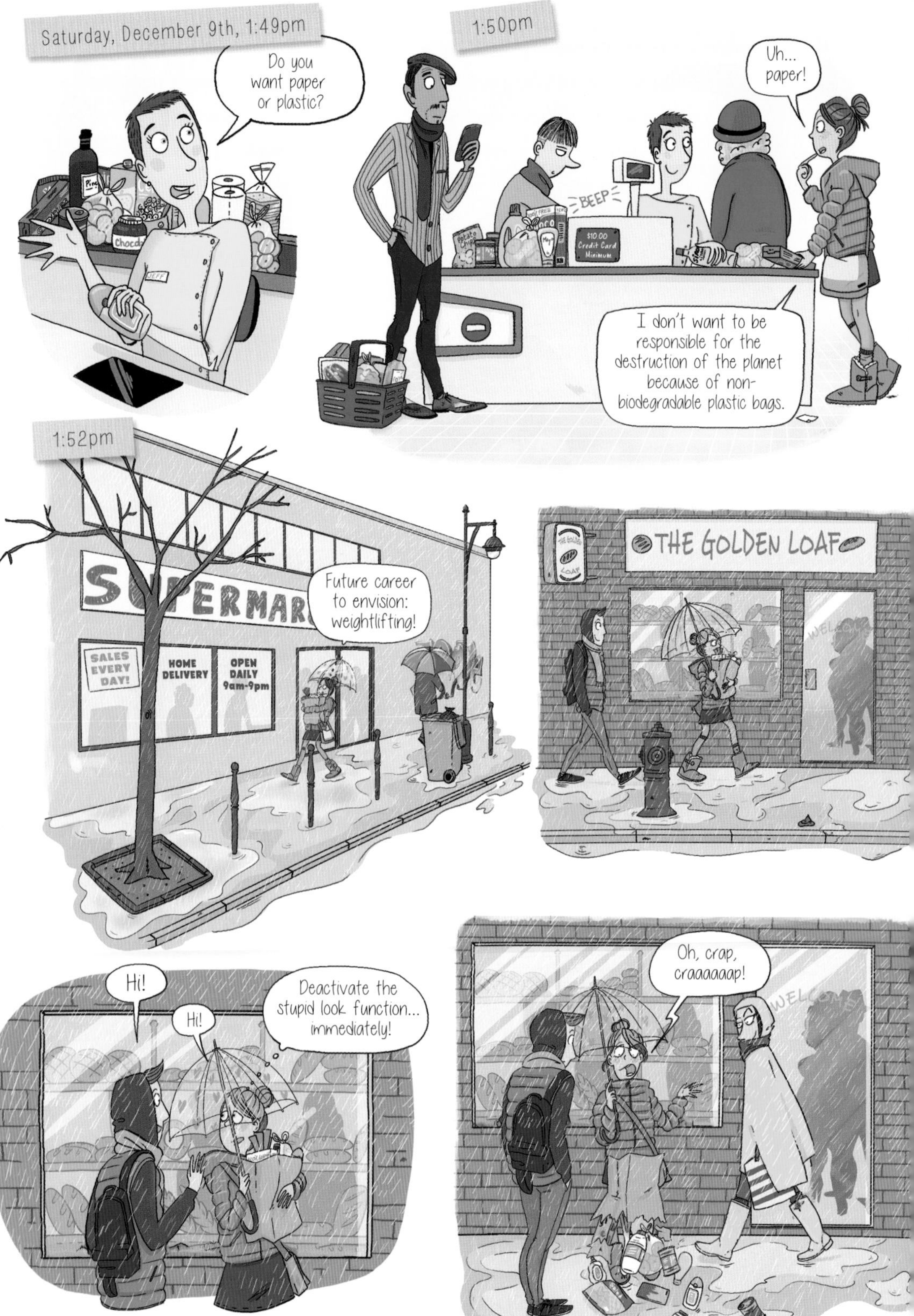
Saturday, December 9th, 1:49pm
Do you want paper or plastic?
JEFF
1:50pm
BEEP
$10.00 Credit Card Minimum
Uh... paper!
I don't want to be responsible for the destruction of the planet because of non-biodegradable plastic bags.
1:52pm
SUPERMAR
SALES EVERY DAY!
HOME DELIVERY
OPEN DAILY 9am-9pm
Future career to envision: weightlifting!
THE GOLDEN LOAF
Hi!
Hi!
Deactivate the stupid look function... immediately!
Oh, crap, craaaaaap!

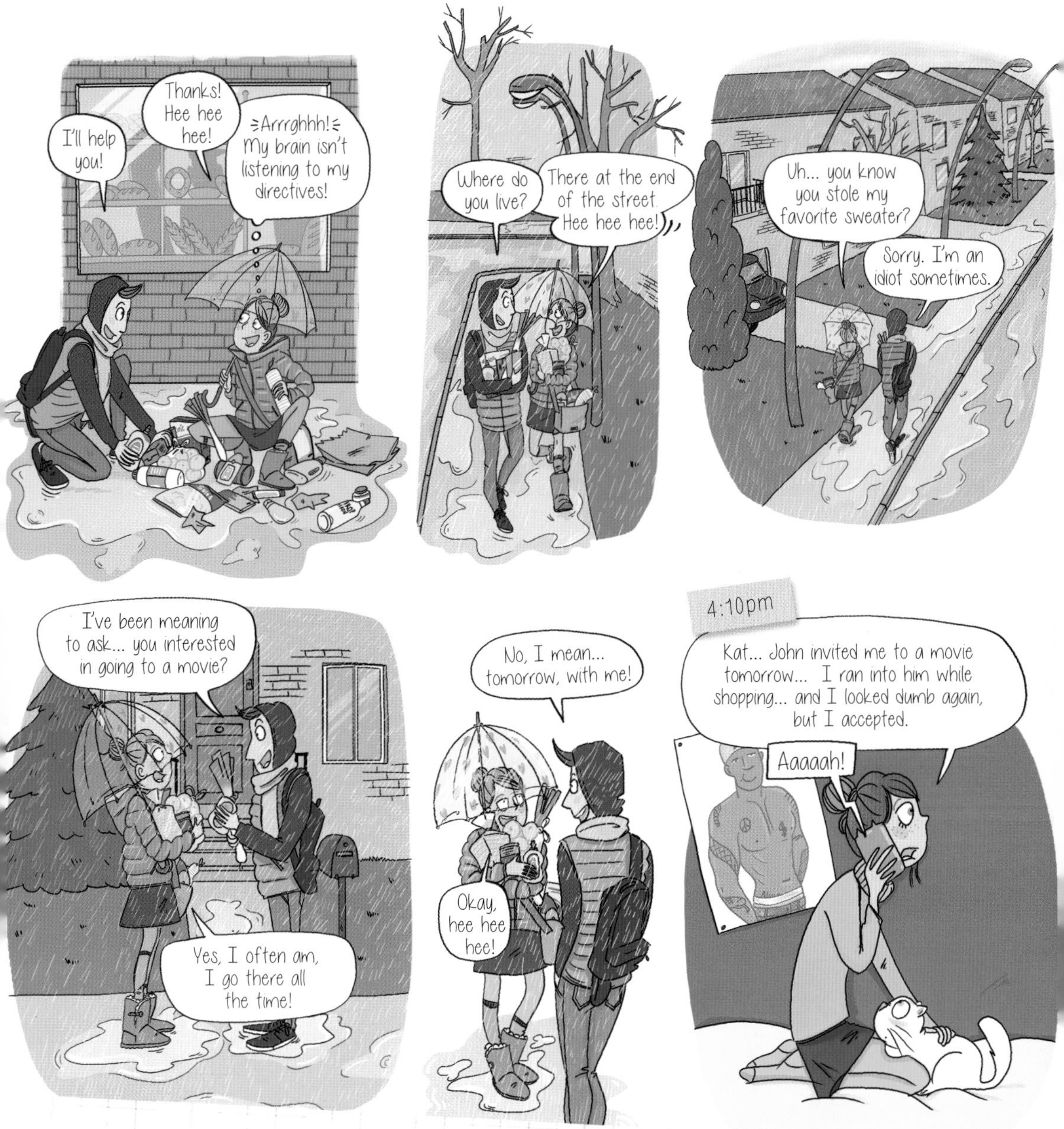
I'll help you!
Thanks! Hee hee hee!
Arrrghhh! My brain isn't listening to my directives!
Where do you live?
There at the end of the street. Hee hee hee!
Uh... you know you stole my favorite sweater?
Sorry. I'm an idiot sometimes.
I've been meaning to ask... you interested in going to a movie?
Yes, I often am, I go there all the time!
No, I mean... tomorrow, with me!
Okay, hee hee hee!
4:10pm
Kat... John invited me to a movie tomorrow... I ran into him while shopping... and I looked dumb again, but I accepted.
Aaaaah!

-Note to myself:

The function "intelligent look" seems officially defective whenever I run into John!!!! But he doesn't seem to notice. Maybe he likes numbskulls and thinks I'm one? But I'm not! (In any case, not as far as I know, but it's true, if I were one, I wouldn't realize it).

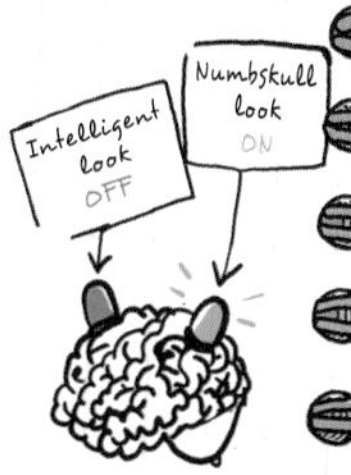
Intelligent look OFF
Numbskull look ON

PS: Try to stop giving myself a headache with random thoughts.

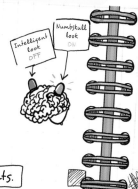

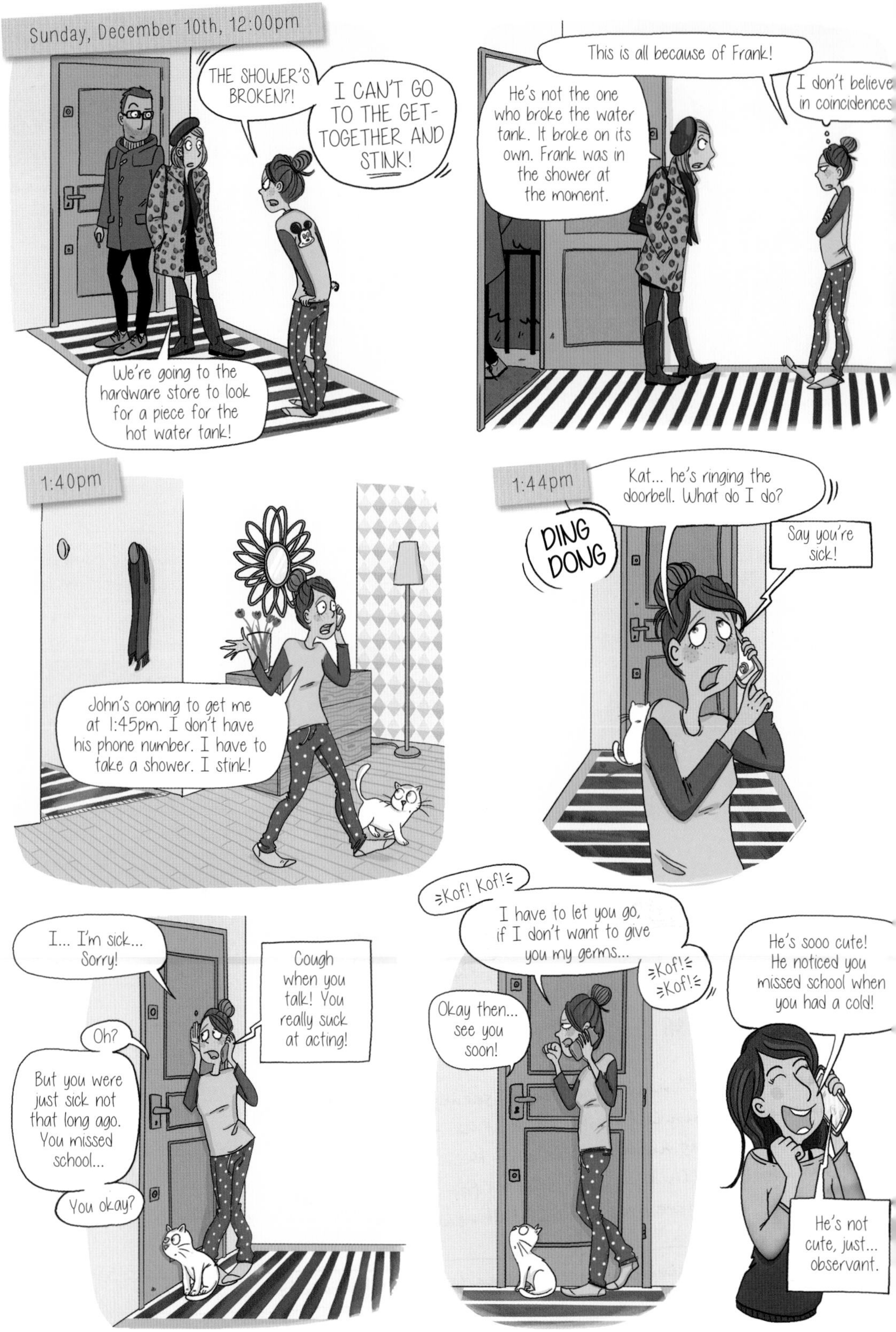
Sunday, December 10th, 12:00pm
THE SHOWER'S BROKEN?!
I CAN'T GO TO THE GET-TOGETHER AND STINK!
We're going to the hardware store to look for a piece for the hot water tank!
This is all because of Frank!
He's not the one who broke the water tank. It broke on its own. Frank was in the shower at the moment.
I don't believe in coincidences
1:40pm
John's coming to get me at 1:45pm. I don't have his phone number. I have to take a shower. I stink!
1:44pm
Kat... he's ringing the doorbell. What do I do?
DING DONG
Say you're sick!
I... I'm sick... Sorry!
Cough when you talk! You really suck at acting!
Oh?
But you were just sick not that long ago. You missed school...
You okay?
Kof! Kof!
I have to let you go, if I don't want to give you my germs...
Kof! Kof!
Okay then... see you soon!
He's sooo cute! He noticed you missed school when you had a cold!
He's not cute, just... observant.

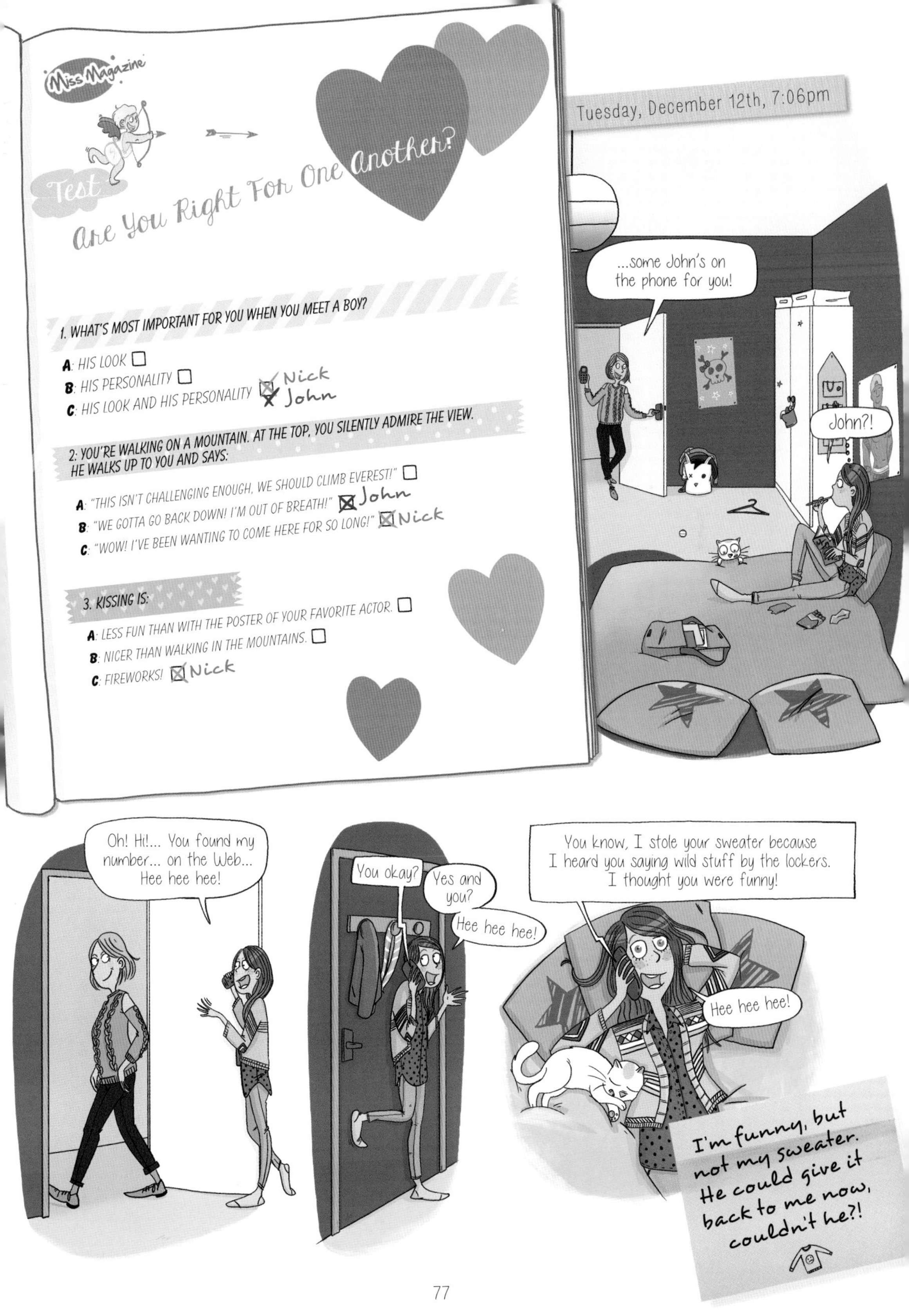
Miss Magazine
Test
Are You Right For One Another?
1. WHAT'S MOST IMPORTANT FOR YOU WHEN YOU MEET A BOY?
A: HIS LOOK
B: HIS PERSONALITY
C: HIS LOOK AND HIS PERSONALITY
Nick
John
2: YOU'RE WALKING ON A MOUNTAIN. AT THE TOP, YOU SILENTLY ADMIRE THE VIEW. HE WALKS UP TO YOU AND SAYS:
A: "THIS ISN'T CHALLENGING ENOUGH, WE SHOULD CLIMB EVEREST!"
B: "WE GOTTA GO BACK DOWN! I'M OUT OF BREATH!"
John
C: "WOW! I'VE BEEN WANTING TO COME HERE FOR SO LONG!"
Nick
3. KISSING IS:
A: LESS FUN THAN WITH THE POSTER OF YOUR FAVORITE ACTOR.
B: NICER THAN WALKING IN THE MOUNTAINS.
C: FIREWORKS!
Nick
Tuesday, December 12th, 7:06pm
...some John's on the phone for you!
John?!
Oh! Hi!... You found my number... on the Web... Hee hee hee!
You okay?
Yes and you?
Hee hee hee!
You know, I stole your sweater because I heard you saying wild stuff by the lockers. I thought you were funny!
Hee hee hee!
I'm funny, but not my sweater. He could give it back to me now, couldn't he?!

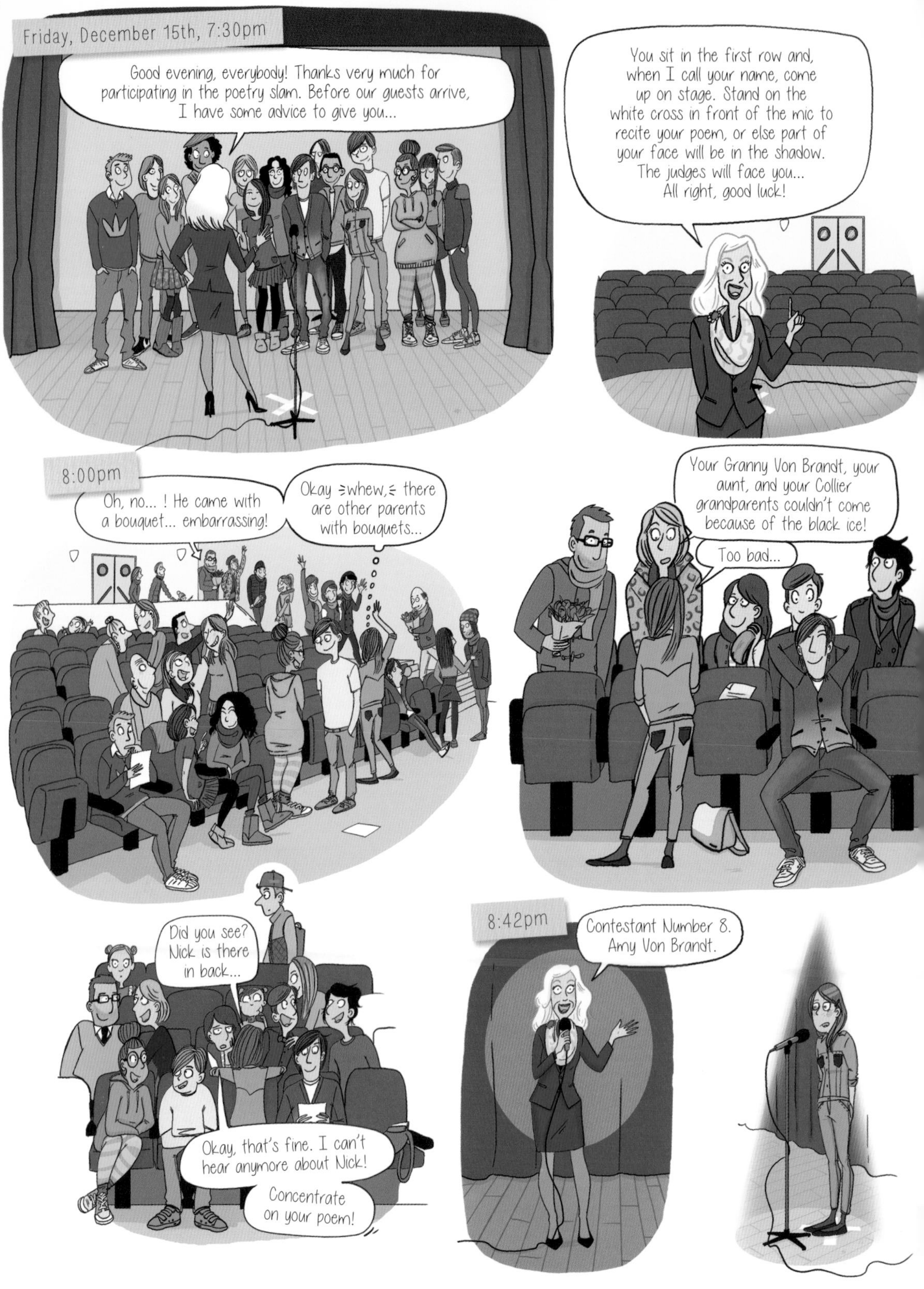
Friday, December 15th, 7:30pm
Good evening, everybody! Thanks very much for participating in the poetry slam. Before our guests arrive, I have some advice to give you...
You sit in the first row and, when I call your name, come up on stage. Stand on the white cross in front of the mic to recite your poem, or else part of your face will be in the shadow. The judges will face you... All right, good luck!
8:00pm
Oh, no... ! He came with a bouquet... embarrassing!
Okay ≥whew,≤ there are other parents with bouquets...
Your Granny Von Brandt, your aunt, and your Collier grandparents couldn't come because of the black ice!
Too bad...
Did you see? Nick is there in back...
Okay, that's fine. I can't hear anymore about Nick!
Concentrate on your poem!
8:42pm
Contestant Number 8. Amy Von Brandt.

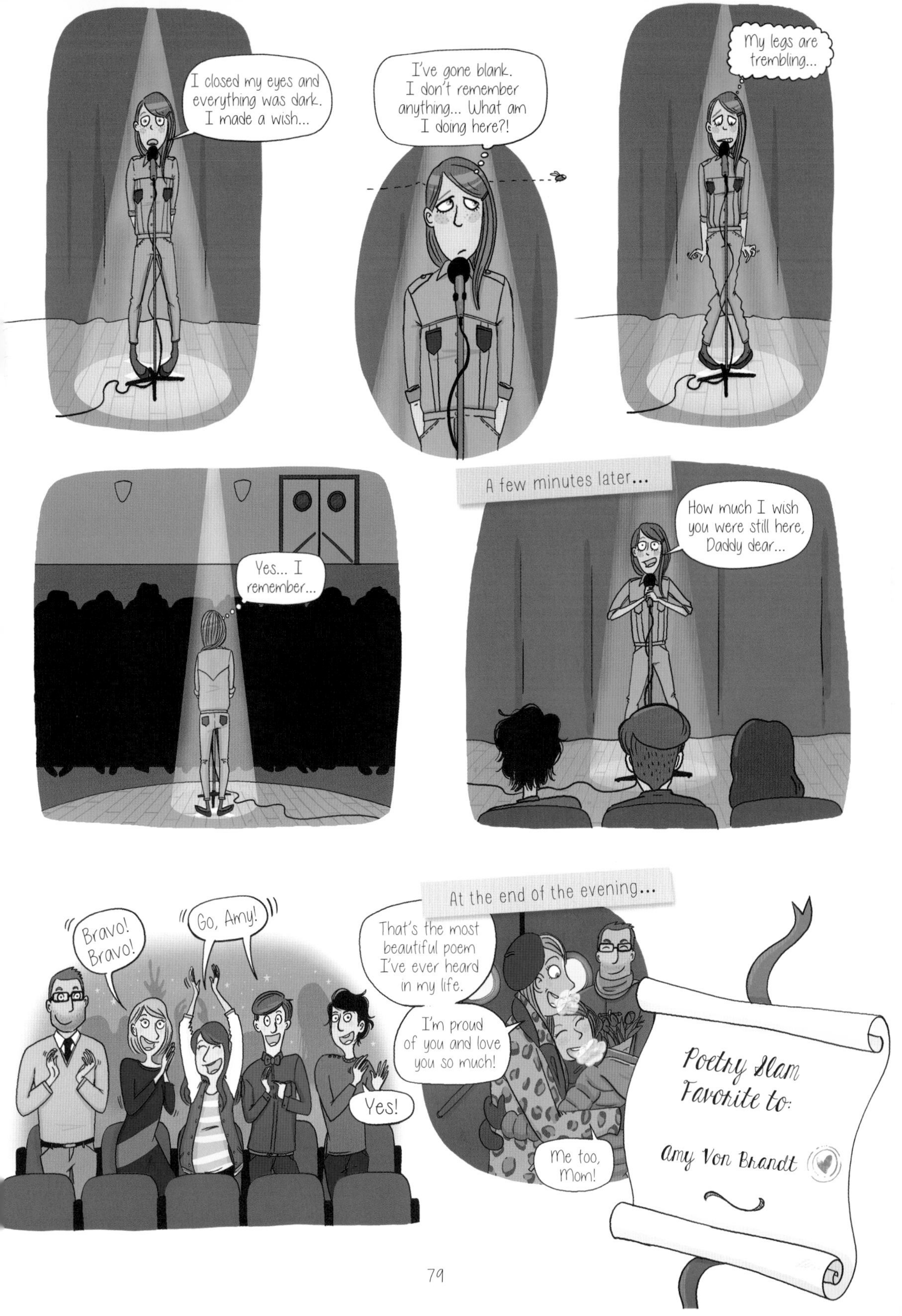
I closed my eyes and everything was dark. I made a wish...
I've gone blank. I don't remember anything... What am I doing here?!
My legs are trembling...
Yes... I remember...
A few minutes later...
How much I wish you were still here, Daddy dear...
Bravo! Bravo!
Go, Amy!
Yes!
At the end of the evening...
That's the most beautiful poem I've ever heard in my life.
I'm proud of you and love you so much!
Me too, Mom!
Poetry Slam Favorite to:
Amy Von Brandt

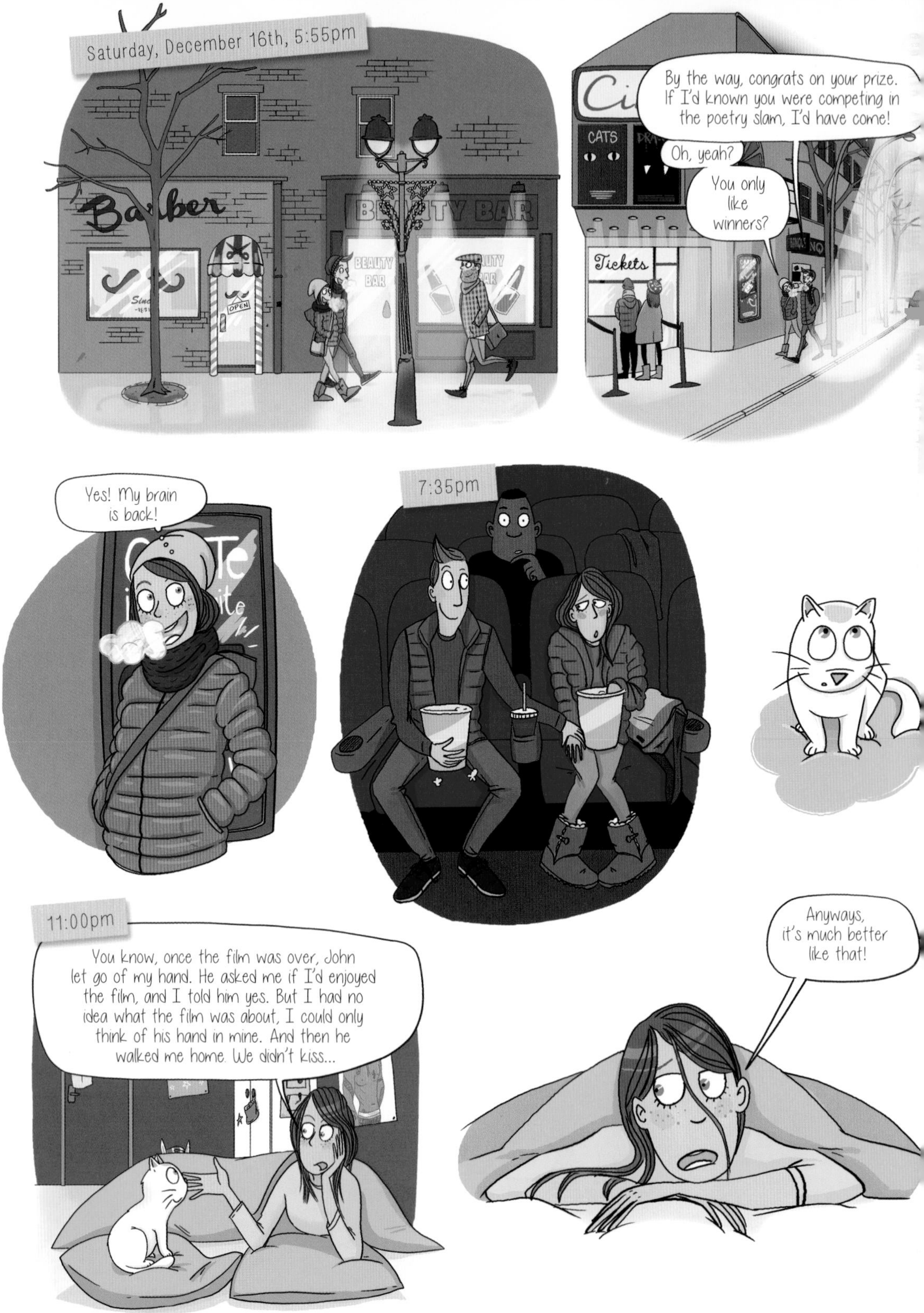
Saturday, December 16th, 5:55pm
Barber
OPEN
BEAUTY BAR
CATS
Tickets
By the way, congrats on your prize. If I'd known you were competing in the poetry slam, I'd have come!
Oh, yeah?
You only like winners?
Yes! My brain is back!
7:35pm
11:00pm
You know, once the film was over, John let go of my hand. He asked me if I'd enjoyed the film, and I told him yes. But I had no idea what the film was about, I could only think of his hand in mine. And then he walked me home. We didn't kiss...
Anyways, it's much better like that!

Clearly my emotions are on a real rollercoaster!
I go from totally-proud-of-myself to
extreme-anger-frustration. The cause?
Nick. I don't understand why I'm so mad at him!
Probably because I understand now I didn't
matter much to him. I asked him if I'd just
been another girl to him.
And he said: No.
That's cool though! But he asked me if we
could be friends... FRIENDS!!! I said yes.
I didn't want to refuse and for him to feel embarrassed
about his proposal. And I wanted to rise above
all that. Love hurts too much.

"I'LL NEVER FALL IN LOVE AGAIN"
(cross my heart!)

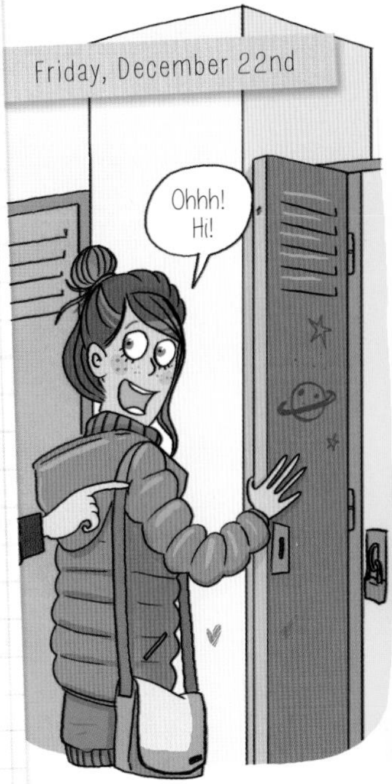

Friday, December 22nd
Ohhh! Hi!

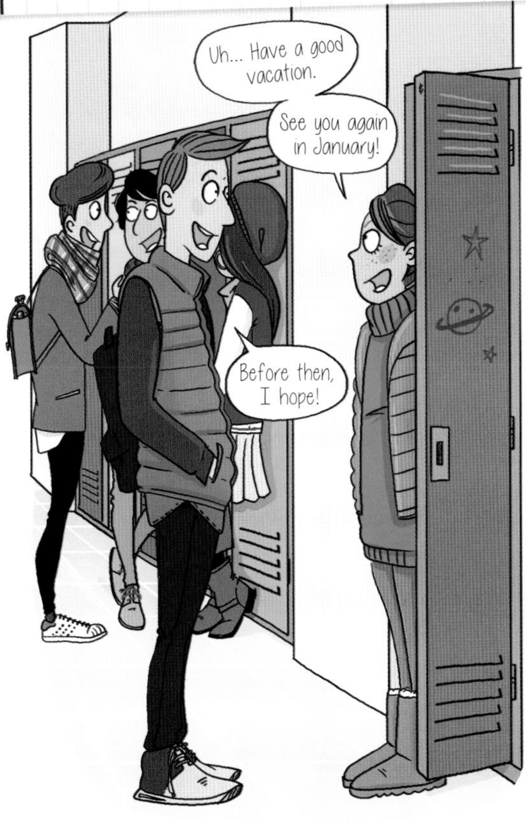

Uh... Have a good vacation.
See you again in January!
Before then, I hope!

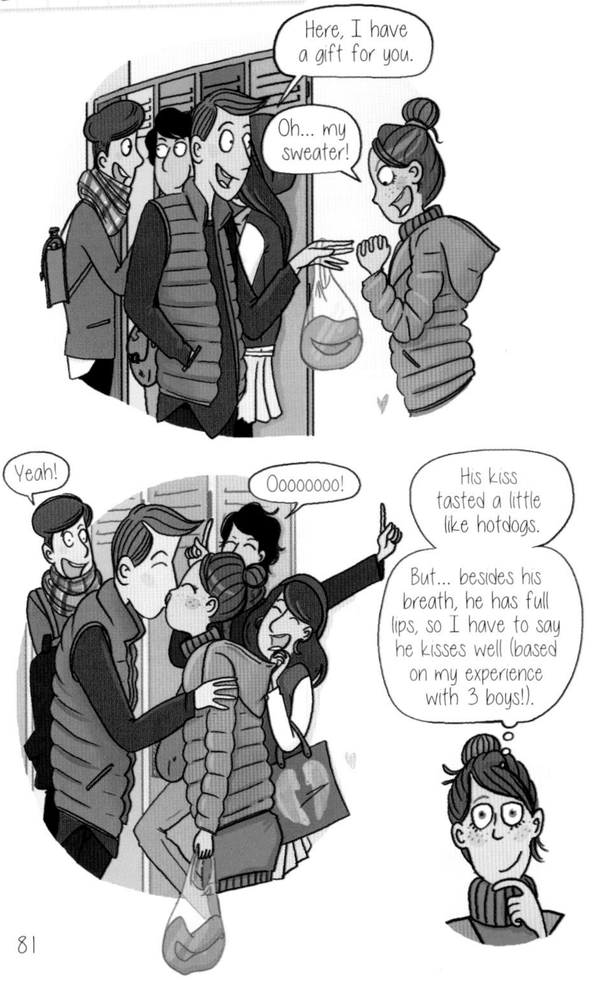

Here, I have a gift for you.
Oh... my sweater!
Yeah!
Ooooooo!
His kiss tasted a little like hotdogs.
But... besides his breath, he has full lips, so I have to say he kisses well (based on my experience with 3 boys!).

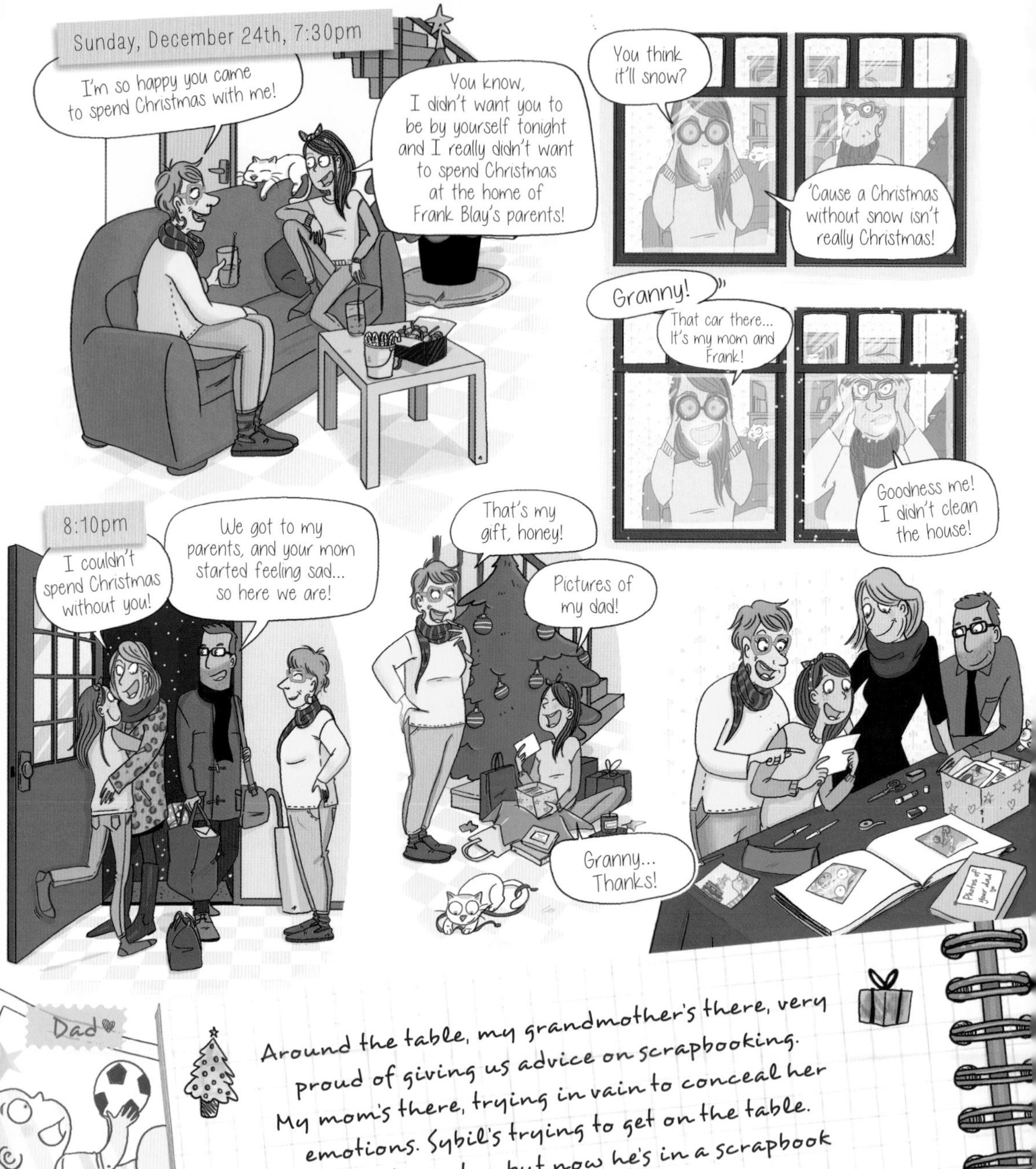

Sunday, December 24th, 7:30pm
I'm so happy you came to spend Christmas with me!
You know, I didn't want you to be by yourself tonight and I really didn't want to spend Christmas at the home of Frank Blay's parents!
You think it'll snow?
'Cause a Christmas without snow isn't really Christmas!
Granny!
That car there... It's my mom and Frank!
Goodness me! I didn't clean the house!
8:10pm
I couldn't spend Christmas without you!
We got to my parents, and your mom started feeling sad... so here we are!
That's my gift, honey!
Pictures of my dad!
Granny... Thanks!
Photos of your dad

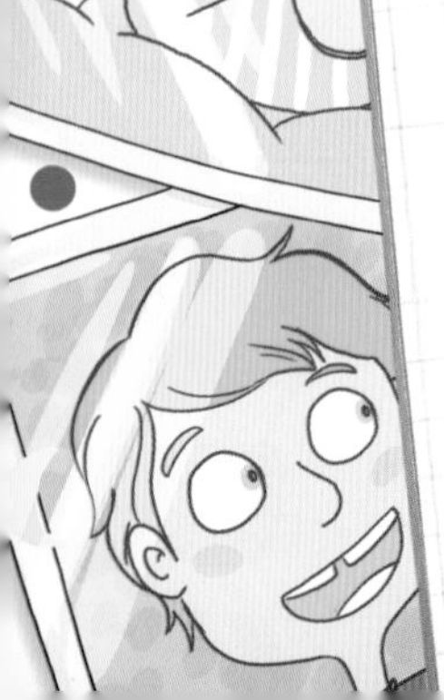

Dad

Around the table, my grandmother's there, very
proud of giving us advice on scrapbooking.
My mom's there, trying in vain to conceal her
emotions. Sybil's trying to get on the table.
My dad's there too, but now he's in a scrapbook
under construction.
(The future "most beautiful scrapbook in the world!").
And Frank's there, my mom's boyfriend, hearty
and alive, who consoles her over seeing my dad
in a scrapbook. And there's me. It's a weird
Christmas. With a weird family.

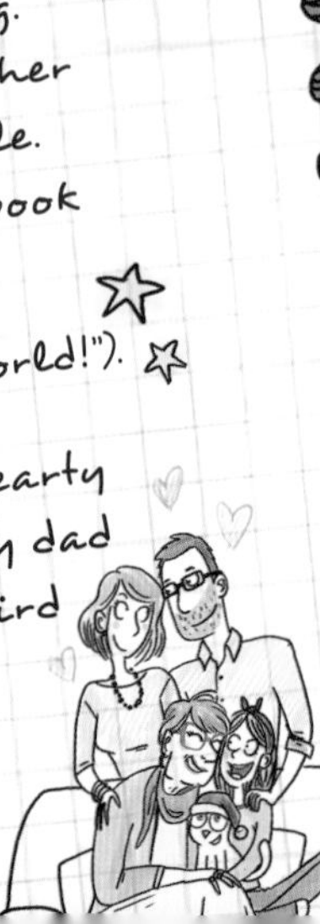

My family.

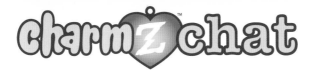

Charmz Chat

Welcome to AMY'S DIARY #2 "The World's Upside Down," based on the novels by India Desjardins, adapted by Véronique Grisseaux, writer, and Laëtitia Aynié, artist. While it may not be okay to snoop and read your friends' diaries, you're more than welcome to enjoy the diaries of Amy Von Brandt. While the response to the first volume of AMY'S DIARY from Charmz has been overwhelmingly favorable, there were a few folks who opined that many of the pop culture references were somewhat dated. Well, not only were those references dated – they were literally dated. This is a diary, after all. But perhaps we were a little too subtle about the fact that AMY'S DIARY isn't set in the present. Nor did we ever say it was. For all the amateur teen sleuths out there, the clues were right in front of you…

The first clue was right on the cover and title pages – that AMY'S DIARY is based on the best-selling novels by India Dejardins. Those novels were first published in 2006, so unless they were science fiction (and admittedly it did mention "Space Alien" in the title), they couldn't possibly be about a girl living in the present.

HANS CHRISTIAN ANDERSEN'S
The Little Mermaid
METAPHROG
PAPERCUTZ

The second clue was that on the very first page of the comics adaptation of AMY'S DIARY there is an actual date: Tuesday, September 13th. As we all know, the same date falls on a different day every year. For example, your birthday may fall on a Monday this year, but it may fall on a Tuesday next year. The most recent Tuesday to be on September 13th was in 2016, but that would've been ten years after the original novel was published. Tuesday, September 13th, 2011, was five years after the original novel was published. But Tuesday, September 13th, 2005 would be a year before the original novel was published – and that's our unofficial guess of when AMY'S DIARY is set. AMY'S DIARY #2 starts on Sunday, May 7th, which works out perfectly, making this volume of AMY'S DIARY take place in 2006. So what may've appeared as "dated" references if you thought AMY'S DIARY was set in the present, are actually totally correct for 2006. Whether it's *Dance, Dance Revolution* or the flip phones depicted, Laëtitia Annié has done her research to get the details right. Of course, *Minions* wasn't released until 2015, but shall we say *Henchmen* was ahead of its time? *The Little Mermaid* was released in 1989, so it all evens out.)

the SMURFS
3 IN 1
THE SMURFETTE
THE SMURFS AND THE EGG
THE SMURFS AND THE HOWLIBIRD
PAPERCUTZ

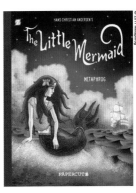

Speaking of details, we couldn't help noticing that one of the graphic novels that Amy's enjoying (see page 58) features Smurfette, from THE SMURFS. Charmz is actually an imprint of Papercutz, the company dedicated to publishing great graphic novels for all ages. We thought it would be fun to feature a short Smurfette story, to provide further insight into Amy's (upside-down) world. So, enjoy "A Kiss for Smurfette," from the Papercutz graphic novel, FOREVER SMURFETTE, on the following pages. And if you'd like to discover where Smurfette originally came from, may we suggest checking out THE SMURFS 3 IN 1 #2 which collects lots of wonderful tales of the Smurfs, including the story in which Smurfette made her debut.

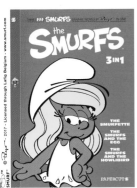

And since we did mention The Little Mermaid, too, we'd be remiss if we didn't mention the beautiful graphic novel adaptation by Metaphrog of the original Hans Christian Andersen classic, also from Papercutz.

But back to Charmz… remember we talked about MONICA ADVENTURES in Charmz Chat and ran a very short preview in AMY'S DIARY #1? Well, we're so excited about MONICA ADVENTURES, we're presenting a special article all about Monica on the following pages. We're convinced if you enjoy Amy and her friends, you'll also have fun hanging with Monica and her gang.

Finally, don't miss AMY'S DIARY #3 "Moving On" coming soon. If there's one thing we can count on in life, is that things change. How we, or in this case Amy, copes with such changes is what makes life, and graphic novels, interesting.

Thanks,

Jim

Editor-in-Chief

STAY IN TOUCH!

EMAIL: salicrup@papercutz.com
WEB: Papercutz.com
TWITTER: @papercutzgn
INSTAGRAM: @papercutzgn
FACEBOOK: PAPERCUTZGRAPHICNOVELS
FANMAIL: Charmz, 160 Broadway, Suite 700, East Wing, New York, NY 10038

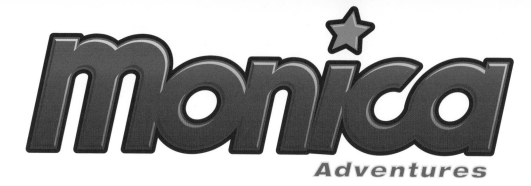

Monica

Adventures

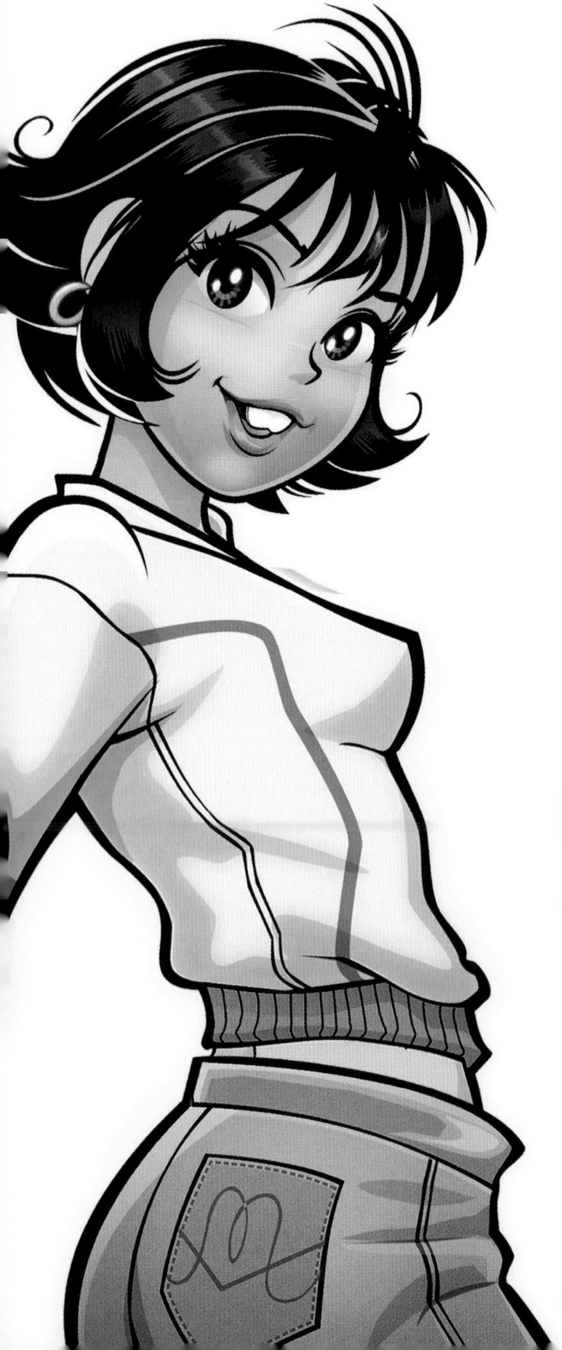

Meet Monica.

She is fierce, confident, and super strong. She won't put up with anyone teasing her or her friends. She's always been like that…

Monica's first appearance in Jimmy Five's newspaper strip on March 3rd, 1963. Even if you don't speak Portuguese, you can see the start of this comic rivalry.

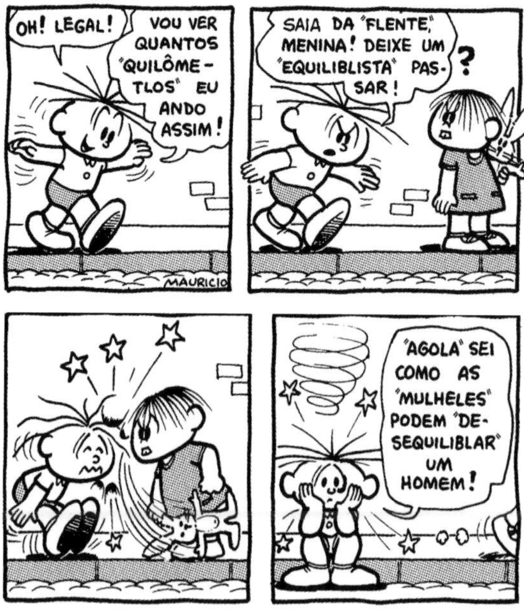

OH! LEGAL!
VOU VER QUANTOS "QUILÔME-TLOS" EU ANDO ASSIM!
MAURICIO
SAIA DA "FLENTE" MENINA! DEIXE UM "EQUILIBLISTA" PAS-SAR!
?
"AGOLA" SEI COMO AS "MULHELES" PODEM "DE-SEQUILIBLAR" UM HOMEM!

Charmz, is proud to publish Monica's adolescent adventures in the United States and Canada for the first time. Monica and her gang have been friends for years, since childhood. Now, join Monica and her gang of friends as they take on all the ups and downs of high school life including dating, social media, crushes, gossip, or just finding the cash to enjoy a night at the movies.

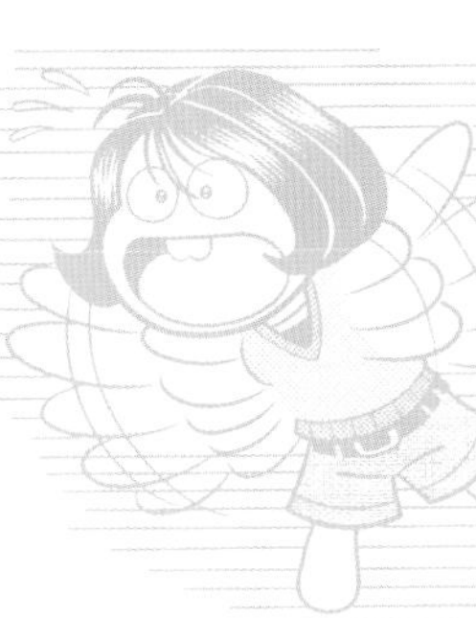

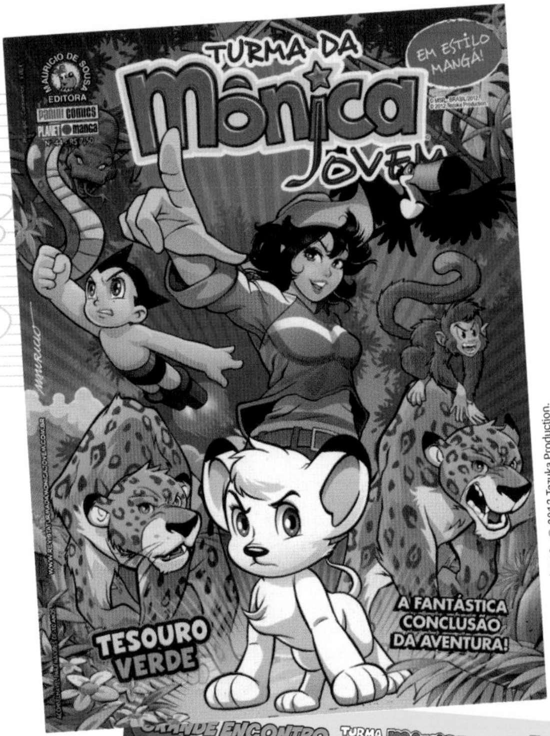
TURMA DA
Mônica
JOVEM
EM ESTILO MANGÁ!
TESOURO VERDE
A FANTÁSTICA CONCLUSÃO DA AVENTURA!

There's a lot to love about Monica. We asked celebrated comics writer Gail Simone for a blurb announcing Monica's arrival on the North American comics scene and here's what she wrote: "The international phenomenon comes to America, with all the charm, fun, and cuteness intact. Monica's here, gang!"

As Gail said, Monica is an international phenomenon. For example, Monica and J-Five have hobnobbed with *Astro Boy* and other classic manga characters such as *Kimba the White Lion* and *Princess Knight*. Mauricio de Sousa, Monica's creator, was a personal friend of their creator, the late master of manga, Osamu Tezuka. He even has a cameo in MONICA ADVENTURES #1!

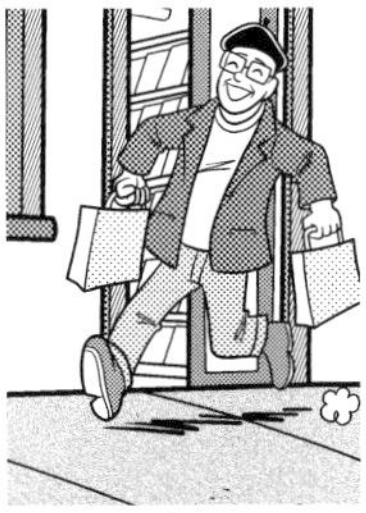

Osamu's cameo.

Not to be outdone, Monica then helped save the universe by teaming up with none other than the *Justice Leaugue*! That's right! Monica has met *Wonder Woman, Superman, Batman,* and all the rest. These adventures are only available in Brazil so far, but who knows what the future may bring?

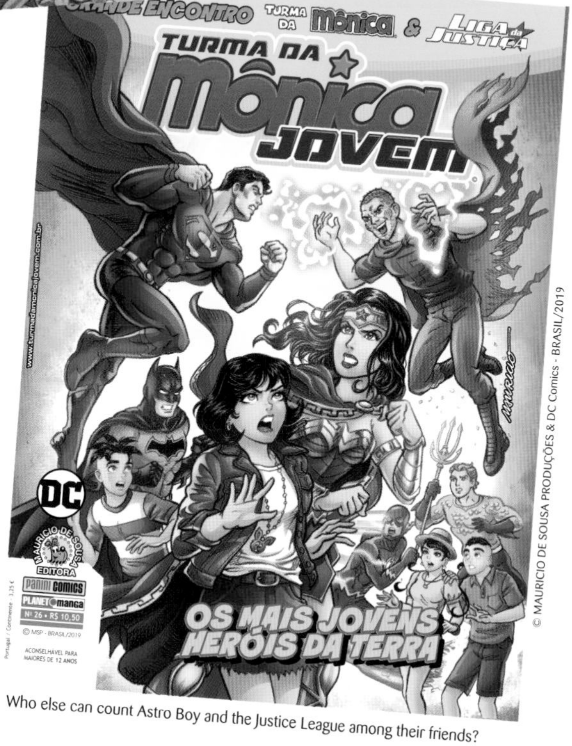
GRANDE ENCONTRO TURMA DA MÔNICA & LIGA da JUSTIÇA
TURMA DA
MÔNICA
JOVEM
OS MAIS JOVENS HERÓIS DA TERRA

Who else can count Astro Boy and the Justice League among their friends?

MONICA is actually one of the first ladies of comics. Created by legendary Brazilian cartoonist Mauricio de Sousa in 1963, her comic adventures as a young, super-strong girl in her neighborhood have taken most of the world by storm since her debut. Monica has been translated to 14 languages and has appeared in 40 countries and counting!

Here's a sneak peek at MONICA ADVENTURES #3:

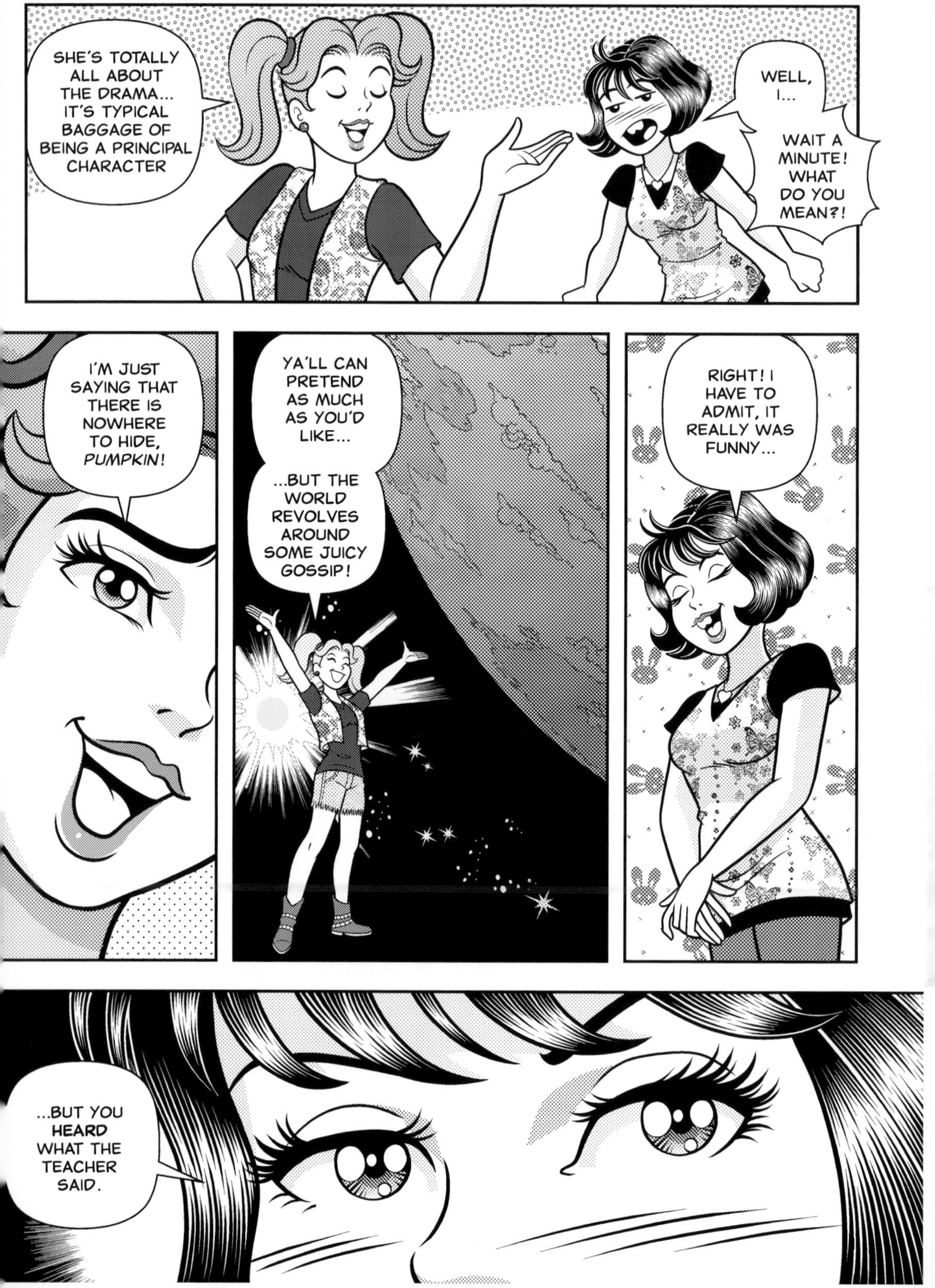
SHE'S TOTALLY ALL ABOUT THE DRAMA... IT'S TYPICAL BAGGAGE OF BEING A PRINCIPAL CHARACTER
WELL, I...
WAIT A MINUTE! WHAT DO YOU MEAN?!
I'M JUST SAYING THAT THERE IS NOWHERE TO HIDE, *PUMPKIN*!
YA'LL CAN PRETEND AS MUCH AS YOU'D LIKE...
...BUT THE WORLD REVOLVES AROUND SOME JUICY GOSSIP!
RIGHT! I HAVE TO ADMIT, IT REALLY WAS FUNNY...
...BUT YOU **HEARD** WHAT THE TEACHER SAID.

Now, thanks to resident Monica fan, managing editor Jeff Whitman, Charmz is bringing Monica to the USA and Canada. "In Brazil, Monica is everywhere you look, from diapers to headlining Comic Cons that rival the big ones here. She is the bestselling brand in Brazil and it is virtually impossible to avoid her influence there," said Jeff. "Her comics are pure enjoyment, with a robust cast of colorful characters you can identify with, zany plots spoofing or parodying all genres, and with a gentle reminder of how it is to be a kid. She is timeless. I knew her adventures as a teenager, presented in a manga-like style, would be perfect for North American audiences.

There's humor, drama, and a whole lot of heart. It is an impressive repertoire that we are just beginning to scratch the surface of. Creator Mauricio de Sousa, his daughter (the real-life inspiration behind Monica!), and the whole studio in Brazil has welcomed Charmz and me with open arms. Bringing these wonderful comics to the United States and Canada was the next logical step for Monica and her friends!"

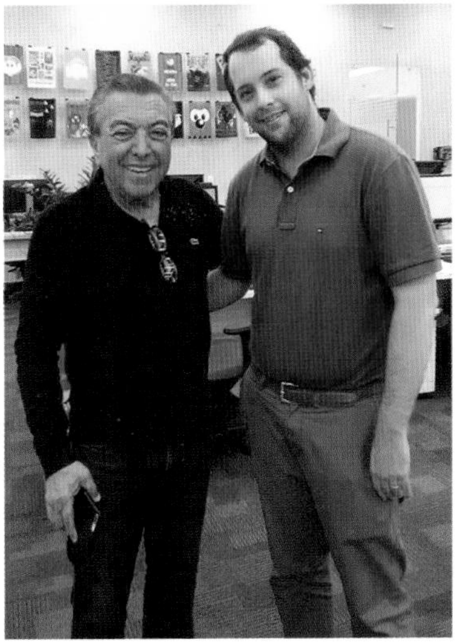

MONICA creator, Mauricio de Sousa, with Monica fan and Charmz editor, Jeff Whitman.

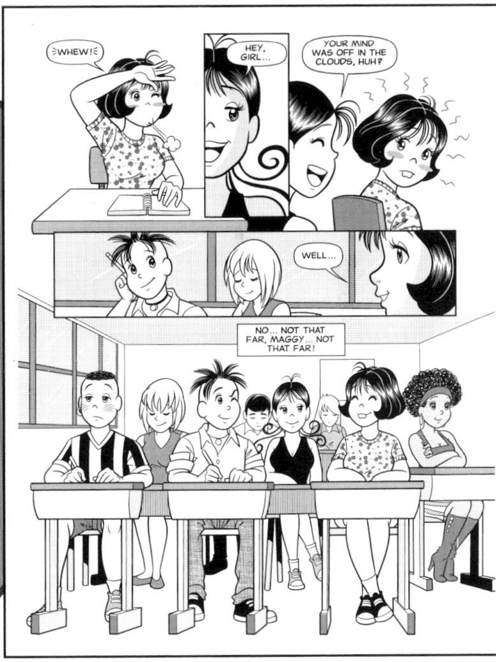
WHEW!
HEY, GIRL...
YOUR MIND WAS OFF IN THE CLOUDS, HUH?
WELL...
NO... NOT THAT FAR, MAGGY... NOT THAT FAR!

Monica and her gang aren't kids anymore in MONICA ADVENTURES. But things haven't changed much as Monica got older. Jimmy-Five now goes by J-Five but still gets tongue-tied around Monica. Instead of teasing her, he pines for her, and hopes to be as successful as her one day. Maggy tries to eat healthier these days, and Smudge has accepted the necessity of a shower, but old habits die hard!

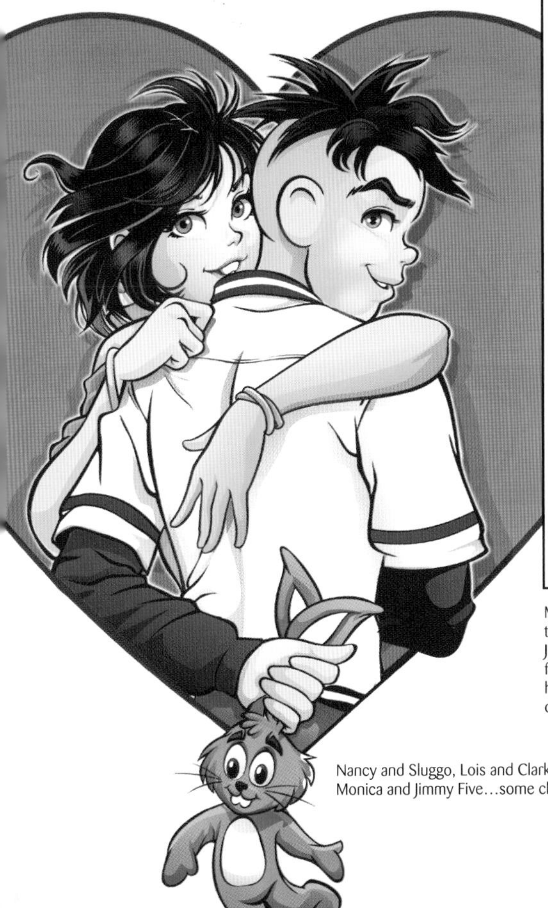

Nancy and Sluggo, Lois and Clark, Jane and Tarzan, Monica and Jimmy Five...some classic comics couples.

Monica first appeared as a young girl in the comics, always running her block as the girl-in-charge. Super-strong, with a short temper and a rather short stature, she was the perfect target for the conniving, but lovable, Jimmy Five (the five stands for the amount of hairs on his head), and his best friend Smudge, who is certifiably afraid of water, to come up with all sorts of maniacal and "infallible" plans to usurp Monica as the leader of their group of friends. Plans, which Monica usually can thwart with her eyes closed and some help from her blue plush rabbit (that doubles as a dangerous projectile), Samson. Add in Monica's best friend, the always-famished Maggy, and some other unforgettable and relatable neighborhood kids and the recipe (calm down, Maggy, not that kind of recipe!) for fun is endless.

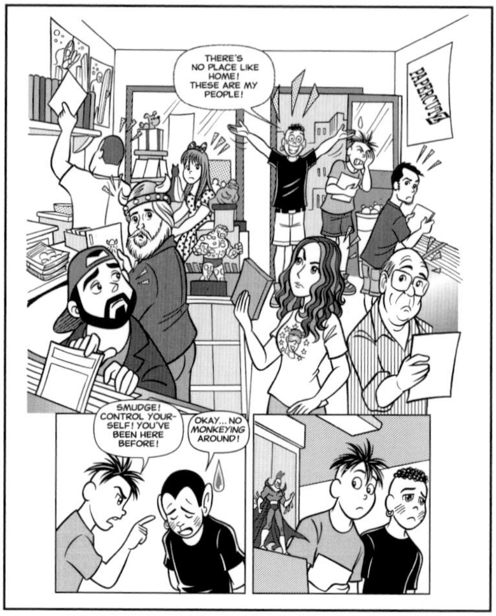
THERE'S NO PLACE LIKE HOME! THESE ARE MY PEOPLE!
PAPERCUTZ
SMUDGE! CONTROL YOURSELF! YOU'VE BEEN HERE BEFORE!
OKAY... NO MONKEYING AROUND!
J-Five and Smudge are bigger comicbook nerds than anyone we know!

Already picked up the first two volumes of MONICA ADVENTURES and want more Monica now without having to take an intensive Portuguese class? Head over to YouTube and check out the "Monica Toy Official" channel to see hundreds of videos of Monica and friends. The best part? The videos have no words! Monica's comedic timing needs no explanation! While you're there, tell them your friends at Charmz sent you!

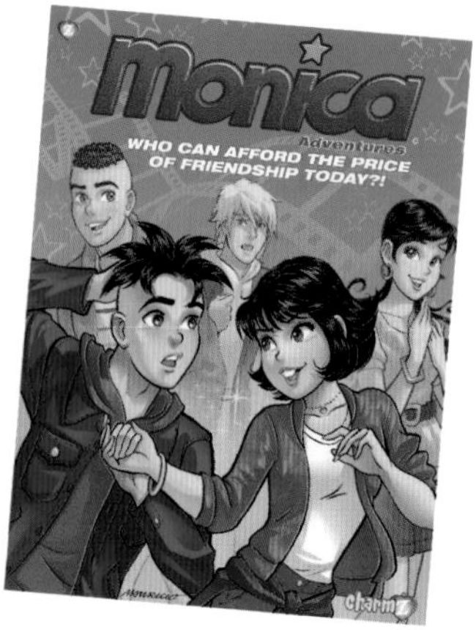
Monica
Adventures
WHO CAN AFFORD THE PRICE OF FRIENDSHIP TODAY?!
Charmz

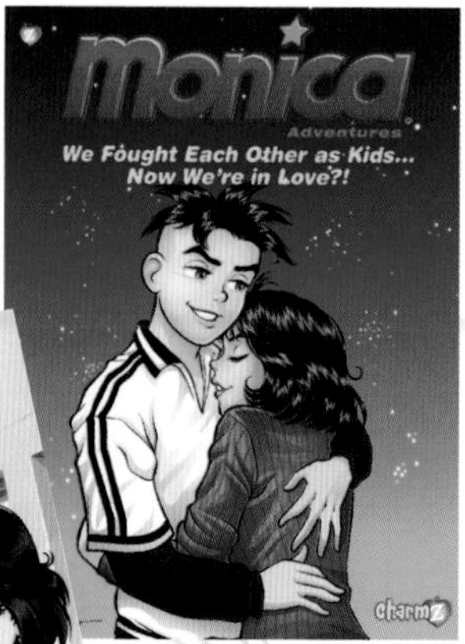
Monica
Adventures
We Fought Each Other as Kids... Now We're in Love?!
Charmz

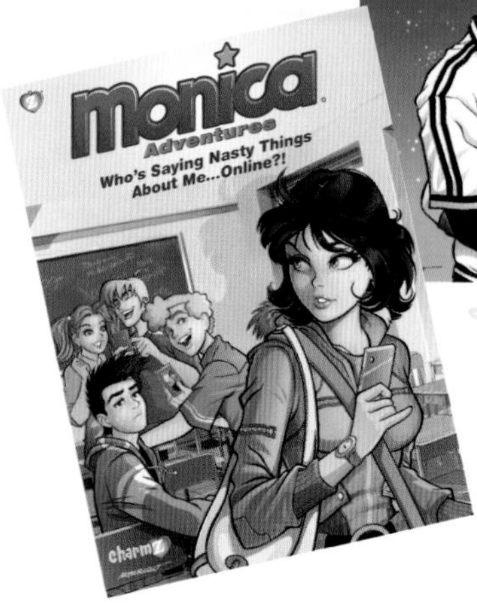
Monica
Adventures
Who's Saying Nasty Things About Me...Online?!
Charmz

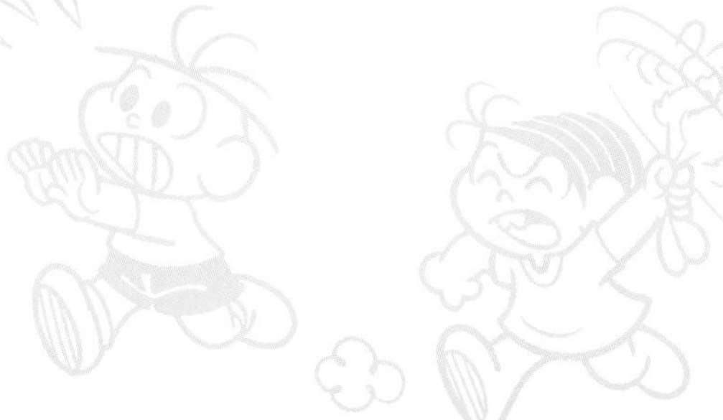

Bonus! Here's a story from FOREVER SMURFETTE...

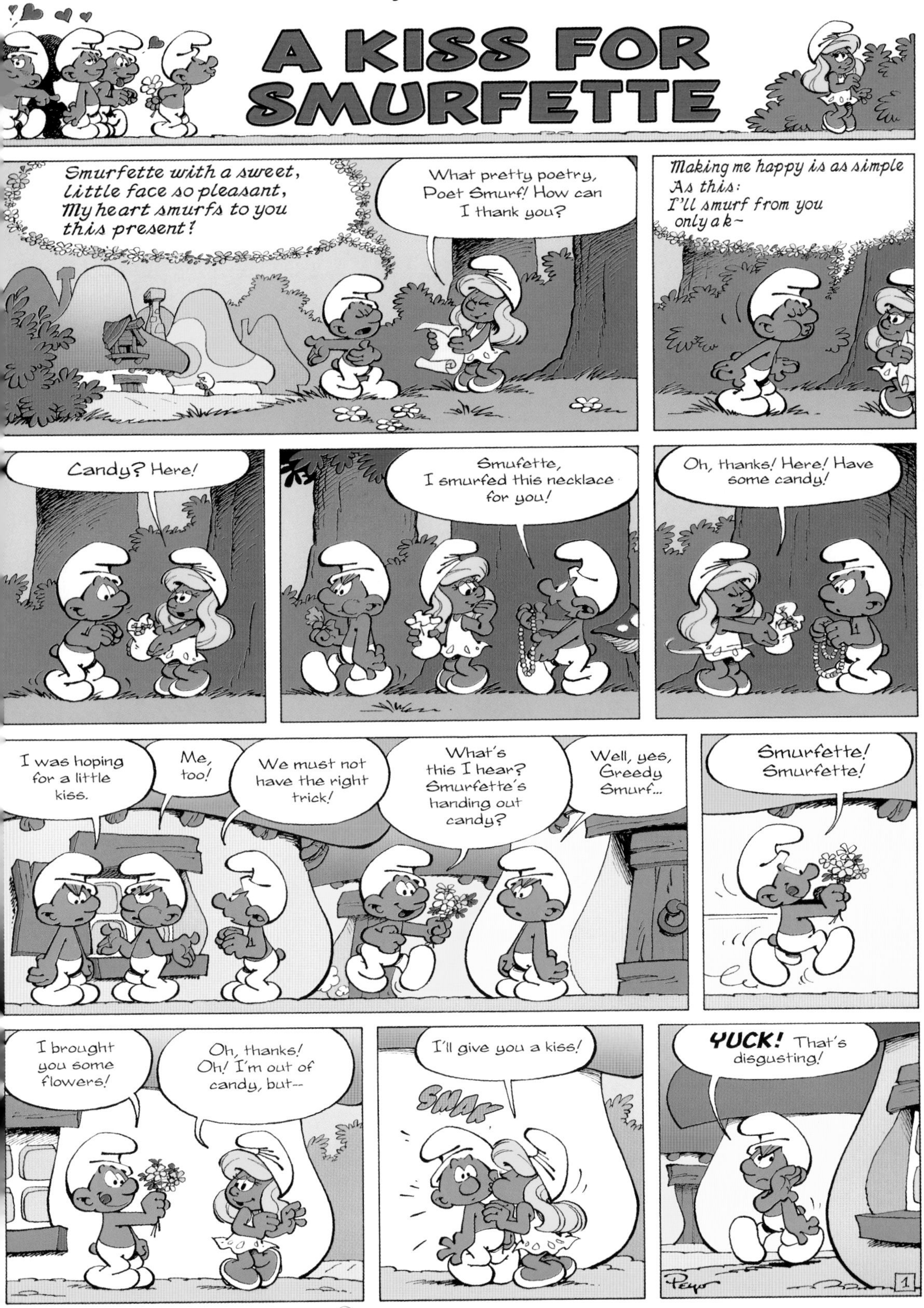
A KISS FOR SMURFETTE
Smurfette with a sweet, little face so pleasant, My heart smurfs to you this present!
What pretty poetry, Poet Smurf! How can I thank you?
Making me happy is as simple As this: I'll smurf from you only a k~
Candy? Here!
Smufette, I smurfed this necklace for you!
Oh, thanks! Here! Have some candy!
I was hoping for a little kiss.
Me, too!
We must not have the right trick!
What's this I hear? Smurfette's handing out candy?
Well, yes, Greedy Smurf...
Smurfette! Smurfette!
I brought you some flowers!
Oh, thanks! Oh! I'm out of candy, but--
I'll give you a kiss!
SMAK
YUCK! That's disgusting!
Peyo
1

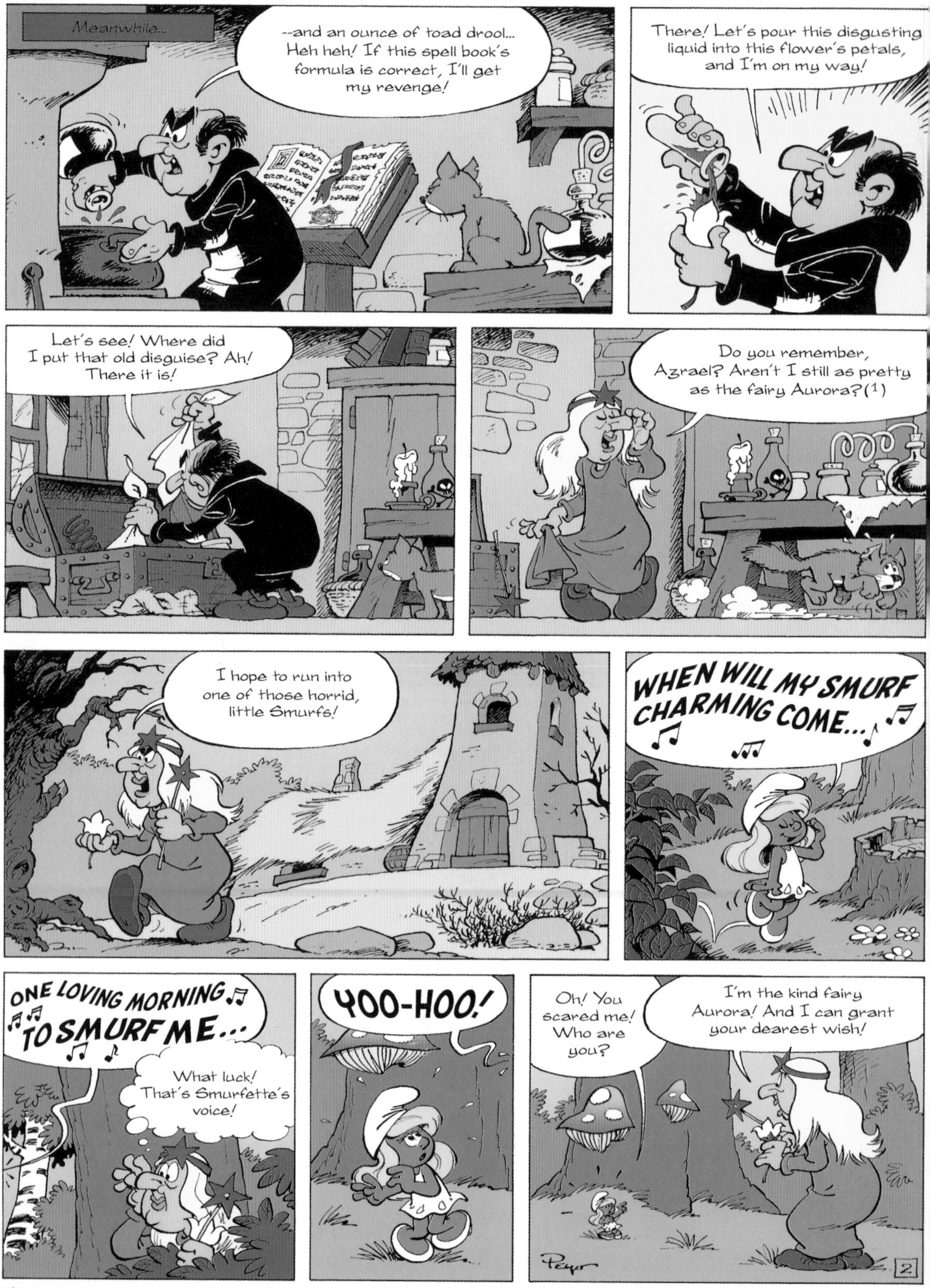
Meanwhile...
--and an ounce of toad drool... Heh heh! If this spell book's formula is correct, I'll get my revenge!
There! Let's pour this disgusting liquid into this flower's petals, and I'm on my way!
Let's see! Where did I put that old disguise? Ah! There it is!
Do you remember, Azrael? Aren't I still as pretty as the fairy Aurora?(1)
I hope to run into one of those horrid, little Smurfs!
WHEN WILL MY SMURF CHARMING COME...
ONE LOVING MORNING TO SMURF ME...
What luck! That's Smurfette's voice!
YOO-HOO!
Oh! You scared me! Who are you?
I'm the kind fairy Aurora! And I can grant your dearest wish!
Peyo

(1) See "The Smurfony" in THE SMURFS #3 "The Smurf King."

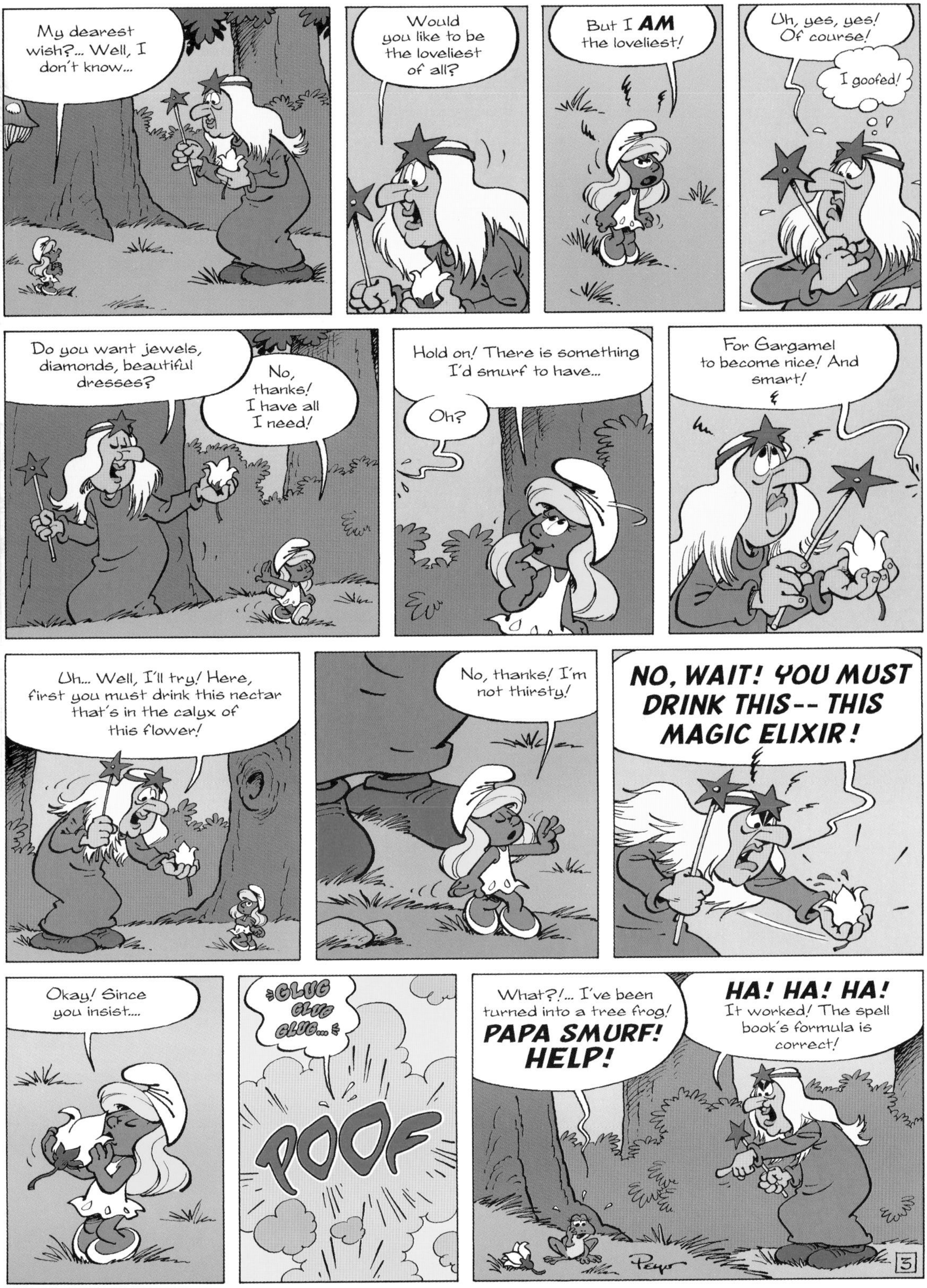
My dearest wish?... Well, I don't know...
Would you like to be the loveliest of all?
But I AM the loveliest!
Uh, yes, yes! Of course!
I goofed!
Do you want jewels, diamonds, beautiful dresses?
No, thanks! I have all I need!
Hold on! There is something I'd smurf to have...
Oh?
For Gargamel to become nice! And smart!
Uh... Well, I'll try! Here, first you must drink this nectar that's in the calyx of this flower!
No, thanks! I'm not thirsty!
NO, WAIT! YOU MUST DRINK THIS-- THIS MAGIC ELIXIR!
Okay! Since you insist....
GLUG GLUG GLUG...
POOF
What?!... I've been turned into a tree frog! PAPA SMURF! HELP!
HA! HA! HA! It worked! The spell book's formula is correct!
Peyo

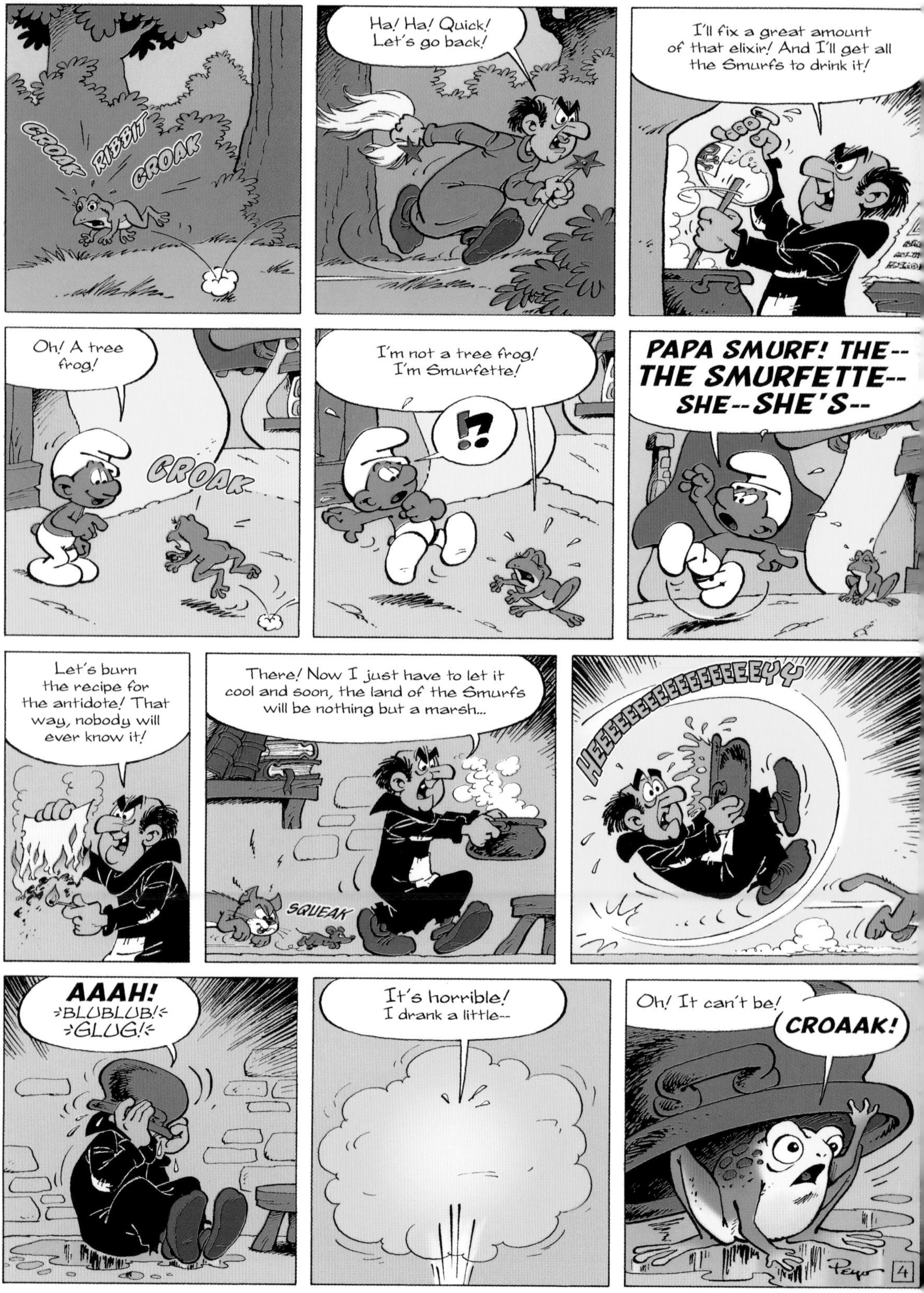

CROAK
RIBBIT
CROAK
Ha! Ha! Quick! Let's go back!
I'll fix a great amount of that elixir! And I'll get all the Smurfs to drink it!
Oh! A tree frog!
CROAK
I'm not a tree frog! I'm Smurfette!
!?
PAPA SMURF! THE-- THE SMURFETTE-- SHE--SHE'S--
Let's burn the recipe for the antidote! That way, nobody will ever know it!
There! Now I just have to let it cool and soon, the land of the Smurfs will be nothing but a marsh...
SQUEAK
AAAH! BLUBLUB! GLUG!
It's horrible! I drank a little--
Oh! It can't be!
CROAAK!
Peyo
4

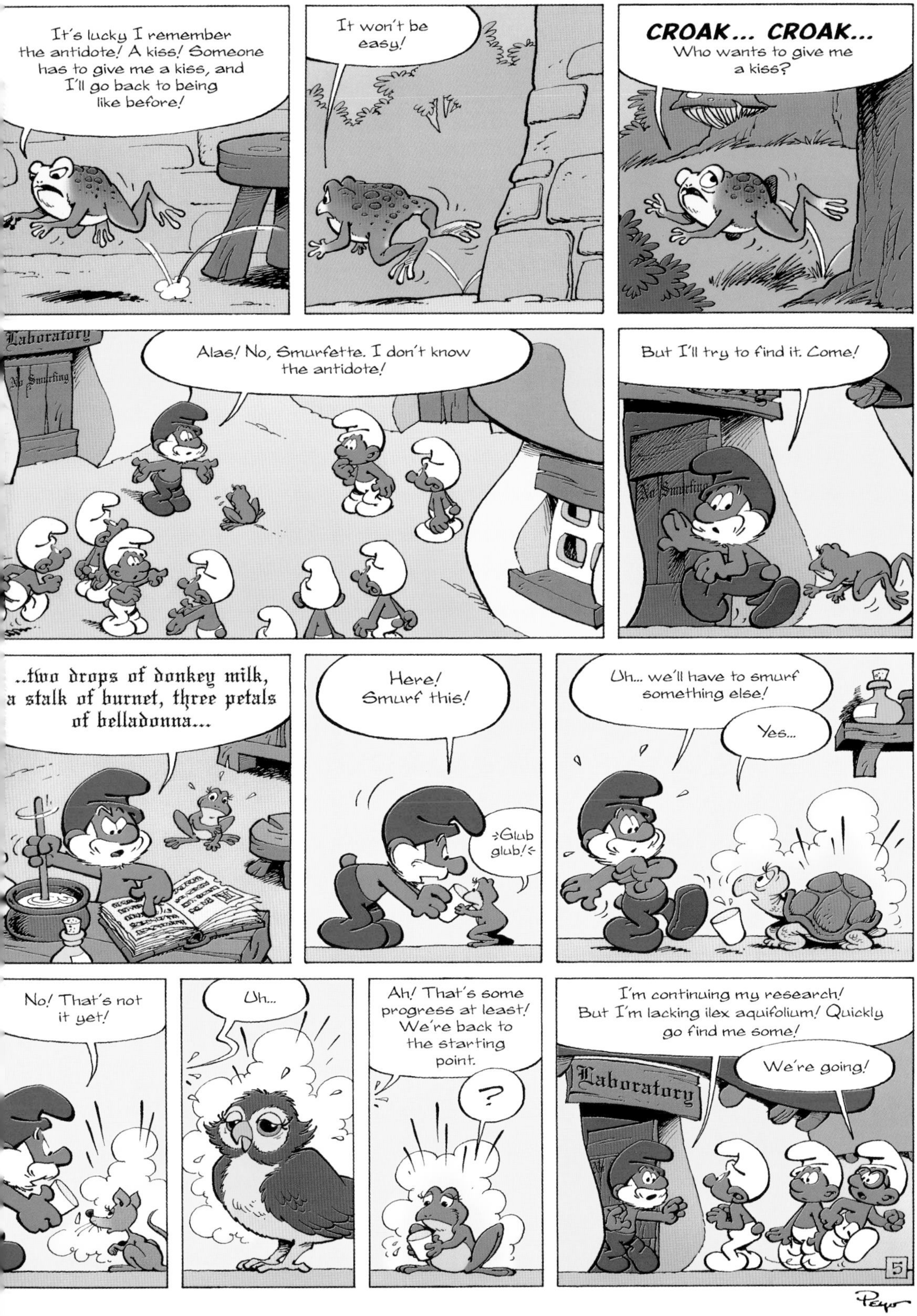
It's lucky I remember the antidote! A kiss! Someone has to give me a kiss, and I'll go back to being like before!
It won't be easy!
CROAK... CROAK...
Who wants to give me a kiss?
Laboratory
No Smurfing
Alas! No, Smurfette. I don't know the antidote!
But I'll try to find it. Come!
No Smurfing
..two drops of donkey milk, a stalk of burnet, three petals of belladonna...
Here! Smurf this!
Glub glub!
Uh... we'll have to smurf something else!
Yes...
No! That's not it yet!
Uh...
Ah! That's some progress at least! We're back to the starting point.
?
I'm continuing my research! But I'm lacking ilex aquifolium! Quickly go find me some!
Laboratory
We're going!
5
Peyo

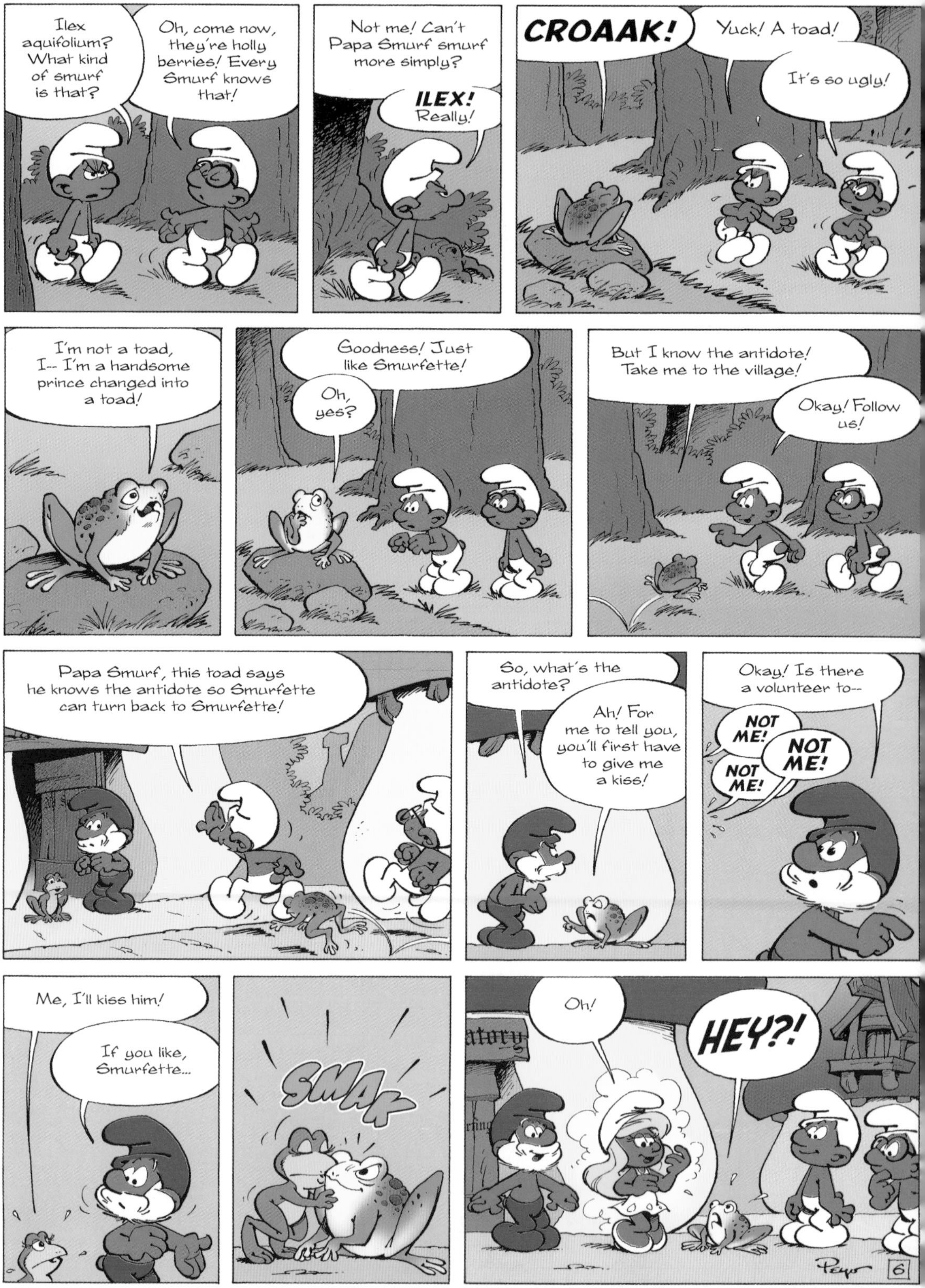

Ilex aquifolium? What kind of smurf is that?
Oh, come now, they're holly berries! Every Smurf knows that!
Not me! Can't Papa Smurf smurf more simply?
ILEX! Really!
CROAAK!
Yuck! A toad!
It's so ugly!
I'm not a toad, I-- I'm a handsome prince changed into a toad!
Goodness! Just like Smurfette!
Oh, yes?
But I know the antidote! Take me to the village!
Okay! Follow us!
Papa Smurf, this toad says he knows the antidote so Smurfette can turn back to Smurfette!
So, what's the antidote?
Ah! For me to tell you, you'll first have to give me a kiss!
Okay! Is there a volunteer to--
NOT ME!
NOT ME!
NOT ME!
Me, I'll kiss him!
If you like, Smurfette...
SMAK
Oh!
HEY?!
Peyo
6

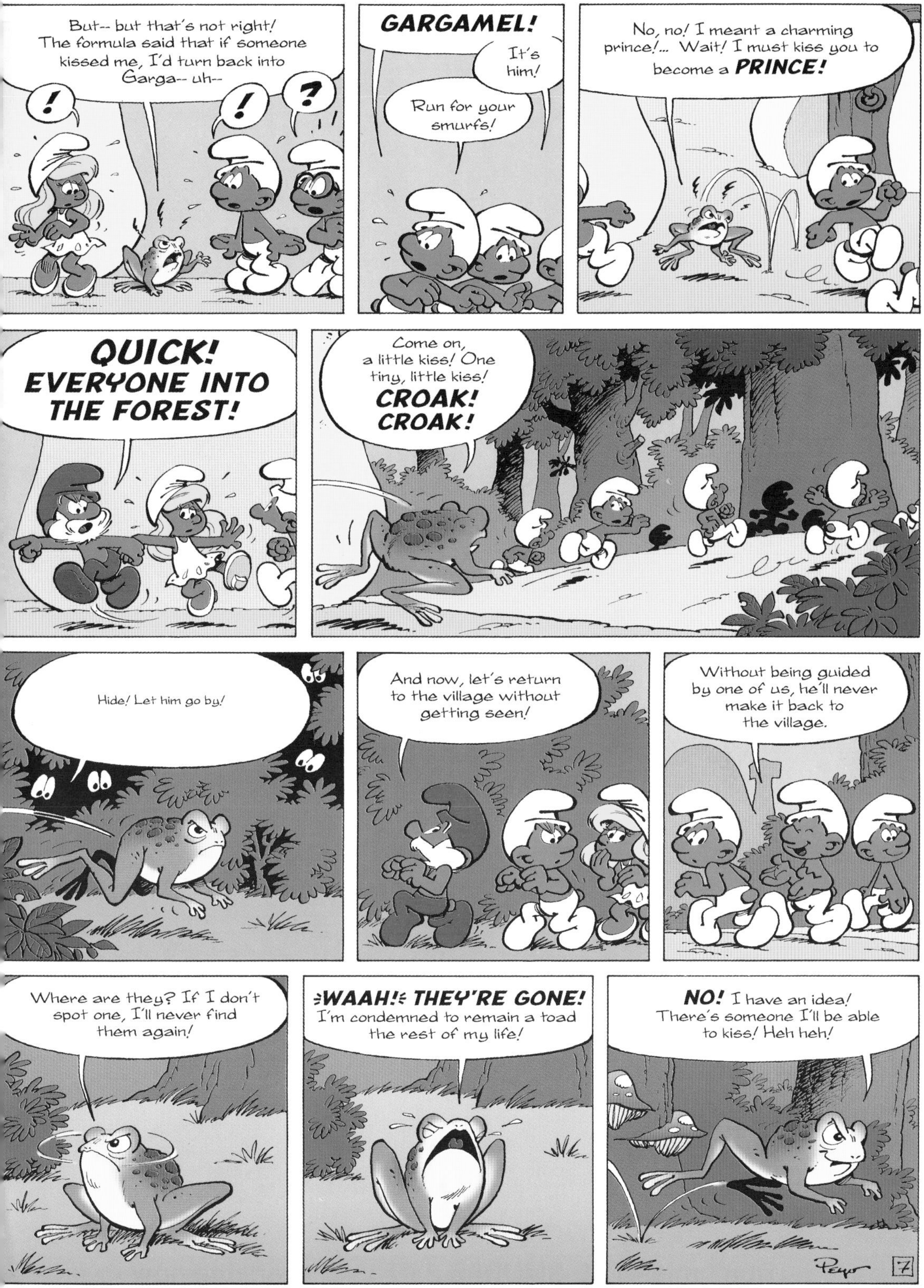
But-- but that's not right! The formula said that if someone kissed me, I'd turn back into Garga-- uh--
!
!
?
GARGAMEL!
It's him!
Run for your smurfs!
No, no! I meant a charming prince!... Wait! I must kiss you to become a PRINCE!
QUICK! EVERYONE INTO THE FOREST!
Come on, a little kiss! One tiny, little kiss! CROAK! CROAK!
Hide! Let him go by!
And now, let's return to the village without getting seen!
Without being guided by one of us, he'll never make it back to the village.
Where are they? If I don't spot one, I'll never find them again!
WAAH! THEY'RE GONE! I'm condemned to remain a toad the rest of my life!
NO! I have an idea! There's someone I'll be able to kiss! Heh heh!
Peyo

That stupid animal better be there!

AZRAEL!

AZRAEL! Come quick!

?

!?

SMAK

It worked! Now I'm my old self again!

PTOOOEY BLECHH

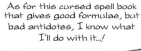

As for this cursed spell book that gives good formulae, but bad antidotes, I know what I'll do with it...!

That'll teach it! Nasty book!

Back at the Smurf Village...

Since I'm so happy, what can I do to make you all happy? Some candy?

NO! A KISS! A KISS!

Hey! I was before you!

Don't push!

-- you should've said so right away!

What a beautiful story!

Peyo ⑧ END

Don't miss THE SMURFS 3 IN 1 #2, available now at booksellers everywhere.